FOXGLOVE COUNTRY

Beautiful raven-haired Sara was trapped by her domineering grandfather in the Pryce ancestral home, brooding Tremannion House in the desolate Welsh Hills. Although she loved and respected him, she feared that the whispered rumours were true – the taint of spilled blood was on his hands. Also someone seemed determined to harm her and she did not know whom to turn to for help – Adam, her grandfather's neighbour at Brennion, or the arrogant, wild and tawny-haired Thaddeus who against her true instinct had aroused her deepest passions...

FOXGLOVE COUNTRY

Foxglove Country

by

Linden Howard

Magna Large Print Books
Long Preston, North Yorkshire,
BD23 4ND, England.

British Library Cataloguing in Publication Data.

Howard, Linden
    Foxglove country.

    A catalogue record of this book is
    available from the British Library

    ISBN   0-7505-1666-6

First published in Great Britain 1978
by Millington Books Ltd.

Copyright © 1977 by Linden Howard

Cover illustration © Len Thurston by arrangement with
P. W. A. International Ltd.

The moral right of the author has been asserted

Published in Large Print 2001 by arrangement with
Rupert Crew Ltd.

Magna Large Print is an imprint of Library Magna Books Ltd.

Printed and bound in Great Britain by
T.J. (International) Ltd., Cornwall, PL28 8RW

Chapter One

It seems strange to be here again, after so
many years, sitting in the high-backed Pryce
pew; the wood shines like dark-brown satin
from years of polishing; the worn prayer
books and fat hassocks are the ones I
remember, and there is even the same fierce
little man in the pulpit, though his hair is
grey now, not black. His sermon is punc-
tuated with a fist smacked down sharply on
the great Bible in front of him, his promises
are simple: Hell fire for the sinner, Heaven
for the penitent.

I think about the way he separates the
sheep from the goats, as I look through the
window beside me; outside in the little
cemetery, amongst the tangled grasses, are
tall foxgloves, their stems covered with pink
bells that sway in the summer wind, and
standing sentinel over the nearest graves is a
marble angel, with folded wings and cleanly
sculpted draperies, one finger pointing to
the sky.

Looking at the graves amongst the
foxgloves, I ask myself: *Who* was most to
blame for what happened, all those years
ago? I have asked myself the same question

many times and never found an answer. I wonder if *he* is thinking as I do? I turn to smile at him and feel the reassuring warmth of his hand in mine. *Don't look back, Sara,* says the touch of those fingers; but yesterday seems so close that it merges with today, and everything is beginning again; although, for me, the beginning was not here, in the shadow of the brooding Beacons, but in London...

My childhood was as placid as a still pool; the only time the waters were violently agitated into ripples was when my grandfather visited my mother. We lived in a quiet Kensington square, my mother, Lily Duffy, and I. There was a cook and a parlourmaid, a woman who came to scrub; Lily looked after my mother, scolded me and sewed for me, took me to bowl my hoop in the park, and let me linger in misty autumn twilights, to hear the muffin man's bell as he walked past with his covered tray on his head.

Lily had been with us since soon after I was born; she was a little bent hairpin of a woman, with a sharp tongue and a kind heart. A daily governess gave me lessons; a tutor taught me to paint and play the piano. My mother took me to see the many famous buildings in London and told me their history; she taught me the Latin names of plants and flowers and liked to hear me read or play the piano to her in the evenings. She

8

took me to the Zoological Gardens and the Crystal Palace, to concerts and to the shops; I loved her and was well content with her company.

My mother was beautiful; tall and stately, with masses of wheat-coloured hair dressed high above her lovely face. Her name was Celia Pryce, and she had married my father, David Pryce, when they were both twenty. He lived with his parents, Rachel and Meredith Pryce, at Tremannion House, in the heart of the Brecon Beacons; my mother was the housekeeper before she married my father.

Tremannion House. The Brecon Beacons. At night, I lay in bed, whispering the words to myself, until they seemed to grow enormous, filling the room with a strange splendour. As long as I could remember, I had yearned to see the place in which my grandparents lived.

My mother had loved my father dearly; there were always fresh flowers in front of the silver-framed photograph of him that stood by her bed.

Once I asked her if she thought I was like him.

'You look a little like him,' she said.

I was too thin; scrawny, Lily said. My hair was dark and unruly, my eyes were brown. Though my father was a handsome man from his photograph, I longed to possess my

9

mother's calm, golden grace.

I scarcely remembered my father; an impression of laughter, of warmth, no more. I was barely four years old when he died; but a vague memory of that last holiday we all spent together often disturbed me. I was aware only that some terrible sorrow and trouble had come upon my parents at that time.

We were at the seaside; Lily had gone to stay with her sister. My grandfather called upon my parents, although I did not see him. I remember hiding behind some velvet drapes, frightened by the sound of angry voices. I heard tears and anguish in my mother's voice and bitterness in my father's, though I did not know what they were saying. After a time my grandfather left; my mother wept for a long time and my father looked old and tired. Next day, they were both calmer. My mother took me to the beach, and my father went out fishing.

A storm rose up, out of an innocent summer sky; the empty boat was washed ashore, and my father's body recovered several miles down the coast, days afterwards. Strangely, my mother did not weep then; there was an ominous quietness about her, a dreadful grief and bitterness in her eyes. In time, she grew calm and more like herself again, although she was never quite the same, never so carefree.

When, in after years, I questioned her about the arrival of my grandfather and all that had happened afterwards, she simply shook her head and said she did not want to talk about it.

My mother had no family of her own; her mother had died when she was born, and her father, a country rector, died when she was nineteen. She was left with very little money and was glad enough to accept the post of housekeeper to the Pryce family.

As I grew up, I became curious; the more so because she answered my questions reluctantly.

'Did my father have brothers and sisters?' I wanted to know.

'One sister, Anne.'

'Then she is my Aunt Anne. Is she older than my father?'

'A few years, yes.'

'Why may we not visit them, Mama?'

Carefully she folded her embroidery; I saw how her hands trembled.

'When you are older I will tell you,' she said.

I coaxed scraps of information from Lily; it seemed that my father had run away with my mother when he wanted to marry her, because it wasn't considered a suitable match. I asked my mother what Lily had meant.

'I was the housekeeper, Sara. Your father

was Meredith Pryce's only son and heir. So your father had to leave Tremannion and live in London.'

'Was Grandfather very angry about that?'

'Yes. Dearest, it is time for your supper.'

When I was ten years old, I grew rebellious.

'Mama, why do you send me out with Lily whenever you know Grandfather is going to call?'

'One day I will tell you.'

'You *always* say that, Mama. One day is *now.*'

Her eyebrows rose and she said quietly:

'Your grandfather treated your father very cruelly. He caused us both terrible unhappiness, but it was your father who suffered the most, and I loved him too dearly to forget or forgive that fact. Anne has never married, and your grandfather has no other grandchild; he is eager to know you and to forget all that he did.'

'You will not let him see me, Mama; is that because you wish to punish him for the bad time when you and Papa were so unhappy?'

She looked startled, but said nothing. I rushed in eagerly:

'Perhaps he really is very sorry for making you unhappy. I would like to see his house and my grandmother and Aunt Anne. May we not go on a visit?'

'Never!' she whispered. *'Never*, Sara! I

shall not return to Tremannion!'

One day, my grandfather called un-expectedly; as soon as the hansom cab stopped outside the house, Lily whisked me hurriedly upstairs on the pretext that my ribbon drawer needed tidying. When she left me for a moment, I tiptoed to the bedroom door. I know well how these visits distressed and angered my mother, and though I had never before been in the house when he came, I could feel his presence when I returned; it was as though an alien force had disturbed our peace and torn the gentle fabric of our days with destructive hands.

Now I was closer to him than I had ever been. I heard his voice; it was rich and resonant, with a faint sound of singing in it – and anger, too.

'I intend to see the child, Celia, whatever you say! I have every right!'

'You have *no* rights!' Her voice was like ice. 'Have you not done us harm enough?'

'Harm? Who pays for her expensive clothes – *and* for yours? Whose money supports this house, pays the wages of servants and a governess to make a fine lady of Sara Pryce? Tell me *that!*'

'You owe us that much. David was your son.'

I heard no more; Lily came back and whisked me from the door.

'Come away at once! Your mama would be

13

most angry! Eavesdroppers never hear good of themselves!'

'It is not fair!' I stormed. 'My grandfather pays for *everything*, yet Mama treats him as though he has done something terrible!'

'Maybe he has!' muttered Lily. 'He causes trouble enough, coming here when she does not want to see him!'

'He wants to see *me!*' I cried importantly. 'And she will not let him!'

'Then she has good reason. Come away, do, child. Don't let your mama hear you talk so, or you will give her one of her migraines.'

Angrily I thrust the ribbons back in the drawer and slammed it shut. I heard Grandfather leave soon afterward, and when I would have run to the window, Lily firmly barred the way. When I went to take tea with Mama, she looked white and exhausted; she kept looking at me in an odd, troubled way. I did not mention Grandfather's visit for – puzzled and curious though I was – I loved her too dearly to want to add to her distress.

When I was sixteen, I put up my hair, and my skirts were lengthened. Still I was not allowed to met my grandfather, and I was growing tired of being fobbed off with excuses and sent out with Lily when he called.

'I *want* to see him!' I told my mother. 'You promised to tell me many things when I was older and I am *sixteen!*'

'Very well,' she said wearily, 'as you are so set upon it, you shall meet him. Perhaps, after all, the time has come.'

My mother had grown much thinner of late and was often too exhausted to go for drives or to concerts with me. I knelt beside the couch and put my arms around her.

'Do you hate them all?' I whispered. 'Grandmother? Aunt Anne? Were they all unkind to you?'

She sighed.

'No, my love. I know that you must go to Tremannion one day, and your grandfather eagerly awaits that time. I have tried to delay it; Tremannion is not the kind of house you imagine it to be, though it looks like a drawing of a castle in a book of fairy tales. Some houses have known evil things, bitterness, great sorrow, and so they are always cold, even on the warmest day, and full of shadows, even when all the lamps are lit. Tremannion is like that.'

I shivered, and she took my face in her hands, her eyes troubled. I thought how frail she seemed, how deep were the shadows beneath her eyes.

'What is to become of you?' she murmured despairingly. 'He holds us all in the palm of his hand still, after all these years. He provides for us. I have nothing of my own.'

She broke off, biting her lip; then she said that Grandfather was coming in two weeks' time, and I was to join them for tea.

As the day drew nearer, I felt a tempest of excitement, mingled with a strange dread I could not explain. Lily scolded me, exasperated, and my governess shook her head over my inattentiveness. When the great day came, I put on my best dress and stood by the schoolroom window to watch for his arrival.

The cab stopped at the front door and my heart beat so painfully that I could scarcely breathe; but all that I saw was the top of Grandfather's head, as he stepped out. He had coal-black hair, thickly streaked with grey, and I cried out in astonishment to Lily.

'He does not wear a hat! I never before saw a gentleman out of doors without his hat!'

Lily sniffed and said dourly:

'What else 'ud you expect, then? He knows no better, living in those wild mountains of his!'

'He is wearing a coat with a cape; he looks big and strong, Lily. I wonder if he is very old?'

'Little girls should mind their own business!' Lily retorted.

I crushed her with a look reminding her that I was almost seventeen, and next year would not have to be told what to do, nor to take lessons in the schoolroom.

At last I was summoned to the drawing-room; my grandfather was standing by the fireplace when I entered and turned eagerly towards me, his face filled with interest and alight with curiosity.

He was so tall and powerfully built that he seemed to fill my mother's dainty drawing-room; he had massive shoulders, his hair was thick and wavy. He had a face not easily forgotten; ruddy-complexioned, with a strong nose, a formidable jaw, and piercing dark eyes that shone brightly from beneath heavy black brows.

Meredith Pryce walked towards me, put his hands on my shoulders in a grip so firm that it hurt, and looked searchingly into my face.

'So this is Sara!' he said softly.

I glanced anxiously at my mother; she was sitting upright on the edge of a small chair, hands clasped in her lap, looking at me as though trying to gauge my reactions to this meeting.

'You are a handsome young woman!' Meredith Pryce said approvingly. 'I like a woman to be handsome – as your mother is – not all buttermilk and peaches and bird bones. One day, Sara Pryce, you shall come to Tremannion!'

I saw the triumphant look he gave my mother; she gazed back at him steadily and without fear. Then she smiled at me and asked if I would please ring for tea.

Throughout tea, my grandfather's talk fascinated me, so that I could scarcely eat. He spoke of the Beacons, on whose great stretches the Pryce sheep grazed; he spoke of farms and cottages that were his, of the coal mines in South Wales that he owned, and I realised that he was a very wealthy man.

When it was time for him to go, he repeated his promise that one day I would go to Tremannion.

'But not yet!' my mother said softly. 'She is still mine, Meredith Pryce!'

He looked grim for a moment; then he laughed and retorted that he would bide his time.

When he had gone, the house seemed to shrink; I dined with Mama that evening. She declared that the afternoon had quite exhausted her, and she declined to discuss our visitor.

Two weeks later, a parcel was delivered to the house; it was addressed to me, and when I opened it, I found a leather jewel case containing a heavy gold locket that was richly chased and set with garnets and seed pearls. The locket hung from a thick gold chain and was the most splendid piece of jewellery I had ever owned. The note with it simply said: 'To Sara, from her grandfather.'

18

My mother's lips tightened when I showed her the locket.

'So he will try to buy you?' she murmured bitterly.

It was more than a year before I saw Meredith Pryce again, but the first edge of my disappointment was dulled as time passed. First, he wrote that he had been ill – a chill that turned to pneumonia. Then my mama became too unwell to receive visitors and he postponed a visit at her request.

The doctor shook his head over Mama and said she must rest as much as possible. The presents continued to come from Wales, always with the same little note: 'To Sara, from her grandfather.' I received a brooch in the shape of a little Welsh harp, a purse of soft kid, a tortoiseshell box, a string of pearls. I knew that my mother was angry about the coming of the gifts, and I thought it was because she feared I might want to go and live with Grandfather.

Mama began to stay in bed or on her couch for days at a time, needing my attention and not liking me to be far from her; so there was little time to think much about Tremannion.

In the year 1897, when I was eighteen, London was decorated with flags and bunting and festoons for Queen Victoria's Diamond Jubilee; a great many special functions and social occasions took place, and Mama – who seemed in better health than she had been for some time – allowed me to attend some of them. I had never seen London look so festive and gay. I was delighted that Mama was able to purchase special seats for us in one of the covered stands lining the route of the Jubilee Procession.

It was a most exciting occasion; the streets were jammed with people, for it was a fine June day. Mama seemed almost like her old self, as we leant forward to see the great Procession, with the Household Cavalry in their magnificent uniforms, the harnesses of their fine horses jingling like a cascade of joy bells as they rode along to the sound of cheers from the crowds; but the loudest cheers were for the small, plump woman holding a parasol, who sat alone in an open carriage, in the centre of it all.

I felt immensely sorry for her.

'She looks lonely,' I said to Mama.

'I daresay she is,' Mama said gently. 'Often.'

It was a long, exhausting day; the streets were so full of people that it took us a great time to travel through them; everywhere the crowds were laughing, singing, jostling one another boisterously on this day of rejoicing.

'You are looking at history,' Mama told me. 'One day you will remember that today you saw a little old lady riding through the streets of London. Sixty years a Queen! It is a long time to have served one's country. She must be very tired.'

Mama looked ill by the time we reached home; I thought it was the heat and excitement. I pulled the shades, took off her shoes, brought cologne. She drank a cup of tea slowly, as though it was a great effort to do so, and said she would sleep for a while.

When I went into her room an hour later to see if she needed anything, I realised that she was dead.

For a moment I could not believe it; then I ran, weeping, from the room.

'Lily! Oh, Lily, Mama is dead!'

It was Lily who comforted me, bore with my storm of grief, brought tea and sal volatile, and made me lie down on my bed. My eyes were swollen, my head ached; I felt helpless and alone, without Mama.

'What are we to do, Lily?' I asked.

'I have sent for the doctor and for Mr Clayton,' she told me. 'Your mama knew, sometime ago, that she did not have much time left to be with you, but she did not wish you to know how ill she was. She gave me Mr Clayton's address and told me I was to send for him when her time came; he is a lawyer, and his firm looks after your grandpa's affairs here in London.'

I had heard Mama mention Mr Clayton; it

was from his firm that a sum of money came every quarter day to provide for us.

When Mr Clayton was announced, I bathed my eyes, brushed my hair, and went to receive him. He was a brisk, pleasant young man, who offered his condolences with great kindness and sympathy, adding that news of my mother's death had been sent to my grandfather. The house in which I had always lived belonged to him; upon my mother's death it was to be sold and I was to go to Tremannion to live with him.

I shivered suddenly, as though a cold hand had reached out and touched me. I had longed, as a child, to visit Tremannion. Now the prospect held no excitement, only an unexpected feeling of dread.

I remembered that all my mother and I had known in the way of comfort and possessions had belonged to Meredith Pryce; though Mama had hated him, she had long since faced the fact that one day Tremannion would be my home.

Grandfather's reply was swift. He wrote to say that as soon as everything was settled, Mr Clayton would arrange for me to travel to Wales. The letter briefly expressed regret for my mother's death, but made no mention of Lily, so I wrote asking if she might come to Wales with me. It would only be for a short time, I pointed out, as Lily had what she called 'a bit put by' and was anxious to go and live with her widowed sister at Southend; but to have her beside me during those first weeks, when life was new and strange, would be a great comfort.

He replied that Lily might come, but I sensed how reluctantly he gave his permission. I would not lack people to look after me, he pointed out. However, since it was my wish, he was prepared to let her come with me.

There was much to be done during the next two weeks, for which I was thankful; it left me little time to brood on my loss. My mother had left me her jewellery; she possessed little, for she had never cared to adorn herself with trinkets. A string of corals, some pretty brooches and bracelets lay in the worn leather box – and a ring I had never seen before. It was obviously valuable, for it was of heavy yellow gold, set with a splendid amethyst surrounded by diamonds.

I showed the ring to Lily, who said:

'Your mama once showed it to me and said that your papa gave it to her. I believe she couldn't bear to put it on her finger after he died; she was so ill then, poor soul, I feared for her reason, Miss Sara.'

Lily had taken to calling me 'Miss Sara' instead of 'Sara' after my mother's death, as though acknowledging the fact that I had acquired a new status.

At the bottom of the jewel case, I found an envelope. It was long and thick, heavily sealed with several impressions in the shape of a small red rose, made in the wax. I had never seen my mother use that particular seal, but the writing on the envelope was hers: 'To be opened only by my beloved daughter, Sara Caroline Pryce, on her twenty-first birthday.'

As I touched the envelope, I felt a shiver go through me, as though a wind had blown through a quiet room. I felt as if my mother stood beside me, a sad, troubled expression on her face. The impression was so vivid that I was quite frightened.

I thrust the envelope back into the jewel case; there was too much to be done to dwell upon these things. Grandfather had set a date for our departure; his last letter, written in thick, flowing script, informed me that Mr Clayton would reserve first-class accommodation on the train for us and would accompany us as far as Brecon, where he would deliver us safely into my grandfather's keeping.

The day of my departure came at last; dressed for the journey, I looked at myself gravely in the bedroom mirror. I had grown thinner, and my eyes were enormous, like those of a child who sees strange things. I wore a new suit, the jacket trimmed with jet buttons, and I had a small, feathered hat on top of my piled-up hair. At the throat of my blouse I pinned my mother's cameo brooch; then I went downstairs, to where Lily and Mr Clayton waited.

From the noise, smoke and confusion of Paddington Station, the westbound train glided as slowly as a ship taking the water with stately dignity. Grandfather had reserved an entire first-class compartment for us, and Mr Clayton was solicitous, providing me with magazines to while away the hours, but I could not read. Instead, I stared from the window at the grimy houses and tall buildings that gradually gave place to green countryside.

Lily seemed ill-at-ease; she had lived all her life in London and distrusted 'foreign' places like Wales.

As we approached the Severn Tunnel, the countryside grew wilder, and Mr Clayton told me tales of the building of the tunnel, with its many delays and difficulties. I marvelled at the tremendous engineering feat that made it possible for us to travel beneath a wide river. The train gathered speed as it raced toward the dark opening that would separate yesterday from today for me.

I thought poor Lily would faint with fright, as, with a whistle and a roar, the train plunged into the tunnel; she shut her eyes

25

tightly, as though we were about to meet a terrible fate. The noise of the engine was like a great heart pulsing in the dark, but when we emerged on the other side of the river, I was disappointed to find the countryside flat and uninteresting.

I remarked that we were now in Wales, but Mr Clayton shook his head.

'Monmouthshire became an English shire in the year fifteen hundred and thirty-six,' he informed me precisely. 'Before that, it was part of the ancient Welsh kingdom of Gwent. Technically we are still in England, Miss Pryce.'

Monmouthshire might be an English county, but we *were* in Wales: I could feel it in my very bones. I was part of this country because of the Welsh blood that flowed in my veins as strongly as the Severn that divided me from all the things I had known.

I was glad when it was time for us to leave the train; arrangements had been made for us to spend the night at a hotel; I was very tired, and glad enough to go to bed, after the meal served to us in our rooms. I wished with all my heart that I was at home again in London.

We continued our journey by hired coach, setting off early next day. It was cool, the sky overcast. We journeyed, at first, through lush green countryside, past swiftly running rivers, prosperous farms, snug cottages. We

26

halted briefly at Abergavenny, a pleasant little town under the shadow of a strangely shaped mountain called the Sugar Loaf. As we journeyed on, the day seemed to grow colder and the countryside became more forbidding. Mists crept low over the tops of dark crags, as though to hide the summits from my eyes. Streams and rivers seemed to hurry away more swiftly, as though anxious to reach the open sea. I saw an occasional waterfall flying in silver foam over great rocks.

I shivered as Lily tucked a rug around me. This place seemed to reject me, as though it wanted to be left in peace to brood upon the secrets of its ancient past.

I was glad enough to reach Brecon, with its narrow streets and busy shops; it stood beneath the frowning Beacons, whose great scarp dominated the north of the county like a great wall.

We arrived early, thanks to the good pace of the horses; Mr Clayton paid off the coach and ushered us into the lounge of a comfortable-looking hotel, where he ordered tea. Meredith Pryce was coming to the hotel to meet us; Mr Clayton would stay overnight and return to London next morning. I had the impression that he would be glad to go.

I heard Welsh voices all around me, with singing undertones to them that I thought most attractive. Some of the people spoke in their own tongue, heightening my feeling of being in a strange country, and increasing Lily's air of gloomy foreboding. Most of these people were small and dark and sturdy-looking; I remembered history lessons, and my governess telling me that they had first come to England from beyond the Caspian Sea, only to be driven by Saxon invaders into the fastness of these mountains.

Tea was brought to us on a big tray, together with small, flat cakes that looked like currant scones.

'Miss Pryce,' Mr Clayton said, 'will you excuse me for one moment? I wish to check that my reservation is in order, for I do not care to leave anything to chance.'

As I nodded, a man sitting alone, nearby, drinking tea, looked up sharply.

He was about thirty, well-dressed in thick country tweeds, and with an air of authority about him. He had a clear-cut, handsome face, with strong, well-defined features. There was a touch of hauteur in the slightly sensuous mouth; his hair was dark brown, with tawny lights in it, curling thick and strong over his head and almost touching his collar. But it was his eyes that most compelled my attention; they were a strange, brilliant green and narrowed slightly as he gave me a leisurely head-to-toe inspection.

Angry, yet fascinated, I looked away from his eyes and studied his hands. They were beautiful; one lay along the arm of his chair, the long fingers seeming to be possessed of a nervous energy as they beat a soft tattoo on the red plush.

A strange feeling overcame me, as I waited for the last and most dramatic part of my journey to begin; an awareness, perhaps, that this man would play a part in my destiny, whether I wished it or not.

He stood up and I saw that he was very tall; he came across and bowed to me, quite unperturbed by my angry glance; his slow smile held mockery and amusement.

Lily looked askance; no gentleman ever accosted ladies travelling alone, and she looked around, uneasily, for Mr Clayton.

The man stood in front of me, and, unwillingly, I raised my eyes to his.

'You are Sara Pryce,' he said; he had a lovely voice, rich and resonant.

I inclined my head briefly in acknowledgement; he was so close to me that I was acutely aware of his strange, mesmeric quality.

'Meredith Pryce's granddaughter,' he added. 'You are going to live at Tremannion. They say you have lived all your life in the city. Perhaps you should have stayed there!'

His smile teased, so that I felt a fresh surge of annoyance for his cool impudence.

'I do not know who you are!' I said shortly. 'I do not think you have any right to–'

'I am a neighbour,' he interrupted me calmly. 'I live on Brennion lands which adjoin those of your grandfather. My name is Thaddeus Flynn!'

Thaddeus Flynn. The words sang through my mind; it was a name to be shouted on the wind, at the top of one's voice, in a lonely place, so that the echoes would tumble back in a waterfall of sound. Indeed, it was not a name at all, I thought, but a statement.

I inclined my head, but not before I had met his gaze fully, and seen that it held both pity and scorn. At that moment, my grandfather came into the hotel, and when he saw Mr Flynn his face became dark with a terrible anger. For the first time in my life, I was aware of being in the presence of a violent, explosive hatred.

'I have been making your granddaughter's acquaintance,' Mr Flynn said. His face was unreadable as he looked at Grandfather, but I saw a gleam of triumphant amusement in the brilliant eyes.

'Why?' my grandfather demanded savagely. 'Do you hope to number *her* amongst your circle of dubious acquaintances? That you will never do. It was outrageous impudence on your part to force yourself to her attention!'

Thaddeus bowed very slightly before turning away; although he did not speak. I felt that he was pleased to have so angered my grandfather. He walked from the lounge, and Grandfather stared after him, eyes blazing; he seemed to be struggling very hard to maintain his self-control.

He turned to me and enquired curtly if it had been a comfortable journey; he seemed in a hurry to be on his way. Our farewells were said to Mr Clayton, and we accompanied my grandfather to the hotel courtyard where the carriage waited.

I looked with astonishment at the horses. There were four of them, huge, powerful animals. They were coal black; the last time I had seen black horses was when the hearse had left the house for my mother's funeral.

For a moment, a terrible anguish clawed at my heart; I struggled to overcome tears. I did not want to ride behind black horses to Tremannion for it seemed like an ill omen.

My grandfather looked at the animals and said proudly:

'The climb to Tremannion is hard and steep; it needs the power of four such mighty horses as these to draw the carriage.'

Roberts, the coachman, was a thin, foxy-looking little man whom I did not like; he eyed me curiously as I was helped into the coach.

Though it was early on a summer evening,

it could have been the prelude to a winter twilight. The skies were leaden and it was beginning to rain, softly and sadly, as though the mountains wept for lost summer. Gone were the green valleys with the little houses cradled safely in their arms. Long strands of mists wrapped themselves around us, as though deliberately seeking to shut out the view.

'The Beacons are a splendid sight on a fine day,' my grandfather told me. 'We shall ride out and look at them together; you will never want to set eyes on London again.'

There was pride and possessiveness in his voice; I felt misgivings. I could feel the horses working hard to pull us up the winding road that seemed to lead nowhere. The scenery was desolate; there were narrow, pebbly gullies laced with thin trickles of water that whispered on their way; stunted trees, crouched low, and half-hidden in the mist; outcrops of rock, strangely shaped and looking as though they had all been tipped carelessly from a giant's wheelbarrow to lie haphazard amongst the furze and scrub; the bleating sheep, who sat by the road, our only living companions, ran away from the sound of the horses' hooves and were swallowed up in the greyness.

'I am angry that Flynn should have forced his attentions upon you!' my grandfather said abruptly. 'Well, he will not trouble you again. He is a penniless opportunist, who rents a cottage from Adam Brennion, living on his wits and on Adam's misplaced charity. He should have been sent about his business long since. Have nothing to do with him! You understand, Sara?'

I looked back into the penetrating dark eyes.

'I understand,' I said.

Again, I felt a force of hatred about me; surely Grandfather could not care so much that Mr Flynn was a waster? There must be some other, deeper reason for his violent antipathy.

We passed a half-ruined cottage, roofless, its door hanging ajar; I had a vague impression of a shape moving at the side of the cottage, almost concealed by the damp curtains of mist and rain; a split second later, something whistled through the air and struck one of the leading horses.

The animal whinnied loudly and reared up on its hind legs, agitating the other horses; the carriage rocked wildly, veering off the road and almost coming to grief upon an outcrop of rock. Lily screamed and Roberts swore furiously; only his skill saved us from being overturned.

My grandfather wrenched open the door, furiously demanding to know what had happened. I sat white-faced and shaken, trying to still the frenzied trembling of my hands. I thought of the bleakness of our surroundings, the black horses, the figure half-glimpsed in the shrouds of mist. I knew there had not been an accident; something had been deliberately aimed at us.

My grandfather returned to the coach, his thick hair beaded with moisture.

'Jasper must have stumbled on a loose stone; the road is treacherous here.'

'I saw someone by the cottage,' I told him. 'I could not say if it was a man or woman, but whoever it was threw something; a stone, I think.'

He stared disbelievingly at me.

'Nonsense! You are overwrought! The cottage has been empty for years!'

'Do you have enemies, Grandfather?' I asked.

'Enemies? What absurd talk! If there are men who envy me my lands and wealth, then I do not fancy that they would hide up here in this weather, simply for the pleasure of casting stones!' he said dryly.

Unexpectedly, he framed my cold face in his hands; it was a grip so firm that I could not move my head, but was compelled to look at him. His face was still, his eyes thoughtful.

'You are tired, Sara! Soon we shall be at Tremannion. Forget what has happened; Jasper stumbled on a stone, no more.'

I knew he was wrong; more, he did not

believe what he said.

We crossed a stone bridge that straddled a noisy stream; the mists ahead of us began to thin out, as though at Grandfather's command.

'Look, Sara!' he said proudly, *'there* is Tremannion!'

The great house stood, proud and arrogant, on a green rise of land just above us. It was built of grey stone, with tall chimneys and many gables; at each end of the house was a square tower.

The windows were set deep in their stone embrasures, reminding me of secretive, heavy-lidded eyes; and in every one of those windows, a lamp had been set, so that the gloom blossomed with golden flowers of light.

The massive front door was iron-studded beneath its stone arch; no walls enclosed this house, which seemed strange to me, accustomed as I was to the neatly defined boundaries of town gardens. Tremannion looked exactly as though it had been violently thrust up through the soil, stones and boulders cast aside, so that a wide area of grass around the house could be tamed into lawns.

The thinning mists curled and wreathed like sad, supplicating ghosts around the walls of Tremannion, the house that sat alone on the roof of Wales.

The carriage turned from the road on to the drive and halted outside the closed door; with great ceremony Grandfather helped me to alight.

'Welcome home, Sara!' he said. 'You should have come long ago; I have often planned how it would be: lights for *you* in every window, sending out a message: Sara Pryce has come to Tremannion!'

I felt as though the clinging mists divided to let the warmth of sunlight envelop me. I looked up at the tall, commanding figure beside me and realised, astonished, that the warmth came from *him;* his love surrounded me, making nonsense of all my fears and forebodings about my new life.

I had never before been enclosed in so compelling a love; even my mother, whose feelings for me had been deep and abiding, had not shown me this intensity of feeling.

I felt puzzled and a little perturbed by such strength of emotion from this man who scarcely knew his granddaughter but I felt reassured by it also, and as I looked at the massive grey house, I knew I would be safe within its walls as long as the master of Tremannion dwelt there.

Chapter Two

'Well, Sara, what do you think of it?' my grandfather asked.

'It is the most splendid house I have ever seen,' I answered truthfully, and he seemed pleased with my reply.

As we moved towards the great door, it was opened by a tall, slender woman with dark hair drawn tightly back from her face into a hard knot on her neck; she had high cheekbones, bright, piercing eyes, and a rather thin mouth.

There was no sound except the rustling of her skirts as she approached us; for all her plainness, she had a graceful walk.

'Well?' my grandfather said abruptly. 'Where is everyone?'

'Waiting in the hall,' she replied, equally abrupt. 'As you instructed. You will see that the lamps have also been lighted as you ordered.'

She turned her attention to me, studying me from head to toe, and then giving me a cool smile.

'I am your Aunt Anne,' she said. 'We were commanded to kill the fatted calf for you, Sara!'

There was mockery in her voice; I said quietly:

'Why? I am not the prodigal son returning!'

'That honour would have been reserved for your father, had he lived!' she replied, looking slyly at Meredith, whose face darkened angrily.

'Mind your manners, Anne!' he told her sharply. 'A husband would have cured you of that pert tongue of yours!'

She seemed annoyed by the rebuke; she turned and walked ahead of us into the house, her back like a ramrod.

'Does Aunt Anne look after the house for you?' I asked my grandfather.

He shook his head.

'No, Sara. I should find *that* too great a trial. Anne looks after your grandmother.'

He hesitated a moment, before he added:

'David, your father, left Tremannion very suddenly. It was a tremendous shock to your grandmother; since then she has been strange and disturbed in her mind. She needs constant vigilance.'

By this time we had reached the hall; I saw the row of servants, lined up to be presented to me, and I felt dreadfully nervous. I turned quickly, to see if Lily was still with me; the sight of her, standing stiffly behind me, reassured me a little.

Aunt Anne stood well away from her

father, watching the scene like a disinterested bystander; another woman came forward to greet us.

She was small, plump, and middle-aged; there was an air of faded prettiness about her. She had lustreless fair hair and wore a heavy gold chatelaine at her waist.

Her eyes assessed me shrewdly, but her smile was kind.

'Sara,' said my grandfather, 'this is your Great-aunt Jessie; her husband was my elder brother, Morgan. She has charge of the servants and all household affairs.'

'Such a tiring journey for you, child!' Jessie fussed gently. 'It is a long way from London. I have been there only once; very noisy it was; too many people. Not to my liking at all.'

'Where is Rachel?' Meredith asked her.

Jessie lowered her eyes and sighed.

'Anne explained that you were bringing Sara here, but she became very confused and upset, insisting that it was Davey who was coming. Anne had to give her a sedative. Such a pity, Meredith, when she has seemed so much calmer of late.'

'And Rowan?' he demanded.

'He is still with the wool dealer from Bradford; I thought he would have returned by this time,' Jessie answered deprecatingly.

Meredith looked displeased; he presented the servants to me with the air of a grand seigneur; the girls from the kitchen, the cook, the housemaids, the parlourmaid, an indoor manservant, the grooms and stable-hands; some of them were English, some of them Welsh, and they all eyed me with great curiosity.

As soon as it was all over, Grandfather said briskly:

'Dinner will be served in one hour, Sara. You will be punctual. I do not like to be kept waiting.'

He sounded remote and formal. His quick change of mood startled me, but I thought that perhaps he was tired.

Jessie took me upstairs. Aunt Anne had already left the hall, melting into the shadows as though she had never been there. It was a big hall, containing some remarkably fine pieces of furniture, and with many oil paintings on the oak-panelled walls. The rugs were old, their colours muted. An Oriental gong stood on a huge oak chest, and there were twin silver lamps, exquisitely chased, at the foot of the shallow, curving staircase.

One of the maids followed us, with a groom bringing our luggage. Upstairs, in the wide hall, Jessie opened a door, and the luggage was placed in a room. When the servants had gone, she led me into the room.

'You have the room next to Davey's old

one,' she said. 'I thought you would like that. The dressing-room has been prepared for your maid.'

There were lamps, books, an arm-chair, a day-bed, thick sheepskin rugs on the floor, and an elegant writing desk in the window. But it was the bed that fascinated me; I had never slept in a four-poster.

A fire burned in the grate, and Jessie said: 'This is a cold house, even in summer.'

Lily did not speak until Jessie left us, reminding me not to be late for dinner as Meredith could not endure to be kept waiting.

'I wish you joy of *this* place, Miss Sara!' Lily said pityingly.

'Oh, Lily, I am sure I shall be happy here!' I told her, but I knew that my voice lacked conviction.

'It wouldn't do for *me;* quiet as the grave. As for Miss Anne, I'd watch out for that one! There's a mouthful of sour apples for you. Not like your father; he was the kindest, pleasantest-spoken man I ever met.'

Lily helped me out of my travelling clothes and poured warm water for me; she found me a dress in soft pearl-grey, trimmed with bands of lavender; she brushed my hair, all the time muttering her misgivings about the Pryce family.

Round my neck I clasped the string of pearls my grandfather had sent me; on an

41

impulse, I slid my mother's amethyst and diamond ring over the third finger of my right hand. I thought it looked very well, the deep purple stone matching the trimmings on my dress; but the ring felt cold and heavy, the diamonds flashing icy fire. I felt as though I had no right to wear the ring.

I was ready to go downstairs when the door of my room was thrust open; the woman who stood in the doorway eyed me with fear and suspicion.

'Who are you?' she demanded.

'I am Sara,' I stammered.

She was a small woman, so thin that the pale dry flesh seemed a scarcely adequate cover for her brittle-looking bones. Her cheeks were prominent, like Anne's, with hollows beneath them, but her eyes were pale and expressionless. The untidy braids of grey hair had slipped their anchoring pins and hung forlornly about her shoulders. She wore an elaborate, crumpled wrapper, in the fashion of ten years ago, and had the appearance of a woman who had awakened reluctantly from sleep.

'What are you doing here?' she demanded. '*I* have never seen you before.'

'I have come to live here,' I explained, 'because my mother is dead. My father lived here once; he was David Pryce.'

'*Davey?*' she whispered incredulously. 'My Davey? So he *is* coming home! They lied to me, you know, and said he was dead, but I know he is alive! He would never have gone away, except for *her!* She was a whore, quiet and sly about it all, enticing him into her bed; with her white skin and her gold hair, and her fine lady airs as if she was too good to be a housekeeper!'

'Mother!' Anne was behind her suddenly, her hand laid firmly on the old lady's arm. 'You should be in your room; come. Megan has brought your supper tray.'

Without a glance at me, she led the old lady away, closing the door behind her. My cheeks were hot; I felt sick and appalled at what Rachel had said.

Lily avoided my eyes; I went downstairs to find my grandfather waiting in the hall.

'You look very well, Sara!' he said approvingly.

'I have just met my grandmother!' I replied shortly, and I repeated to him what she had said.

His face was like stone.

'You must pay no attention to her, Sara. She never forgave your mother for taking Davey away; she idolised him to the point of possessiveness.'

'Then perhaps he was glad to escape!' I said wryly.

'No doubt he was,' my grandfather agreed quietly. 'Think no more about the whole business. I explained to you that Rachel's mind was disturbed. She spends most of her time in her own rooms.'

He took my arm and led me into dinner.

The magnificence of the dining room at Tremannion was a great surprise to me. Heavy curtains of red velvet were pulled across the windows to shut out the rainy dusk. A maid waited to serve us from an array of silver dishes on the vast mahogany sideboard. The table was laid with white damask, set with beautiful silver and sparkling crystal; in the centre of the table, ornate silver candelabra supported tall red candles.

There was a splendidly carved chair at the head of the table; the chair on its right was vacant; behind two other chairs, Jessie and Anne waited for the master of the house to take his place and gave them the signal to be seated. Jessie looked nervous, her eyes continually checking the table appointments; Anne stared straight ahead, her face expressionless.

It all seemed terribly formal after the cosy intimacy of supper in Kensington with Mama. Rowan's chair, I guessed, was the one at the far end of the table. Grandfather glanced briefly at it before he gave us the signal to be seated.

'Rowan is the devil of a time with the wool buyer!' he said impatiently to Jessie.

'He returned a few moments ago,' Jessie

replied soothingly. 'He'll join us as soon as he has changed, Meredith.'

We were halfway through the second course when Rowan arrived; he was not much taller than me, dark and compactly built, with an air of being much more at home outdoors than in this lavishly appointed dining-room. He had hazel eyes, a tanned skin, and a shock of unruly dark hair.

'Sara,' said Meredith, 'this is Rowan, your Great-aunt Jessie's son and your father's cousin.'

Rowan's smile for me was tired and had a hint of strain.

'Hello, Cousin Sara,' was all he said.

I saw Anne look at us both with sly malice before she returned to the closed circle of her own thoughts.

'Well?' said Grandfather sharply to Rowan. 'How did it go?'

'Sprake and I finally agreed on the figure; he argued, mind, said the price was too fierce. Dug my heels in, I did; well then, I said come to the auction and bid with the rest, but no, he wanted the contract. So he will pay the price, and I told him you would be down to sign in the morning.'

'He will be getting value; mine is the best wool in Wales,' my grandfather retorted. He turned to me, pride in his voice.

'Tremannion sheep are the finest on any

mountain, north or south, east or west. The best wool, the best meat. Tomorrow, when I have come back from signing the contract at the Brennion Arms, I will show you.'

'It is coarse wool, Sara,' Anne said. 'Fit only for carpets and rugs, thick quilts and blankets. Not like Shetland wool that is so fine and soft you can pull a shawl made from it through a wedding ring.'

'My sheep provide you with soft living!' my grandfather replied. 'As to a wedding ring, what has that to do with you? You are scarcely likely to see one on *your* finger!'

I thought it was a cruel taunt, but she *had* provoked him, I reminded myself. She bent her head; I saw the way her knuckles shone as they gripped her knife and fork.

Grandfather turned his attention to Rowan and they discussed the contract, the quality and number of the fleeces which, I gathered, were to come from a specially bred flock. Jessie made light, pleasant conversation with me, about London and the Diamond Jubilee celebrations; she did not mention my mother.

As soon as the meal was over, Anne left us; my grandfather looked at me from under his heavy brows.

'You look tired, Sara; go to bed. Tomorrow night you shall play for me. No one has played the piano in this house since your mother left.'

I hesitated.

'Might it not distress Grandmother, if she hears me play?'

'*I* am master in this house, Sara,' he said, his face cold and forbidding. 'Do not forget that, and do not concern yourself with things that happened a long time ago, before you were born.'

He bade me good night and walked away.

When I reached my room, I found Lily unpacking my trunks, bemoaning the fact that most of my gowns were crushed and would need to be pressed. I asked her how she had enjoyed her supper with the staff.

'Oh, well enough,' she conceded grudgingly. 'Some of them chatter away in Welsh and a strange language it is, to be sure. The cook does very well, but they're a close lot. Not a word out of them about the folk upstairs!'

I smiled, thinking how disappointed she must have been; she left her unpacking, helped me to undress, and went to her own room, saying she was bone-tired. As for me, I no longer felt sleepy; the day's events had been so strange that my brain would not be still. I decided to go through Mama's lap desk, a task I had not found time to perform since her death. I thought I might discover there the answer to some of the questions that buzzed in my mind.

I put the lamp on a table and set about my

task. The beautifully polished little desk bore her initials; underneath the slope was a tray containing her pens, a few bills, a small birthday remembrance book, and a photograph of my father, young and dark and solemn, against a background of hills. There was a picture of my mother as a girl, looking so carefree that tears came to my eyes. I found also a painted miniature of me as a baby and a love poem, written in a strange hand, addressed to my mother and signed 'David.' It was a delicate, passionate poem and I felt like a trespasser. Beneath it was a large, unsealed envelope that crackled stiffly when I picked it up.

The enveloped contained my mother's birth certificate; her marriage lines: 'Celia Grace Heriot to David Owen Pryce.' There was also my birth certificate: 'Sara Caroline Pryce, born October the Thirty-first, Eighteen Hundred and Seventy Nine.'

I had never known the exact date of my mother's marriage – until this moment; checking the certificates, I realised that she had been married to David only six months before I was born.

I compared the dates again, hoping to discover that the error was mine, but it was not. I felt a burning sense of shame and dismay, understanding the reason for the hurried elopement.

Everyone in his house must have known

the truth, I thought bitterly.

I thrust the certificates back into their envelope, and felt resistance to the paper as I tried to push it under the pen tray. I put my hand into the recess and found something small and hard jammed there; I worked it free and when it lay on the palm of my hand I saw that it was a small gold seal, with the shape of a rose cut in its base.

I took the sealed envelope from my mother's jewel box and looked closely at the seals in the wax; the impressions had obviously been made by the seal I held.

I was tempted to break the seals, to read the letter, for then it might answer my questions; but my mother's firm handwriting made disobedience impossible. I could not do it. I loved and trusted her – I had done so all my life; the tell-tale dates on the certificates made no difference to that fact.

I slept soundly, after all; the bed was comfortable. I did not draw the curtains around it, and when I awoke I saw the pale morning sky coming alive with faint colour in the east. Gone was the mist and the rain; the great, bare Beacons lay like lazy giants, tawny shoulders towards the heavens.

I looked at the Beacons for several minutes; they dominated the whole landscape, looking as though they had been shaped by a great hand, smoothed and patted into place, a curve sliced away here, the rounding of a headland there, long fingers scoring the turf to make the deeply indented gullies with which the Beacons were seamed.

I threw off my nightclothes and dressed myself in a warm skirt and blouse, thick stockings, and stout shoes. Lily was a sound sleeper and the communicating door between our rooms was closed. I tiptoed out, along the corridor, and down the stairs. As I reached the bottom, a clock dropped five sonorous notes into the silence. The vibration shivered all through me; the house was utterly still, not even the servants were astir. I looked at the great door and wondered how I was going to draw the bolts.

However, I managed it, though they were stiff, and I had to stand on tiptoe to reach the topmost one; it took all my strength to ease back the great door and then close it as quietly as I could behind me. I would be back before the servants were up, I reasoned. I had an hour; I wanted to taste the morning, keeping a secret rendezvous with hilltop and cloud and breeze. I could go to the east, west, south, or north; I chose the northwest path that ran beside the house and climbed into the Beacons.

Halfway up the path, I turned back to look at the house. It stared at me, dark and brooding, silent but never asleep; I felt its eyes on me, until the path veered away behind a hump of rock and turf, so that I could no longer see its forbidding outline.

I had never before been out alone in the early morning; a great sense of freedom possessed me. I found a dry stone wall, crumbling in places, and growing beside it, the pink, bell-like flowers that I knew were foxgloves from the illustrations in my botany book. They were pretty flowers, like bevies of crinoline-skirted ladies who had all fallen backwards in a heap. I gathered an armful of them for my room.

I stepped through a gap in the wall; beyond it was what seemed to be the remains of a sheep-pen, with a rusty, broken gate leading to a curious-looking ditch, lined with smooth stones and only a few feet deep; the ditch ended in a small slab of stone overhanging a still, blue pool. I dipped my fingers in the water and it was icy; I knelt and looked down. The water was quite deep but so clear I could see the stones at the bottom.

There was no one about when I pulled off my shoes and stockings. I stood on the stone slab, feeling like God, looking at the world spread below me, a green and brown quilt of Welsh tapestry, trees, farms, villages, reaching to the farthest horizon, beyond which the Severn divided me from England

and the yesterday to which I could never return; but I did not want to think about that.

I held my skirts in my hands and began to dance an Irish jig that one of my mother's maids had taught me. My hair tumbled about my shoulders, the air tasted fresh and sweet; when I stopped dancing for want of breath, I heard the sound of clapping.

Thaddeus Flynn stood by a cluster of trees in a small wooded dell just below me; he was wearing a shirt open at the neck, tweeds, and glossy leather boots; as he sauntered towards me, I saw how the early morning sun made an autumn splendour of his thick, reddish-brown hair.

I stood there feeling very foolish as he smiled up at me, showing strong white teeth. It was an appraising smile, as his long, slow glance raked me over from my head to my feet.

Had his hair or his eyes been a shade darker, I thought suddenly, he would have looked like a gypsy or a buccaneer.

'Does Meredith Pryce know that his granddaughter dances barefoot above the old sheep-dip?' he mocked.

I tossed my head, and answered him sharply.

'Turn your back whilst I put on my shoes and stockings, Mr Flynn!'

'Why should I?' he demanded with lazy

impudence. 'You have a pretty ankle. A very fine pair of legs, too. If you don't wish such details to be noticed, then you shouldn't lift your skirts so high when you dance!'

I blushed furiously, outraged by his cool mockery.

'You were spying on me!' I cried furiously.

'I could scarcely miss seeing you!' he retorted, laughter in his voice.

I saw how strongly the muscles rippled beneath his shirt; he shrugged lazily, as I stood there, glaring at him.

'No wonder my grandfather doesn't wish me to know you!' I told him, trying to sound aloof and dignified.

His face was suddenly scornful.

'Meredith Pryce is a man who under-stands only two things: how to breed sheep and how to possess people. Each in his own tongue, so the saying goes; I find HIS tongue very unmusical in my ears! I pity YOU – for you are now his possession. Per-haps you are also the instrument of his revenge!'

'Revenge? On whom?' I demanded, startled.

'You must ask him to tell you!' The voice was cold. 'Poor little Sara Pryce! Never again will you be free to come and dance up here in the early morning, and feel as though you hold the whole of Wales in your hand!'

'What nonsense!' I retorted, amused.

'Remember this is not London, tucked warm and cosy as a quilt around you!' he said softly. 'This is wild country and if it breeds fine sheep, it also breeds strange people!'

'I shall be very happy at Tremannion!' I insisted.

'Until you see how deep the shadows are, how dark its secrets!' he retorted.

I tossed my head; he was trying to frighten me, I thought. Nevertheless, my hands were trembling as I picked up my shoes and stockings and the flowers I had picked.

The turf felt cool and springy under my bare feet, as I jumped down from the stone slab. Thaddeus Flynn looked at my flowers and said, with a smile:

'Foxgloves grow everywhere in this part of Wales; especially in the cemetery – *there*, they seem to grow best of all.'

Without another word, he turned and walked away from me, with long, purposeful strides; not once did he look back.

Slowly I put on my shoes and stockings; as I set out for Tremannion, I thought about his strange words.

Coming near to the house, I saw that the front door was open; Cousin Rowan stood outside, lighting his pipe.

I looked at the brown, blunt-fingered hands, the shock of hair that would never be tamed; his eyes met mine thoughtfully.

'Good morning, Cousin Sara; you are up early,' he said formally.

'It was such a lovely morning that I wanted to be out of doors,' I explained. 'I found a sheep-pen and a little ditch, lined with stones, that led to a pool. The water was icy cold when I put my hand into it.'

'You have been to the old sheep-dip,' he replied. 'That water is always cold because the mountain springs feed it. Once, the sheep were put into the pen, then the gate was opened and they were driven along the gully that you call a ditch, so that they could not escape; when they reached the stone slab, they were thrown into the pool.'

'How cruel!' I protested.

He looked amused at my ignorance.

'Cruel? The sheep came to no harm, silly! They swam across the pool to the far side, where it is shallow, and then trotted away, bleating and making a great fuss about nothing!'

'Why throw them into the pool?' I asked, still baffled.

'To wash them,' he explained. 'The buyers who come to the Wool Auction will not pay good money for dirty fleeces, full of grease and sweat. So the sheep are all washed before their fleeces are shorn. That is the old dip, where you went this morning; no one uses it since a woman was drowned there.

Your grandfather has a much bigger pool, a mile to the east. If you had come last week, you could have seen the dipping there!'

'Who was the woman drowned in the old pool?' I asked curiously.

'Nancy Flynn, Thaddeus Flynn's mother,' he replied, nodding towards the path along which I had come.

'You have no need to learn sheep-farming, Cousin,' he added shortly. 'One thing, though, you need to learn, soon; Meredith Pryce will be very angry if he knows you have been with Thad.'

'I didn't go out to meet him!' I replied, colouring with embarrassment. 'I met him, by accident, near the dip!'

'*I* shall not say what I know,' Rowan replied softly. 'I mind my own business, Cousin! But take care! Always take care what you do!'

I ran past him into the house and up the stairs, my heart beating loudly. In my haste and anxiety I passed the room that was mine, and unthinkingly opened the door of the one next to it.

As soon as I stepped inside, I realised that this was my father's old room; curiously I looked around me.

The room was as comfortable as my own. There was the same kind of tapestry quilt, although the bed was a narrower one; not a four-poster. There were ebony-backed brushes on a chest of drawers, a leather-framed mirror on the wall above it. There was a deep arm-chair near some shelves of books and a big desk.

Clean towels had been placed beside the jug and basin on the marble-topped wash-stand; to my amazement, I saw a curl of steam rising from the jug. I dipped my fingers in and found that the jug was full of hot water.

I looked at the fresh flowers placed in a vase on the desk; there were matches beside the oil lamp, and near it, a photograph of a group of schoolboys, framed in silver.

I opened a book that stood on a table beside the bed; a name was written on the fly-leaf in flowing script: 'David Owen Pryce.'

This place was uncannily alive, I thought; it was like a room whose occupant has just left.

Blindly I turned towards the door, but I was too late. The door was just closing, and I heard the sound of a key being turned in the lock.

Chapter Three

I dropped my flowers, ran across the room and rattled the door-knob, shouting loudly; I put my ear to the door, but I heard no sound outside, and realised that the thickly carpeted corridor would muffle the sound of departing footsteps.

The walls of this room, like the door, were strong and thick; one could remain a prisoner for a long time, I reflected, as I took off my shoe and beat upon the wall that divided my room from this one.

There was no reply to my frantic knocking; I glanced at the small clock ticking on the mantel shelf and saw that it was ten minutes past six; Lily arose punctually at half-past six, so I would not long be imprisoned here, I reasoned; nevertheless, I fought down panic with the greatest difficulty. All my life I had feared being shut in a room alone, with no means of escape; my mother had once told me that she possessed exactly the same fear, and had once been accidentally locked in a room at Tremannion, to her horror; she had been distraught when she was finally released.

Whoever had closed this door and locked

it had seen me standing in my father's room; had someone who had known and hated my mother played such a cruel trick?

The minutes ticked away with painful slowness. Determinedly, I focused my attention on a shelf of schoolbooks near the window. All of them had my father's name written on the fly-leaf; as I picked up one of the books, a sheet of paper fluttered to the floor.

I picked it up and read the words written in neat copperplate; it was the beginning of an essay entitled: 'The House Where I Live.'

It is a big house, high up on the Beacons. It has a lot of rooms and so there is plenty of space to play, but I do not like it much and I shall not be a sheep-farmer, like my father, when I grow up. I shall live in a little house, in a town, not here where it is very lonely...

'What on earth are you doing here?' Anne asked coldly, from the doorway.

I spun around guiltily, the sheet of paper fluttering from my fingers; I had been too engrossed to hear her unlock the door. She stood there, looking at me as though I was a trespasser.

'I have no wish to be here,' I retorted, with as much dignity as I could muster. 'I mistook this room for mine and was standing here when someone locked the

59

door behind me.'

She looked scornful and disbelieving.

'Who would do that?' she said.

'Someone with a strange sense of humour!' I retorted, my voice trembling.

Angrily I stepped past her, thankful to escape from a room that was so haunted.

'You have forgotten something,' she said.

She bent and gathered up the foxgloves, handing them to me with a cold little smile.

'So you have been out?' she added, with raised eyebrows.

'Yes,' I replied. 'Tell me, Aunt Anne, who uses this room?'

'No one, Sara.'

'Yet, there are fresh flowers here; a clock that keeps time; the water in the jug is so hot that it must have been placed there only minutes before I entered the room.'

'Megan brings hot water each morning,' Anne said precisely. 'She is my mother's maid; the water is placed here, and the flowers kept fresh, at my mother's request.'

'Perhaps Megan locked me in here!' I retorted.

'I hardly think so; she is a good servant and not given to practical jokes!' Anne said, with a rather malicious smile.

'Why does Grandmother keep this room as though it still has an occupant?' I asked.

'Because she refuses to believe that David, her only son, is dead; she says that he will one day return and must find his room ready for him. If these beliefs bring her comfort, why should I destroy them?'

She did not wait for an answer – if, indeed, I could have found one. Trembling I went into my own room and found that Lily was awake; she came through the communicating door from the dressing-room where she slept, looking in consternation at my white face.

Because I needed to talk to someone I could trust, I told her the story of my morning's escapade; she shook her head, lips pursed.

'It's my opinion Miss Anne Pryce locked you in there,' she said angrily, when I had finished. 'Didn't I tell you to watch out for her? And you've no business to go wandering off out of the house at such an hour! It's no way for a young lady to behave, and well you know it, Miss Sara! You don't know what might happen to you,' she hinted darkly, 'especially with people like Mr Flynn hanging around, up to no good! What were you thinking of to let him see you dancing up there in your bare feet!'

'I didn't KNOW he was there!' I cried, exasperated. 'He is no gentleman, Lily!'

'That he is not, my lamb,' she murmured consolingly. 'I wouldn't trust him no further than I could see him!'

She poured hot water for me, found a

clean blouse, and pinned the little Welsh harp brooch to it; I was feeling much better by the time I went down to breakfast.

When I entered the dining-room Anne was lifting the cover from one of the dishes on the sideboard; her eyes flicked over me briefly and without much interest.

Rowan was standing with his back to the window, looking ill at ease as he always did inside the house.

'Good morning, Cousin Sara,' he said briefly.

Jessie finished checking the table before she wished me good day; she never trusted the maids where the table appointments were concerned, although she had trained the girls herself.

'Did you sleep well, Sara?' she asked.

'Yes, thank you, Aunt Jessie. I have never before slept in a four-poster bed, but I found it very comfortable.'

'Did you draw the curtains around you?' she asked, smiling.

I shook my head; pride would not let me admit my fear of being shut in, even by the draperies around a bed.

'I have slept in that bed,' she told me. 'On winter nights I enjoyed pulling the curtains around me, so that I felt as though I was shut up safely in my own world. I liked to lie there and listen to the storms. We do have very bad weather here in the winter-time;

when the wind blows up here, it seems as though it is trying to tear this house apart.'

'What a pity it doesn't succeed!' said Anne, to no one in particular.

Rowan ignored her remark and said to me: 'Winter is hard for the sheep; it is bad when the lambs are born too soon and are weakly. If we have not had time to get the sheep down to the pens, then we must go out and look for them.'

At that moment, Meredith came into the room, filling it with his tremendous vitality; he came to me, took my chin between his thumb and forefinger, and looked at me searchingly.

'Well, Sara? You have had a good rest, I see. Your eyes are bright and you do not look tired, as you did yesterday.'

His smile grew wider, as he glanced down at the brooch pinned at my throat.

We took our places behind our chairs; Meredith went to the head of the table and signalled for us to be seated. He did not say grace, nor did we have prayers. I felt a sharp stab of homesickness, remembering my mother's soft voice, reading from the big black Bible, and asking for a blessing on our food.

The fresh air had made me hungry; Anne toyed disinterestedly with her food, for all the fact that she had shown an interest in breakfast before her father's appearance.

He asked her, suddenly, if she intended going out during the morning.

'Yes,' she said defensively. 'I am going down to the village.'

'Roberts is driving me to the Brennion Arms at nine-thirty,' he said formally. 'There is room for you in the carriage.'

To my surprise she looked flustered, and avoided his eyes.

'I prefer to walk. It will be pleasant to be out of this house, enjoying the fresh air and exercise.'

He looked at her from beneath his heavy black brows, his smile sardonic.

'Surely if you have an errand in the village, it could be undertaken by one of the servants?' he suggested.

'Dr Evans has left me a prescription for Mama,' she replied unwillingly.

'Ah! So you need to visit to apothecary!' he retorted, vastly amused.

She gave him a furious look, her cheeks pink; I saw her hand tremble as she lifted her cup to her lips.

Jessie, ever a peacemaker, fluttered nervously into the breach, asking Meredith if he would be returning in time for lunch.

'Certainly,' he said crisply. 'I do not imagine that Sprake will dally over the signing of the contract. I have some other small matters to attend to, before my return. Serve lunch at the same time as usual.'

'Shall I show Sara over the house this morning?' Jessie asked eagerly.

'By all means.' He turned to me and smiled. 'This afternoon, you and I will go out together, Sara. This evening, we are having guests to dinner: Adam Brennion and his cousin, Catherine Grey, who keeps house for him.'

He looked at his sister-in-law and added:

'I expect Rachel to be present, as we are having guests.'

Anne looked up sharply, her face distressed.

'Mama is not well enough!'

'Nonsense! The specialist that Evans brought from London declared that it was not good for Rachel to sit alone in her room so much; he insisted that it would be of the greatest benefit to her to take a more active part in the household affairs. You know this very well, yet you encourage her to remain apart from us and evade her duties.'

Anne stood up and thrust back her chair.

'I will not be responsible–' she began.

'I have not asked you to be; Adam and Catherine understand the position very well,' Meredith replied.

Jessie was an excellent guide; she asked me if I had seen the emblem out on the stone-work over the front door. I had to admit that I had not noticed it, my attention having been centred on the occupants of the house rather than its adornments.

'It is a carving of a ram and a ewe,' Jessie explained. 'The tale concerning it goes back to the time of your Great-grandfather. A poor house this was in those days, with no money to keep it as it should have been kept, trouble amongst the tenants, and a strange sickness killing off the sheep. Then, it is said, the Devil rode this way and made a bargain with your great-grandfather. Give me the prettiest maid in the county of Brecon, he said, and I will give you a ram and a ewe like you have never seen. The ram will sire a flock that will make your fortune and put an end to all your troubles. A fine choice *that* was for a man who was be-trothed to the prettiest girl in the county!'

'What happened?' I asked, fascinated.

'They say the Devil was seen riding away on a black horse that night, with a young maiden riding behind him. Some said she went willingly, preferring the Devil himself to your great-grandfather. Next morning, a strange-looking ram and a ewe were seen grazing outside the house, and the emblem was seen over the front door, freshly cut, though no one knew who had carved it there. The girl who was to have wed your great-grandfather was never seen again; years later, when his sheep had made him a rich man, he married a widow who was said to be the ugliest woman in Swansea, and she bore him two sons!'

The story sent small shivers along my spine, as I remembered the four black horses that had pulled the coach up the steep hill to Tremannion.

As Jessie conducted me through the many rooms in the house, I realised that my grandfather was a man of culture and good taste. The library was full of books, many of them with rich bindings and obviously valuable; there were ornaments of silver and porcelain, oil paintings in heavy gilt frames. The drawing-room was large and gracious, with a grand piano placed at one end of it; from it led a smaller drawing-room, and then a morning-room. Eventually, we reached a large room in the east tower which was my grandfather's study.

I walked across to the window; from there, I looked down the valley to the roofs half-hidden by the trees and a silver loop of water girdling the green countryside.

'Your grandfather has his suite of rooms entirely in this tower,' Jessie explained. 'His bedroom and dressing-room are above this one. Your grandmother's rooms are in the west tower.'

'So the whole house separates them?' I murmured, turning from my contemplation of the peaceful scene below me.

Jessie waited for me by the door; as I

passed the massive desk near the window, I looked down at the heavy silver inkstands, the leather blotter, and an ebony tray containing an assortment of pens and pencils, sealing wax and a small gold seal.

I picked up the seal and looked at it; there was a rose cut into the base, making it the exact replica of the one in my mother's desk.

Jessie was eyeing me curiously. I put down the seal and followed her from the study.

We looked in at the kitchens and the servants' hall; upstairs, there were many fine bedrooms, though none of them had a four-poster like the one in my room. Jessie's rooms were comfortably furnished and contained some fine china and pretty ornaments.

Rowan's rooms were austere by comparison with the others.

'My son does not care for what he calls a muddle of bits and pieces,' Jessie told me. 'Well, he spends little enough time here, after all. Mostly he is out of doors, where he likes best to be. There's enough to do; he is answerable to Meredith for everything connected with the breeding and selling of the sheep. Rowan was but a babe and David a schoolboy when we came here. The two of them grew up together, but it was Rowan, not David, who wanted to breed sheep. A great disappointment it was, indeed, to

Meredith; but he has treated Rowan handsomely, I will say that for him.'

When we reached the door of Rachel's room, Jessie bit her lip and gave me a troubled look; guessing the reason, I told her that I had met my grandmother the previous evening and that she had behaved very strangely.

Jessie looked relieved.

'Then you will know what to expect; although there are days when poor Rachel appears to be almost normal.'

When we entered Rachel was sitting on the broad window-seat, her hands folded in her lap; her hair was neatly dressed, her face composed. Only her eyes were expressionless.

Jessie introduced us, and Rachel repeated my name, a flicker of interest in her eyes.

'Sara. So *you* are Celia's child? For all that, you look more like a Pryce. Dark as a gypsy. The first Pryce to live here was a gypsy who seduced a rich man's daughter; history repeats itself, sometimes, does it not, Jessie?'

Aunt Jessie made a non-committal reply; Rachel went on looking intently at me.

'I did not like your mother,' Rachel told me calmly. 'She was too quiet, too soft, altogether. In the end, I hated her. Davey was all I had, and she took Davey away from me.'

She waved aside her sister-in-law's embarrassed protests. I said boldly:

'My father was not compelled to go away with my mother; he went because he wished to do so.'

'She was expecting his child.'

Jessie darted Rachel a quick, horrified look and then glanced uncomfortably at me.

'I know that she was expecting his child, Grandmother,' I replied. 'But they loved one another very much and would have wed, in any case.'

'He will not end his days with *her*,' Rachel retorted, staring unseeingly over my head. 'He will come back to Tremannion.'

Hastily Jessie plucked at my sleeve and motioned me from the room. She asked me if I would like to see my mother's old room, and I nodded, unable to speak.

Our route led us past the old nurseries; I looked at a painted wooden rocking-horse, trying to imagine my father and Rowan riding on the broad wooden back. There was a doll's house that must have belonged to Anne, a mahogany high-chair, a scarred desk with several sets of initials scored on its surface. Beyond it was the night nursery, with a carved crib on rockers and a nursing chair; but I could not imagine Anne and David and Rowan inhabiting these rooms as carefree children.

My mother's old room was as impersonal as all rooms that are unused; it was quite big and overlooked the path I had taken to the old dip; I thought suddenly of Thaddeus Flynn, whose mother had been drowned in its icy waters.

'You have seen it all, now,' Jessie said. 'Except for the servants' bedrooms and your Aunt Anne's room, which are below your grandmother's. She does not like anyone except Megan to go into her rooms. You must not pay any attention to the things your grandmother says; nor to Anne.'

'Why does Aunt Anne dislike me so much?' I asked.

'Perhaps because your grandfather makes much of you,' Jessie pointed out gently. 'And, even as a child, Anne did not please him. She was always stubborn and wilful. She is clever, also, and a clever woman is a thorn in a man's side, for it is men who manage the affairs of the world and women must submit to them, not question their wisdom.'

'Was my father a clever man?'

'Not in the way that Anne is clever; she is quick and her brain is sharp. Your father was kind and even-tempered, which is a more comfortable thing to be,' Jessie answered dryly.

'Why does not Aunt Anne go away, if she is so unhappy?'

'Where would she go, child?' Jessie demanded, bewildered. 'And who would care

71

for Rachel? She finds Anne a great comfort.'

After we had toured the house, I was left to my own devices until lunch-time. There were only three of us for lunch: Meredith, Jessie and myself.

Grandfather was in high spirits, for his business in the village had been satisfactorily dealt with, and he was pleased with the contract that Mr Sprake had signed.

'Do you ride, Sara?' he asked briskly, after lunch.

'Yes. I often rode in Hyde Park. I was well taught. Did you not know, Grandfather? After all, you paid for my lessons.'

'How do you know that?'

'Once, when you came to the house, I heard you demand to see me. You told Mama that your money paid for *everything*. I was hiding; I wanted to see you.'

He smiled slowly, and once again I felt the warm, out-reaching love that had enclosed me the previous night when we had arrived at Tremannion.

I changed into my riding habit, and we went to the stables; the mount chosen for me was a pretty chestnut mare named Sheba; my grandfather mounted a spirited-looking horse named Solomon, and I was reminded of the legend about Tremannion; as we rode from the stable-yard, I remarked that Aunt Jessie had told me the tale, and he said it had always been a favourite of his.

We rode to the top of a slope that rose behind the house; above us the sky was clear blue and the sun lay warmly upon us. A breeze whispered amongst the grasses and I heard the lazy murmur of water from some nearby rocks. From this high point, I could see not only the village, but the little white-washed chapel with the graveyard beside it, and pink splashes of foxgloves amongst the tombstones. To the right and left of us, the countryside rose and fell like great seas that had been stilled in motion. In the distance, beyond a crumbling stone wall, I saw a house; it was not so big as Tremannion, but it was comfortably tucked against a shoulder of green countryside.

'That is Brennion,' Meredith told me, pointing with his riding-crop. 'You will like Adam Brennion, Sara. He is a fine young man and will make a splendid husband, when he marries.'

I glanced swiftly at him, wondering what was in his mind, but he was pointing his crop towards a great flock of sheep, far below us. They looked like little white clouds running before the wind on a blustery day. There was a man on horseback with them, and I realised it was Rowan; two dogs were with him, and the sound of their barking rose on the still air, blending with the plaintive bleating of the sheep. The dogs worked the sheep expertly, running fast and low to the ground, racing back and forth, rounding up stragglers, keeping the flock together with no more guidance than an occasional whistle from Rowan.

'These are my sheep,' Meredith said proudly. 'You see but a small part of them down there. I count my flocks in thousands.'

The words of Thaddeus Flynn came back to me, whispered on the breeze.

'He understands only ... how to breed sheep and how to possess people.'

I dismissed them as the words of a ne'er-do-well, jealous of another man's success. We turned our backs on Brennion and made our way along the top of a ridge so high that we seemed to be poised between earth and Heaven. We cantered over the turf, past the outcrops of rock and stunted bushes until we came to the Tremannion sheep-dip. Beyond the wide, still pool were farms and cottages that belonged to Tremannion; but there was no time today, Meredith declared, to visit all his tenants.

As we turned homewards, I asked jestingly:

'Do you own the village, also?'

'Most of it,' he replied matter-of-factly.

At the Home Farm, the farmer and his family were presented to me, and we were offered refreshment, which Meredith declined, saying that we must be on our way. I enjoyed the importance of being stared at, with curiosity and deference, as the grand-daughter of the master of Tremannion; it was a delightful sensation, such as I had never known before.

There was a find herd of cattle at the Home Farm; also a dairy, poultry, and a large kitchen garden; from this place, I was told, came most of the food for the table at Tremannion.

The afternoon's outing ended on an unfortunate note. We made a detour on the way home, in order that I might have yet another view of the magnificent scenery. This detour brought us out on the road near the ruined cottage where we had narrowly escaped disaster on the previous evening; by the cottage, we saw Thaddeus Flynn, grazing his horse.

The sun gleamed on his long leather boots and tawny hair; his eyes were the colour of emeralds; he looked completely relaxed as his horse cropped the turf and did not seem at all put out when he saw us.

So we met for the second time that day, and his fine, careless bearing commanded my attention. My heart raced furiously as I recalled our previous encounter as, unwillingly, I felt myself forced to meet his laughing eyes.

'Good day to you both!' he said, with mocking courtesy.

Meredith stared straight ahead, as we rode by; his mouth was an angry line. Above us, in the blueness, a hawk hung motionless on a thread of air; the bird reminded me of the man by the cottage.

As we rode on, I glanced fleetingly over my shoulder; he was still watching us and lifted a hand in a salute that had an air of familiarity, an acknowledgement that we had shared an illicit adventure.

Guiltily I looked away; as for my companion, the straightness of his back and his silence were eloquent. He said nothing until we reached the stables.

'Sara,' he said softly, 'wear your most becoming gown tonight.'

Lily laid out my gown; it was a new one, bought just before my mother's death, and I felt sad as I looked at it. I was to have worn it to a ball given to mark the Queen's Diamond Jubilee celebrations.

'It is not a brightly coloured gown,' Lily pointed out. 'And your dear mama would wish you to look your best as there are guests tonight.'

The gown was of white lace over shell-pink taffeta; it was cut low on the shoulders, its edging of filmy white chiffon edged with tiny pink silk rosebuds. A little posy of rosebuds was sewn near the hem of the gown, as though it had fallen from a careless hand. My slippers matched the pink under-skirt and had tiny roses on them.

It had been a very costly outfit, but I remembered that Mama had been delighted with it, remarking on how well the white lace became my dark hair and eyes.

I was ready to go downstairs when I heard a tap at the door. Lily answered, and I saw that it was Megan, Rachel's maid, who stood there. She was a small, dark, wrinkled woman, whose age I could not guess.

Megan handed Lily a long leather case, saying that my grandfather had instructed her to hand it to me.

As soon as she had gone, I opened the case; on a velvet bed lay the most exquisite necklace I had ever seen, composed of tiny diamond and turquoise flowers linked on a fine gold chain. The note with it said simply: 'To Sara, from her grandfather.'

Lily clasped the necklace around my neck and stood back to admire the effect.

'I haven't never seen you look so beautiful, Miss Sara,' she said, awe in her voice.

'Mama always said that fine feathers made fine birds!' I reminded her; but the mirror confirmed that I did, indeed, look my best, and I felt happy and excited.

I met Aunt Anne on my way downstairs; she looked quite splendid in a rich, rustling gown of dark-red taffeta, with garnets at her throat and in her ears. She looked at me in silence for a moment, then said:

'You are the sacrificial lamb, Sara! How well you look the part!'

'I do not know what you mean!' I retorted.

'Then I shall not enlighten you,' she said, eyes dancing. 'You must find the answer for yourself – as you will, soon enough.'

Grandfather and Rowan were already in the drawing-room when I arrived; Meredith looked magnificent in evening clothes, but Rowan seemed uncomfortable, as though he was out of his element; he was very silent, though I was conscious of his eyes on me.

Jessie's plump little figure was encased in golden-brown satin; she kept glancing anxiously at Rachel, who sat stiffly on the edge of a chair, taking no notice of any of us. She wore grey chiffon, threaded with velvet ribbons, and her thin fingers toyed ceaselessly with the diamonds at her neck. When she and Grandfather spoke to one another, they were as formal as two strangers who were forced to be polite to one another.

Oh, the joy in Grandfather's face when he looked at me! The love in his eyes, the proud possessiveness in his smile! After all these years, I remember it as clearly as though it was yesterday.

I thought of how we had ridden together under the summer sun, and how happy I had been with him; all my fears and forebodings concerning Tremannion seemed suddenly absurd. For what was there to fear? Meredith was kindness itself to me and full of loving concern for my well-being. As for Aunt Anne, she was an embittered spinster, and Rachel, a pathetic creature, groping through the mists of yesterday. Rowan and Aunt Jessie were normal enough and kindly disposed towards me.

Adam Brennion and Catherine Grey were announced and my grandfather presented me to them.

'This is Sara,' he said with pride.

Adam Brennion was a pleasant, quietly spoken young man in his mid-twenties. He had a fair skin and fair hair; his eyes were a bright blue and altogether he was very English-looking.

'I am delighted to make your acquaintance, Miss Sara,' he said with formal courtesy and a look of approval in his eyes.

His cousin, Catherine, seemed to be a few years older; I glanced at her fingers and saw that she did not wear any rings. She was quietly dressed in a blue gown with a single string of pearls at her throat; she had a gentle face, dove-grey eyes, and soft brown hair simply dressed in a knot. She seemed colourless, as though she could easily merge with the background and not be noticed; but she reminded me of the cool sound of water splashing over stones.

She added her greetings to Adam's, her voice low and sweet; but I saw a brief flicker of curiosity and surprise in her eyes.

Meredith escorted his wife into dinner; the room was entirely lit with tall candles, and flowers and plants had been massed in the great fireplaces. There was a manservant to wait upon us, as well as a maid. I remarked to Rowan that his mother must have worked very hard to make the room and table so attractive.

'Yes,' he agreed, 'but, then, it is woman's work.'

'I saw you this afternoon,' I told him. 'You were busy with the dogs, rounding up the sheep; I was out riding with your uncle.'

'I would rather be out *there!*' he declared emphatically, with a derisive glance at the elegant table. 'Not in here, dressed up in these clothes!'

'Don't you care for parties?' I asked, surprised.

'No. Parties are a great waste of time. A lot of people in fancy clothes, very empty in their talk, eating and drinking and laughing at nothing. It is all very stupid.'

I looked at the hard brown hands, the wild hair above the tanned face. Wanted to tease him a little, I whispered:

'We met Mr Flynn on our way home this afternoon! Your uncle was most put out, and would not say "good afternoon" to him!'

He nodded solemnly, as though pleased that he had been proved right.

'What did I tell you this morning, Cousin? Did Mr Flynn smile at YOU, then? He has a sweet tooth for women; he keeps a mistress down in the village and another in Brecon. There is a man who knows how to enjoy himself, now!'

Hastily I turned my attention to Adam, who said to me:

'I do hope that you will let me show you something of our countryside, Miss Sara. It looks its best at this time of year. You must come and visit us at Brennion; it is an old house and has an interesting history.'

I nodded and smiled; I looked at Rachel, whose eyes seemed utterly empty. She spoke to no one and ate her food mechanically. Anne seemed restless, though there was colour in her cheeks, and her eyes were bright. I wondered why she had called me a sacrificial lamb; was it because I was dressed in white?

In the drawing-room, the ladies were a rather silent group, until the men joined us.

'Play the piano for us, Sara,' Grandfather commanded.

I was nervous at the thought of playing in front of so many people; however, I could scarcely refuse.

Rachel looked on in disbelief as Meredith unlocked the piano.

'No one plays it now!' she cried.

'A piano should be played,' Meredith retorted, unperturbed. 'It is in excellent condition; the tuner comes regularly from Brecon.'

'I would rather it was not played!' she insisted vehemently.

'Nonsense!' Meredith's voice was curt. He beckoned to me and I went most unwillingly. I did not want to play the piano if it was going to cause trouble between my grandparents.

However, Meredith moved the stool into position for me; his face and manner allowed no arguments. I saw that Adam and Cathy and Jessie wore bright, fixed smiles. Rowan was looking at Meredith with disgust and contempt in his face.

It was not a good beginning, and I stumbled unhappily over the first few bars, before I recovered my composure and began to play properly. I chose a light-hearted waltz, then a Chopin melody, sad and dreamy; finally, I played a ballad that had been a favourite of my mother's.

To my horror, Rachel rose to her feet, and, before anyone could stop her, she ran across to me; but, in the split second before she tried to bring the heavy lid crashing down on my hands, Meredith forestalled her, holding her wrists in an iron grip.

'Go to your room, Rachel,' he said coldly.

Rachel stared at him defiantly; with an angry glance at her father, as though she blamed him for what had happened, Anne led her mother from the room.

Jessie, looking worried, murmured something about heating milk for Rachel as Megan had gone off duty for the evening; she followed Anne from the room, as though glad to escape. Catherine stared at the toes of her shoes, and Adam asked me if I had enjoyed the Jubilee celebrations in London, while Meredith and Rowan discussed the coming sheep-shearing.

After a few moments, Meredith suggested that Rowan might like to take Catherine for a walk outside in the fresh air, as the night was warm; he added that he had a book of old prints he wished Adam to see and would fetch it from his study.

I knew that it had been a deliberate manoeuvre to leave me alone with Adam; I felt annoyed and embarrassed.

'I wish he had not asked me to play,' I said bitterly, as soon as Meredith had left the room.

'I am sure he did not realise how much it would upset your grandmother,' Adam said soothingly. 'Please do not upset yourself, Miss Sara. We all understand that Mrs Pryce is a little – unwell. I do not see why she should object; you played very prettily, I thought.'

I smiled, grateful for his kindness, but aware that there were too many things in the house that I should never understand.

'Tomorrow, I must visit cousins in Abergavenny,' he added, 'but I shall be free on the following day and should consider it an honour if you would come for a drive with me; with your grandfather's permission, of course.'

I knew that Meredith would give his consent readily; I smiled and said that it sounded delightful.

'I understand that Mr Flynn rents a cottage from you,' I added. 'I met him, when I was in Brecon, on my way here; Grandfather and I met him today when we were out riding.'

'Your grandfather disapproves of Thaddeus Flynn,' Adam said.

'Do tell me why,' I begged.

'There are many reasons. I do not think we should discuss it, Miss Sara,' he said with surprising firmness.

'Is that because Mr Flynn is your friend?'

'Yes. It makes things difficult. Your grandfather thinks it foolish of me to allow Thaddeus to rent the cottage.'

He changed the subject; I felt vexed and frustrated; as soon as Meredith returned, I jumped to my feet, saying that I was going to ask Lily for some cologne, because my head ached.

I was at the top of the stairs when I saw Anne. I darted back into the shelter of a doorway, not wanting to be seen, for I knew she would say something bitter and unkind to me.

However, she did not see me, but hurried away to a small staircase that led to a passage near the servants' quarters; but she was near enough for me to see how different she looked from the woman who had sat at dinner earlier that evening.

Her hair hung loosely about her shoulders; she had changed into a simple blouse and skirt and looked as carefree as a young girl.

Astonished, I stood in the doorway, wondering where she was going; I forgot that I had intended to ask Lily for cologne. After a few minutes, I went back to the drawing-room, still puzzled by the change in Anne.

I sat with Adam and Grandfather, looking at the book of prints; Jessie did not return, and it was some time before Catherine and Rowan reappeared. There was colour in her cheeks and she looked more alive, as though she had enjoyed her walk.

Adam and his cousin left the house soon afterwards; when they had gone, Meredith put his hands on my shoulders and said:

'You look beautiful, Sara; and you behaved most becomingly. Your mother would have been proud of you; Adam has asked my permission to take you for a drive and, afterwards, to have tea at Brennion with Catherine and himself.'

'Are you pleased?' I asked.

'Of course,' he said. 'Adam will look after you very well; he is a splendid young man, and I hope that you will both be great friends. He has taken a great fancy to you, Sara.'

'But we have only just met!' I said, my cheeks pink.

He laughed softly, as though he was pleased.

'What of that? I tell you, Sara, you are a beauty; and you play the piano most prettily.'

'Grandmother–' I faltered unhappily.

His face looked so dark and forbidding suddenly that I dared say no more; he bade me good night, and I went slowly upstairs.

When I opened the door of my room, the lamp was burning on the table by my bed; the jewel box that had been my mother's lay open on the dressing-table where I had left it. The door between my room and Lily's was wide open but Lily was not there.

She lay on her back on the floor of my room, her head against the heavy brass fender; her eyes were wide open and staring at the ceiling.

'Lily!' I cried in horror; I knelt beside her and put a hand beneath her head to try and raise her, but I could not. My fingers felt suddenly wet; I drew my hand back so sharply that it brushed against the skirt of my gown.

Horrified, I saw the bright red stain of blood against the bridal-white lace. I looked down at the still figure on the floor and realised that Lily was dead.

Chapter Four

I closed my eyes to shut out the sight of the small, crumpled figure; I felt sick and faint with horror, and it seemed as though dark, unhappy forces swirled around me as I knelt there.

There was no sound save the rhythmic voice of the clock that seemed to keep time with the heavy drumming of my heart. I forced myself to open my eyes, scrambled to my feet, and ran, sobbing, from the room.

In my confusion and distress, I turned towards Rachel's room, instead of towards the stairs; she opened the door just as I reached it and stood staring at me; she wore the crumpled wrapper in which I had first seen her, and in the lamp-light, her face looked ravaged and bitter.

'Lily is dead!' I sobbed.

'Lily?' she replied indifferently. 'There is no one of that name in this house.' Her eyes travelled down to the stain on my dress, and she drew back, her eyes wide and terrified.

'Did Meredith try to kill you?' she whispered. 'As once he tried to kill *me*? He said that it was an accident.'

I turned away and ran weeping down the corridor; as I reached the bottom of the stairs, Grandfather came from the drawing-room with Adam.

I sobbed out my news; his arms went around me, strong and comforting. I heard Adam's swift, indrawn breath and saw his shocked face. Then, mercifully, the wild drumming of my pulses became a roaring in my ears and a black tide of unconsciousness washed over me.

When I awoke, I was lying in my own bed, with the sunlight streaming into my room. I lay there puzzled for a moment, and then memory caught at fragments and held them fast in my mind: I recalled being lifted by gentle hands; a short, grey-haired man held a glass to my lips; someone drew the blankets around me, and I remembered that Jessie had been quietly crying to herself.

I raised myself on one elbow and stared at the fireplace; the brass fender with its heavy knobs had been removed and replaced by a smaller one; there was a new rug in front of it. Beside my bed, in the arm-chair, Jessie dozed, her face tired and wan.

I cried out to her; she opened her eyes at once and came to my side. Her hand was cool on my forehead, her face troubled.

'Lily *is* dead, isn't she?' I whispered forlornly. 'It wasn't just a bad dream?'

Her lips trembled as she spoke.

'Lily tripped and fell and fractured her skull, so Dr Evans says. The edge of the rug was rucked, and the strap of her shoe was broken. He said she would have been unconscious at once and suffered no pain. You must try to remember that, Sara.'

She poured something into a glass and held it to my lips; I did not want the drink, but she coaxed me gently, and afterwards I drifted into sleep again. Next time I awoke, Dr Evans was by my bedside.

'Most unfortunate, Miss Pryce,' he said sympathetically. 'Your maid fell heavily and sustained a fractured skull. A nasty shock for you, finding her as you did. She may have been overcome by faintness or stumbled over a broken shoe fastening; who can say? She would not have suffered, I assure you. You must try not to brood upon it.'

When he left me, Grandfather came and asked:

'Would you like me to arrange for you to have another room?'

'No,' I replied firmly. 'I will stay here.'

'I have arranged for Olwen, Megan's sister, to take Lily's place. You must rest today, Sara.'

'I shall come downstairs to tea,' I insisted, with an effort.

'You have courage,' he said approvingly.

Courage? I sighed, as the door closed behind him. Lily's death had cut the last tie that bound me to my carefree childhood and made me feel much older than the girl who had journeyed from London such a short time ago.

'You look tired, Aunt Jessie,' I said. 'Please go and rest.'

Her face was puckered with weariness and worry; she went, without a word, as though she could not trust herself to speak.

Olwen brought me some soup at lunchtime; she was a plump, rosy woman in her late twenties, pleasant of manner, her singsong voice very soothing. She brought hot water, helped me to dress, brushed the tangles from my hair; I looked at my listless face and heavy eyes, knowing how much I was going to miss Lily's good-natured chatter and gentle scolding. I remembered how grudgingly Meredith had given his permission for her to accompany me to Tremannion – I still had the letter he had written me about Lily; as soon as Olwen had left me, I went to the jewel box that had been my mother's and was now mine; in it, I had placed the sealed envelope my mother had left to be opened on my coming of age and my grandfather's few letters to me.

I found Meredith's letters; but the long, sealed envelope was not with them. Frowning I searched my mother's small lap desk, thinking I might have put it there, but there was no sign of it.

Trembling, I sat down on the edge of the bed; I felt tired and confused – the result, no doubt, of Dr Evans' sedative. The envelope must be somewhere in this room, and I would have to search for it later when my mind was clear. I had obviously hidden it and forgotten the hiding place.

Reading Grandfather's letter, I realised that he had only given his consent to Lily's presence at Tremannion in view of the fact that she planned to stay such a short time. Why had so small a thing mattered so much to him, I wondered?

I felt quite composed when I eventually went down to the drawing-room. Meredith was not alone; Catherine Grey was with him.

She rose to her feet as I entered the room and came across to greet me, her quiet face full of sympathy.

'Dear Sara!' she said kindly, 'we are all so distressed by what has happened. I called to see if there was some way in which I could help you.'

She put a small posy of flowers into my hands, her cool fingertips brushing mine; so soft she was, so like a dove amongst the eagles, I thought. Yet, last night, when she had returned from her walk with Rowan, there had been a lively sparkle about her and colour in her cheeks that was not there today.

I thanked her for the flowers, touched by her thoughtfulness. 'Will you pour tea for us, Sara?' Grandfather asked.

I nodded; I was beginning to feel better.

He pulled the heavy tassel by the fireplace, and two maids brought in an embroidered linen cloth, a heavy silver tray, and fine china. I looked at the stand of dainty sandwiches and the tiny cakes; it seemed strange to be dispensing tea as though I was mistress of Tremannion.

'Adam has asked me to convey his sympathy to you,' Cathy told me. 'He says that he will quite understand if you do not feel equal to a drive with him tomorrow.'

'Nonsense!' Meredith said briskly, before I could answer. 'The drive will do Sara a great deal more good than if she stays indoors.' He turned to me. 'It will take you out of yourself. You must not let this business make you too unhappy, my dear. Lily was your maid, and she would have been leaving here within a few weeks, after all.'

'That is not the point!' I protested. 'She

has looked after me since I was a baby and I was very attached to her.'

He patted my hand and said:

'Nevertheless, as Dr Evans says, you must not brood. Adam will call for you after lunch, as I arranged with him last night.'

He could be very high-handed at times, I thought, with a touch of resentment; Meredith Pryce was a man used to ordering other people's lives.

'I shall enjoy entertaining you to tea, after your drive with Adam,' Cathy told me eagerly. 'Brennion is not so large nor so splendid as this house.'

She smiled fleetingly at Meredith and added:

'It is much older, though; I think you may find it interesting.'

We had almost finished tea when Rowan came into the room; I saw Meredith's disapproving look, for his nephew was in his working clothes, wearing boots and thick breeches. His shirt was crumpled and his hair tousled; for all that, he brought a breath of outdoors into the quiet room.

He greeted us all and said, formally, to me:

'I trust you are feeling better, Cousin Sara?'

'Yes, thank you,' I replied.

He nodded and said no more; he was a man of few words, as I knew, and I suspected that he found it difficult to find the appropriate remark for the occasion. He was far more at home with his sheep and his horses than with us. The thin, rose-wreathed cup that I filled for him seemed incongruous, like the postage-stamp sandwiches.

'I understand that you were to spend the day arranging for the hiring of the shearers,' Meredith said brusquely.

'It is done,' his nephew replied, equally brusque. 'Joss Dando will come, and Glyn's sons, as usual; also the Thomas cousins, and the other men we hired last year.'

'It will be a busy time for us all,' Cathy said, 'though Tremannion flocks far outnumber ours. Will you have the traditional supper this year, Mr Pryce?'

'Of course; it will be a great novelty for Sara. We shall use our two largest barns and that will scarcely hold them all; we shall have our own celebrations in the house, as usual; but it is several weeks away, yet.'

'Jessie will be planning it already,' Cathy said.

I saw the look Rowan gave his uncle; it was hard, almost calculating. Then he turned to Cathy and said that he would accompany her back to Brennion.

'There are some matters on which Adam has asked my advice,' he said.

'You will need to make yourself presentable if you intend to accompany Miss Grey,'

Meredith told his nephew. 'Look at the dust on your boots. You are not a farm-worker, Rowan.'

'A man cannot work in his best clothes,' Rowan retorted, colouring. 'Only those who live like fine gentlemen and do no work can go about their business in good clothes.'

He and Cathy left soon afterwards; the maids cleared away the tea things, and I was alone with my grandfather. I walked across the room and looked out of the long window. The later afternoon was fine and sunny; patterns of sunlight and shadow made the Beacons amber and purple; in the clear sky overhead, a lone bird hovered.

Grandfather came up behind me, put his hands on my shoulders and turned me round until I was facing him. His eyes were bright and piercing under his heavy brows, but the forbidding face was more gentle than usual. Again, I could sense the quality of his love that reached out to me; it was deep, fierce, protective. Surely, I reasoned, no harm could come to me whilst I was so loved?

'Do not let the sight of death distress you unduly,' he said briefly. 'It is merely something to be faced and accepted, that is all. In this instance, you have behaved with dignity – as a true Pryce. Do so always, Sara!'

It was like a command, I thought; he was willing me to be the person that he wanted me to be.

'I feel as though there is nothing left of my yesterdays,' I replied. 'All the years I spent with my mother seem so far away, now.'

'Look forward! Never look back; it is foolish and useless. There are many to-morrows; but remember – life will only give you what you want if you *demand* that it shall do so – as *I* have demanded always, Sara! Life gives nothing to those who hesitate or falter or beg favours! One day you will have power. You must know how to use it and make it serve you!'

I stared at him and shivered, feeling cold.

'A woman cannot have power!' I faltered.

'You are wrong; be guided by me, Sara, and you will have all you desire!'

I searched for a meaning behind the words; finally, I said slowly:

'Is not Cousin Rowan the heir to Tremannion?'

'Indeed my nephew is my heir,' he agreed calmly. 'When David died, there was no other.'

'Is Cousin Rowan a good farmer?'

'An excellent one. He understands sheep and horses and cattle and how to handle them. But, as the nephew of Tremannion's master, it is his job to direct and control men, not work with them, like a labourer.'

'Do you mean that he is not a gentleman?'

'I educated him as one; to no purpose, it

seems. He will never care for the things I have gathered here; the old, the rare, the beautiful. Paintings, good wine, a quality in clothes and appointments mean nothing to him. Let us hope that *his* heirs have greater regard for such things; but I doubt that it will be so.'

'Why has he never married?' I asked curiously.

'How should I know the answer to that?' he replied irritably. 'When he weds, he will doubtless take a dairymaid or a farmer's daughter for his bride, and think himself well served. He is like his father; Morgan was dull and stupid, content to follow the herd. As the elder son, Morgan would have inherited Tremannion, had not the old prophecy been fulfilled.'

'What prophecy?' I asked, fascinated.

'It is said that the Devil left behind more than the ram and the ewe that he gave to found our flock; for his gifts never come without attendant curses,' my grandfather said sombrely.

'What is the curse?' I asked impatiently.

'He decreed that the eldest son in each generation of Pryces would never inherit Tremannion. My father was the younger of two sons – *his* elder brother was killed when his horse threw him. A stone was flung at the horse and it shied; no one knew who had thrown it. Morgan was killed in a brawl,

by a man who he had cheated at cards – yet
the man who killed him was never traced.
David died far away from here, drowned at
sea.'

'That must have been very sad for Grandmother, too,' I ventured.

'Rachel?' he retorted contemptuously.
'Your grandmother and I have long been
bitterly divided, Sara, by events that need
not trouble *you*. "David's death has made
her strange," they all whisper knowingly. It
is the soft excuse on all their lips; but I tell
you, her strangeness of mind began long
before then. Her wild, irrational moods are
growing worse and more frequent; have
nothing to do with her – she hates you and
will cause you harm if she can!'

'Is that because my mother took David
away from here?'

He nodded curtly and added:

'Leave Rachel to Anne's ministrations;
those two understand one another very well.
There is no bond between Anne and myself;
it has always been so.'

'Last night,' I whispered, 'Grandmother
said that you once tried to kill her and pre-
tended it was an accident.'

He looked so fierce that I wished I had not
spoken.

'Her mind feeds on sick fancies, as I have
told you! You dwell upon these things much
more than is good for you. I did not achieve

wealth and power by being diverted from my purpose. Let no one divert YOU!'

Flustered, I said the first thing that came into my head.

'I am not to be diverted by Mr Flynn, either; is that not so?'

His hand shot out and gripped my shoulder with such strength that I cried out.

'You are to have no contact with him; do you understand that?' he said furiously.

'What has he done?' I asked, sheer curiosity ousting the fear that questioning might arouse him to greater wrath.

'He is a waster; a man who is too easy with women. Adam is a fool to be soft towards him because of their childhood friendship. Flynn lives in idleness in Adam's cottage, whilst better men work. He knows better than to trespass on Tremannion lands. Why give him further thought, Sara? He is of no use to you – or to any decent woman. Look, rather, at Adam. *There* is a man who is honest and diligent, and a good farmer. If I had a son, I would wish him to be like Adam; I would trust you with Adam, Sara,' he added persuasively.

He made Thaddeus sound exciting – and Adam dull. It was a traitorous and unfair thought, I decided, one to be firmly resisted. Meredith was looking at me as though he wanted me to say something.

'I like Adam very well,' I told him sedately.

'Good! You two will be great friends,' Meredith prophesised.

Suddenly I recalled how I had watched the dogs work the sheep; driving them tirelessly, alert, watchful, moving this way and that, missing nothing. I felt as though I was being driven, gently, but with great firmness and determination by my grandfather.

'Were you very unhappy when my father died?' I asked.

'Naturally.' His voice was flat. 'He was my only son, my heir. Though it is true that all I had worked for meant nothing to him. He had no ambition to farm Tremannion. His heart was set on the cities.'

'So he wanted to go to London with my mother? It wasn't just that—'

I broke off, colouring furiously. Meredith looked at me searchingly.

'Just that what, Sara?'

There was no evading the question.

'I have seen my mother's marriage certificate,' I murmured unhappily, 'and my birth certificate.'

'You must not feel a shame that is not yours, Sara,' he replied with great gentleness. 'No one outside this house knew the truth.'

'Am I like my father?' I asked.

'I think not! You are like ME! We are not simple people, you and I! *Our* characters have strange twists and turns, we have a fire

100

and spirit that people like David never knew; and we have a determination to make life yield up what we most want to us! There are people whom life shapes; and those who shape life. WE are the ones who shape life for ourselves, Sara!'

I stared at him, fascinated. He had a blinding honesty, and it was a facet of his character that few people probably ever saw. Coupled with his singleness of purpose, it had turned him from a moderately successful man into an immensely wealthy one. The idea of being like him appealed to me.

'The Pryces are a strange people!' I murmured. 'They seem to have a stormy history!'

'You are part of that history!' he murmured. 'Come, Sara!'

He took me to his big study in the tower and showed me the portraits I had only glimpsed briefly during my tour with Jessie. He pointed out the swarthy, laughing gypsy Seth Pryce, who had seduced a rich man's daughter and won himself Tremannion as part of her dowry. His wife was a merry-looking woman who had borne him many sons and daughters. I saw that other Meredith, who had made his pact with the Devil; he was like a hawk, with a strong cruel face. Yet he had a sensuous, passionate mouth, and I was suddenly reminded of Thaddeus Flynn.

There was a portrait of the widow from Swansea, prim-mouthed, pallid, with heavy-lidded eyes; she stared down haughtily at me from her gilt frame, as though anxious to assure me that I was an interloper.

There was a painting of Grandfather as a handsome young man, with a devil-may-care look about him. Rachel as a bride, pretty, but with an emptiness in her face, as though it was a page on which nothing had been written. I saw Morgan, with his dark mane of hair, his weak mouth; Anne, chilly and unsmiling in an elaborate evening gown, diamonds at her throat and in her ears; and, finally, a painting of my father as a child, a sturdy, smiling boy with candid eyes.

'This is your family!' Meredith declared proudly. 'You are part of all this. You belong here!'

'What if I marry?' I asked. 'Surely I shall do so, one day? I shall go from here and you will be lonely again.'

'Oh, you will marry!' he agreed calmly. 'But you will not leave me!'

'How can that be, unless I marry Cousin Rowan?' I asked.

Anger flickered in his eyes, like a flash of summer lightning, and was gone.

'Rowan? No, Sara. Let him have his dairy-maid or village girl. I have other plans for YOU!'

And with that I had to be content, for he would say no more.

In spite of my assurance to Grandfather that I did not want to change my room, I prepared for bed rather uneasily that night; Olwen helped me and then returned to her own room in the servants' quarters. The door between my room and the dressing-room where Lily had slept was firmly closed; the silence lay thickly about me, and even the clock had stopped.

Determinedly I sat down and wrote a letter to Lily's sister, explaining as best I could what had happened. It was a sad, difficult task; I wrote that I would send Lily's possessions on to her, and as I sealed the envelope I remembered the missing letter.

When I lifted the lid of the box, I saw it lying there.

I pressed my hand to my damp forehead. It had NOT been there this morning, I told myself firmly! I would have seen it, confused and unsure of myself though I had been. Someone had taken it and had now returned it.

With shaking hands, I carried the envelope over to the lamplight. The seals were intact; but if someone had broken them and read the letter, it would be a simple matter to refix the envelope – provided that the thief had a small gold seal with a rose cut in it and a supply of wax.

I searched my mother's lap desk and found *her* seal. Only one other person in this house owned its twin, so far as I knew: Grandfather.

Why should *I* not open this envelope, I thought? After all, whatever it contained was meant for me and might tell me much about this house and the strange people who lived in it.

Tempted, I ran a thumbnail beneath one of the seals; the wax cracked and a minute red flake fell to the floor. How simple it would be to break all the seals and draw out the sheets of paper that I could feel!

My finger moved towards the seal again; once I had completely prised away the first, I would find strength of purpose enough to break the others, I assured myself. After all, Grandfather had said that one should never be diverted from one's purpose; and no one need ever know what I had done.

Slowly I turned the envelope over and looked at the neat, upright handwriting. I thought I saw my mother's face, calm and kind, firm of mouth and chin. She was smiling, with all her love for me, all her pride in me showing in the eyes I remembered so well.

I could not do it; angrily I thrust the envelope aside. I was a coward, and Grandfather scorned such cowardice. I had given no promise to my mother, yet I would have felt as though I had broken one with every seal I shattered.

It was hard to fight down the almost overwhelming temptation; I sat for a long time, thinking, listening to the murmurings that an old house makes when it frets and sighs in its sleep; there was a gentle creaking in the wainscot, the soft complaint of a little breeze at the window, like a lost soul seeking refuge. I looked at the four-poster bed, unwilling for sleep, recalling how Jessie had said she liked to pull the curtains around her on winter nights, so that she was shut away in her own world.

I could not have slept with those soft, clinging curtains trapping me in that great bed, I thought.

I heard an owl cry; I walked across to the window and looked at a world whose beauty took my breath away; I blew out the lamp so that I could see it better.

The Beacons slept peacefully, clothed in the glory of moonlight, with silvered hollows in them, like frozen lakes, and deserts of black shadow stretching to the horizon. Every tree crouched low to the ground, every stark boulder and every soaring outcrop of rocks were clearly defined in that soft, silver light washing over the whole countryside.

I had never seen anything so wonderful; so

still, so utterly peaceful, I thought.

The owl hooted once again; it was a double note, twice repeated, and it sounded as sad as a ship at sea calling a warning through the fog; then, from a dense patch of shade some distance from the house, a figure moved swiftly, and I realised that the owl's cry was a signal made by a human voice.

I strained my eyes, trying to discover the identity of the figure, which was moving towards the tower in which Rachel had her apartments. I realised that it was a man; whether he was short or tall, I could not tell, for he crouched low as he ran.

Anne's apartments were on the ground floor of the west tower, I remembered.

Well, that was her affair; her mother, no doubt, slept soundly, for Anne had the means to make sure she did so; but I was intrigued. I was also restless. I had been indoors all day and needed some kind of action. Lily's death still lay depressingly upon my mind.

Looking back after all these years, I realise that I made excuses to myself, because I wanted to taste again the freedom I had known the day before when I had danced up above the old sheep-dip; the sheer pleasure of being entirely alone, whilst the rest of the world slept.

I told myself I merely wanted to satisfy my

curiosity concerning Anne. I knew other ways of leaving Tremannion than by the front door, for Jessie's tour of the house had been thorough, and my memory was good.

I pulled on some clothes and left my hair hanging loose about my shoulders; I crept along the corridor until I reached a narrow staircase that gave access to a small passage downstairs near the servants' sitting-room. At the end of the little passage was a door that gave directly to the stable-yard and to a path leading around the side of the house.

I drew the bolts without difficulty and felt the cool night air run sweetly against my hot cheeks. Stepping outside, I kept close to the walls, where the shadows were deepest, and, as I rounded the corner, I could see a faint chink of light between thick velvet curtains, drawn across the windows in the ground floor of the tower. I heard a woman's laughter, low and full of pleasure. A happy laugh, I thought; if Anne had a lover, would that not make her happy...?

I stood there, irresolute, for a few moments. I did not want to go back into the house. I cannot explain what happened to me then; perhaps it was a spell, com-pounded of moonlight, the softness of the breeze, the sweet taste of the air, and the knowledge that the house was oppressive, with its burden of old sorrows. I know only that a strange compulsion sent me walking past the house, down the green slope, along the road to the village. It was like being drawn to a destination by a force stronger than oneself; I shivered, but it was not with cold nor fear.

I reached the place where the water foamed under the bridge. Here, a stone had been flung at my grandfather's carriage, with its four coal-black horses. Tonight, there was nothing sinister about the place; the water laughed to itself, at some secret joke of its own. It foamed over into spray that was like myriads of crystal beads. The scene was so beautiful that I was entranced and realised, for the first time in my life, that great beauty creates a pain inside oneself almost too deep for tears.

I ducked beneath the rotting wood of the lintel and entered the tiny cottage; the floor was of earth, dank and sour-smelling; there was a pile of rubbish in one corner. The window openings were so small that they admitted very little light; only dwarfs could have lived in such a place, I thought, and I was glad to come out again.

A path ran at right angles to the cottage, and I decided to explore it. It became steeper, curving sharply into the heart of the Beacons, and still climbing, until, to my surprise, I found myself at the top of a small, disused quarry.

The place looked weird and uncanny in

the pale light. The turf had been gouged away to show the bare bones of the Beacons; the stony slope glimmered white beneath me, but tiny bushes had begun to grow again, clinging to the stone face as though determined to cover the scars in the green countryside. At the bottom of the quarry lay a pile of boulders, little heaps of shale, and some rusted ironwork like the skeleton of an ancient animal.

How secret and remote it all seemed; just beyond where I stood were two more cottages, like the one by the stream, both of them abandoned. One was a mere pile of stones; the other, joined to it, still had most of its roof intact. There were no gardens at the back of them, for they were built against a buttress of turf and rock that rose sheer to the sky.

I climbed the last few yards and leant, breathless, against the cottage wall; below me, beyond the bottom of the quarry, the ground sloped away to farms and cottages, where a few lights still twinkled like glow-worms.

I was alone in the world, or so I thought. The path went on, past the cottages, its twists hidden by a mass of boulders; from somewhere along the path, I heard the unmistakable sound of footsteps.

My blood ran cold; frightened, I pressed my back against the rough wall of the cottage, trying to make myself one with the shadows. The cottage door was closed, and there was no way I could escape, except along the path I had just climbed, where I would have been clearly visible.

The footsteps grew louder; from the screening rocks a figure emerged, striding along. For one awful moment I believed it was the Devil, coming back to Tremannion to strike another bargain, for the man who was walking towards me was very tall and wore a black cloak.

Then I realised that the man was Thaddeus Flynn.

I felt a curious pleasure in taking him by surprise. I stepped from the shadows as he reached me, tossing my hair back over my shoulders; he stopped abruptly and regarded me with astonishment. Then, before I knew what was happening, he laughed and pulled me against him.

'Look what a gift the gods have sent!' he cried gaily; and he put one hand under my chin, forcing my face up to his.

To the end of time, I shall not forget that kiss; it was wild and sweet and terrible, without tenderness, his mouth holding mine as though he would never set it free. No man had ever kissed me with that arrogant insistence before. I struggled wildly, knowing it was a token protest, for desire and exultation soared in me, flaring like a rocket; only to die in a shower of sparks as he let me go.

'Still looking for adventure, little Sara Pryce!' he mocked. 'You should be sound asleep in your bed. Do you know where you are? Have you not heard the tale of Seth Pryce, who kept a gypsy mistress at Tremannion and turned her out of doors when he tired of her? She was said to have lived in this cottage, on Brennion land! You look like her, with your hair all loose, as though you had been tumbled in the hay!'

I put the back of my hand against my bruised and swollen lips.

'How dare you!' I choked.

'You enjoyed being kissed! You found it more interesting than the chaste pecks of the young men of London! You are not at all the prim young lady you pretend to be!'

It was as though he could see into the dark, secret places of my heart; I hated him for his knowledge and the way he used it.

'I came out for a walk,' I said coldly.

'At this hour? It is past midnight!'

'I did not know there would be anyone about! I would sooner have met the Devil himself!' I cried.

I did not know what made me say such a thing, but Thaddeus laughed delightedly.

'I am sorry to have disappointed you! Would you like me to prove that I am every bit as able as he?'

I backed away; the emerald eyes narrowed, his voice was scornful.

'You are safe enough with me! I kissed you to teach you a lesson. You should not be here – the quarry is dangerous at night, unless one knows all the footpaths.'

'YOU seem to know it well!' I retorted. 'I see you are wearing evening dress under your cloak. Were you going to dine up here, alone?'

'No; though I find it an interesting idea. Or perhaps not alone, but with the right companion. I have dined in Brecon with a charming woman who keeps an excellent table. As it was a fine night, I sent the Brennion coach ahead and decided to walk the last few miles; I like the view from here, especially by moonlight.'

'I have heard that you keep a mistress in Brecon!' I said scornfully. 'Rowan says you have a sweet tooth for women!'

'Some women; not for Meredith Pryce's granddaughter!' he mocked, his eyes gleaming wickedly.

'Why do you hate him so much?' I demanded curiously.

'Because he killed my mother.' His face sombre, the light gone from his eyes.

I thought of the icy waters of the sheep-dip, and shivered.

'Wasn't it – an accident?' I whispered.

'Ask HIM! He will give you the answer! It

112

should make an interesting tale to listen to, when you are bored with that great house of his.'

'He has been kind to me!' I cried. 'He has cared about me all these years, yet he need not have done so; he has given me a home! He wants me to be happy!'

'Come and tell me that when you are as old as Anne!' he retorted, with quiet bitterness. 'I fancy you will say it with less conviction. He is utterly ruthless when he wants something! Once, Anne was like you; young, full of fire! Oh, her face was not so pretty as yours, I daresay!' he added mockingly. 'But she had dreams – ambitions – ideals! He took every one from her. Because she had escaped him and Tremannion, he brought her back to nurse Rachel; THAT was his reason.'

'It seems a perfectly good one to me!' I retorted.

'How little you understand, as yet. Do as he wishes, and he will give you everything! Deny him, and he will crush you – as he crushed Rachel, and Jessie, and as he has tried to crush Anne. Now – it is time you returned. You cannot wander alone at this time of night. I will come with you.'

'I can go alone, as I came!' I retorted.

Angry, I turned from him; I was astonished at the storm of emotion I had experienced. I AM like Grandfather, I thought proudly! I am not a doll, stuffed with sawdust, as Thaddeus Flynn would like to think!

I had not gone half a dozen paces before I stumbled and fell heavily to my knees; bruised and shaken. I was already scrambling to my feet when Thaddeus reached my side.

'You see?' he said. 'You are only fit to ride in a carriage along the streets of London!'

I said nothing; his hands had not been clumsy or rough when he helped me to my feet.

'Are you hurt?' he demanded, exasperated.

I shook my head; there was not room for the two of us to walk abreast. He went ahead of me, telling me curtly to keep close and hold on to his cloak. I felt humiliated; he probably knew, and enjoyed that fact, I reflected miserably.

We made the journey in silence; long before we reached the bridge, I could hear the sly chuckle of the water.

'This bridge marks the beginning of Tremannion land,' Thaddeus told me, when we reached it. 'I have no wish to come further with you.'

'There is no need,' I assured him stiffly.

He stood looking down at the sparkle of water for a moment.

'I heard of the accident,' he said quietly. 'I am sorry.'

114

This change of mood was so unexpected that the tears came suddenly to my eyes.

'I shall miss Lily,' I replied, hoping he could not see that I was crying. 'She has looked after me all my life; she was kind and pleasant.'

'It cannot have been easy for you!' he said abruptly. 'But, then, it can never be easy, here. You should have stayed in London.'

'What could I have done?' I asked. 'I was not trained, I had no money. I could have been a governess or a seamstress, that is all.'

'Perhaps it is a more comfortable thing to be the granddaughter of a rich man, no matter what payment is exacted!' he commented dryly. 'Well, I am told they have given you another maid: Olwen, Daughter of Hawthorn, King of the Giants!'

'What on earth does that mean?' I asked, bewildered.

'It is part of an old Welsh legend; every rock and cave, every mountain and lake and river in Wales, has its tale of enchantment. I have filled a book with the tales and not heard them all yet!'

I stared at him in astonishment; he was an eagle come down to earth, to flutter on my hand for a moment, I thought; but before I could reply, he wrapped his cloak around him, gave me a curt nod, and strode off into the night.

Slowly I went home to Tremannion, knowing that I was not the same person who had left its shelter only a little while ago. I came within sight of its walls and saw it as an enchanted castle in the silver light. My mother's voice drifted down the years to me:

'Tremannion is not the kind of house you imagine it to be, though it looks like a drawing of a castle in a book of fairy tales...'

I knew she was right; and I wondered if she had been unhappy there.

There was no light burning in the ground floor of the west tower; I stood outside for a moment, the magic of the night all about me still. My senses were alive as they had never been before; the imprint of Thaddeus Flynn's kiss was burned into my mind, my body ached with a longing and torment, a desire and delight, that frightened me.

There were emotions I could scarcely control; so, I thought, I must be careful never to see him alone again; for the terrible attraction he possessed for me could only bring disaster in its wake, unless I stamped it out ruthlessly.

Once inside the house, I bolted the door quietly behind me and ran lightly up the narrow flight of stairs; the lamps had all been put out – there should always be a lamp left burning in these long corridors, I thought indignantly.

Fortunately, I had the soft, pale flood of

moonlight to guide me, as it filtered through a window near the top of the stairs; then, like a dark cloud moving over the moon's face, a tall, powerfully built figure stepped in front of the window, almost filling the space, blotting out the light.

I stood quite still, my hands shaking, my heart racing violently.

'Well, Sara?' Meredith Pryce said softly, 'where have *you* been?'

Chapter Five

For a moment I was shaking too violently to speak.

'I asked you where you had been, Sara,' he repeated.

'For a walk,' I stammered.

'At such an hour? You have been about from this house for a considerable time. I saw you go, from my window. The master of Tremannion never sleeps!' he added softly.

I had known those windows were so many watching eyes, I thought bitterly! I dared not tell him that I had met Thaddeus for he would never have believed me if I told him it was an unpremeditated meeting. I knew he would explode into violent rage at the very mention of the name. Neither did I

117

dare tell him I had walked to the old quarry, for he would tell me – with justification – that it was not the place in which to take a walk alone late at night.

I was learning to be deceitful, I reflected miserably. That fact troubled my conscience.

'I went down to the stream,' I murmured.

His voice was ice cold with suppressed fury.

'You sneak out of the house by a back staircase like any kitchen maid bent on an hour's frolic with a village lad – YOU, Sara Pryce of Tremannion! You know perfectly well that a young woman in your position does not behave so! Quite apart from this, the countryside is unfamiliar to you; your behaviour has been foolish and undignified, and I am extremely displeased with you, Sara!'

I was silent, knowing that I deserved the reprimand.

'Come!' he said shortly. 'I will take you back to your room.'

He moved away from the window; in silence, I followed him along the moonlit corridor. For so tall and powerful a man, he moved very softly and agilely, I thought; perhaps he was well used to making his way around Tremannion whilst the household slept, I reflected. At least Anne had been more fortunate than I, for Meredith had apparently not noticed the arrival of the visitor to the west tower.

Meredith opened the door of my room and stood aside for me to enter.

'Are you going to lock me in?' I asked resentfully.

'Don't be foolish, Sara. I shall leave it to your good sense not to repeat tonight's escapade,' he retorted coolly. 'I trust you will enjoy your outing with Adam tomorrow. I shall leave Tremannion early tomorrow morning, for I am going down to the Five Valleys to visit the Pryce mine.'

'I should like to visit a coal mine,' I said. 'I have never seen one.'

'You are not likely to visit one; it would be as unsuitable an outing as your walk this evening,' he replied dryly. 'Coal mines are rough and dirty places, and the men regard the presence of a woman as a bad omen.'

I hesitated, and then said, with a sigh:

'I am sorry that I have displeased you, Grandfather. It is a beautiful night, and I longed to be out of doors.'

'Had you told me so, I would gladly have accompanied you on your walk,' he replied, closing the door behind him.

He would never understand the need I had to be alone sometimes, I thought despairingly; I went to bed in a state of turmoil such as I had never known. For eighteen years, my life had been lived calmly and peacefully, in the shelter of my mother's love, without great heights of passion or black depths of despair to trouble my days. Now I felt like a frail boat tossed on a merciless sea.

My last waking thoughts were of the man who had held me in his arms, aroused such longing and pain with his ardent kisses, and then mocked my confusion.

On my way to breakfast next morning, I met Anne.

'Good morning, Sara,' she said briskly. Her hair was neatly dressed, her manner reserved. It was impossible to believe that she was the same woman whose soft, happy laughter had floated to me on the still night air.

'Mama and I are going for a long drive,' she added. 'We shall take a picnic lunch. It will be a great joy to be out of the house for a day!'

'Do you dislike me?' I asked impulsively.

'Perhaps I pity you!' she retorted. 'Have you ever seen a tree bending in a great wind?'

'The tree that does not bend must break,' I pointed out.

'*I* did not bend!' she retorted. 'Nor did I break! My father will be able to keep me in this house only so long as my mother needs me. YOU will bend to him, always! YOU will stay here and grow old, as I have done!'

'What nonsense! I shall marry one day!' I told her firmly.

'Only if you allow Meredith to choose your husband for you! He wants you to marry Adam, because he can manipulate him as he manipulates you! Meredith Pryce thinks he has the power to shape his world and its inhabitants to his liking. He thinks of himself as God – master of Tremannion, lord of the Beacons! Ah well, little Sara, you have a new maid to look after you, to cosset you and fetch and carry at your bidding; the rest of us must manage as best we may. Nothing is too good for Meredith Pryce's granddaughter, is it?'

Her voice was sharp; she laughed at my discomfiture as she swept past me.

When I reached the dining-room, Aunt Jessie was there, listlessly eyeing the breakfast dishes.

'You still look unwell,' I told her.

'I'm well enough,' she said, not looking at me.

'Couldn't you rest today?' I suggested.

She shook her head.

'There is always much to do in a house like this,' she told me. 'I cannot sit idle; it frets me. Rowan has been up for most of the night with a sick ewe; she is one of the finest in your grandfather's flock, and he is deeply concerned. He has sent for Mr Williams, the veterinary surgeon.'

I helped myself from the array of dishes on the sideboard, but I did not feel hungry. Anne's words and the shadow of Lily's death lay coldly over me, though I tried to put unhappy thoughts from my mind.

'Grandfather told me the old prophecy about the eldest son never inheriting,' I said. 'If it had not come true, then you would be mistress of Tremannion today; how strange!'

'It causes me no sorrow that I am house-keeper, not mistress here,' she replied quietly. 'Morgan hated Tremannion; we had a fine house in Tenby and we lived happily there. Your grandfather has called Morgan a thriftless man and a gambler, who squan-dered much of the Pryce fortune. That is true; but a woman does not always love a man for great virtues, nor hate him for weaknesses, Sara.'

I turned the phrase over in my mind; I had never before thought of reasons for loving.

'I was almost penniless when Morgan died,' Jessie added. 'Meredith gave me a home here, for Rachel needed a companion. Also, she did not train the servants nor run the house efficiently. Meredith has treated me generously, and Rowan was never treated differently from David.'

'Why did my mother come here as house-keeper, Aunt Jessie?'

'I could not manage the house as well as

attending to Rachel; she was both difficult and demanding and she and Meredith quarrelled constantly over her methods of housekeeping. So your mother came; *I* thought she was too young, but she did her job well enough, and your grandfather liked her.'

'My mother fell in love with David,' I said, watching Aunt Jessie.

She nodded.

'No one guessed. There did not seem to be anything between them. They saw one another constantly, of course, as they were both under this roof, but...' she broke off, colouring, and then added bluntly:

'It is a shameful thing for an unmarried young woman to bear a child. Men say that the woman should be strong when the man tempts her and tries to seduce her; yet women are expected to be pliant and submissive to men in all other ways, to please them and be obedient to them. People will say that it is a man's nature to be hot-blooded and the woman must check his ardour; they never say that a man bears equal blame with the woman for the child they have begotten between them. A child without a father's name is a constant reproach to a woman.'

'Did my mother feel – bitter – about what happened?' I asked.

'I don't think so, child, for your father was

more than willing to marry her. They both went away, very quickly and quietly, and were married. David should have prepared his mother for what he intended to do; it was a great shock to her, and she was ill for a long time afterwards. Dr Evans declared that the illness was in her mind and would grow worse. So Meredith made Anne give up the school to look after her mother.'

'What school?' I asked.

'Anne was in charge of the village school. She liked her work there, and the children all thought that the sun shone out of her eyes. Even the dull ones seemed to get a fair amount of learning in them, and Anne was engaged to a schoolmaster from Carmarthen. She was different then; happy enough, though she never got on with Meredith; sometimes I think he was jealous of it all, Anne leading her own life like that. She fought him, all the way, on the matter of teaching, for he said it was unfitting that a Pryce should be village schoolmistress.'

'How could he force her to give it up?' I asked impatiently. 'If a nurse had been found for Grandmother, then Anne would have stayed at the school.'

Jessie shook her head and looked at me with pity for my ignorance.

'Meredith was Chairman of the Board of School Governors. His influence went as far as Carmarthen,' Jessie said dryly. 'The schoolmaster was dismissed. He left the district in a hurry and that was the end of his engagement to Anne. Make no mistake, child; nothing stands in Meredith's way when he wants something.'

'Yet you said he had been generous to YOU, Aunt Jessie.'

'Because I have neither reason nor wish to oppose him,' she replied calmly. 'My son will be master of Tremannion one day – that cannot be altered, for with David's death, there was no other male heir.' She gave me a quick, direct look. 'No woman can inherit Tremannion, for the name of Pryce must continue also. I have served Meredith and his household for many years now; my greatest joy will come on the day that I see *my* son in possession here. He is a good sheep farmer, Sara; he has worked as hard as Meredith and deserves his inheritance.'

'Surely it is time Rowan was wed?' I said. 'For he must have sons…'

She gave me a thoughtful look.

'Yes. It is time he found a suitable wife,' she agreed.

I ate my breakfast in silence, aware of her eyes still regarding me with a strange look in them; I felt vaguely uncomfortable.

Meredith had said contemptuously that Rowan would take a farmer's daughter for his bride; perhaps he was wrong. There were other women: Catherine Grey, for instance.

She would make a splendid mistress for this house.

Rowan came in just before lunch, looking defeated and weary; I met him in the hall.

'The ewe died,' he said. 'We could not save her.'

'I am sorry,' I murmured. 'I wish it had lived.'

'What is it to you?' he asked bluntly. 'Just a sheep, no more.'

'I can still understand how sad it must be to fight for a life and lose the battle,' I replied. 'Especially if it is a valuable animal; your Uncle Meredith will be upset.'

'Williams will make tests to see if he can find the cause of it,' Rowan told me. 'One of Adam's ewes died in just such a manner, some years ago, and it was the beginning of a strange illness that wiped out half of the Brennion flock.'

'Did they not find the cause of it then?' I asked.

'Not to this day, Cousin!' He looked at me with a curious, half-amused look in his eyes. 'I never yet met a woman born and bred in a big city who cared a jot for sheep!'

'If I am to live here, then I want to understand all these things,' I replied earnestly. 'Tremannion flocks are of great interest to me; this is my home. The Pryces are my family.'

I spoke with a small thrill of pride; Rowan

126

threw back his head and laughed.

'It is not all summer-time here and peaceful grazing for the sheep. Come winter it is hard and cruel. The snows are thick and if they have come suddenly, the sheep may be lost in the drifts. If we do not find them quickly, they will die, suffocated by the snow. There is no sun then, there are no foxgloves for the gathering. The women stay in the house, and the roads are impassable over the Brecons.'

I felt dismay at the thought of being shut up indoors with Rachel and Anne; as for Thaddeus Flynn, what would he do if he could not go down to Brecon to his mistress?

'In winter,' Rowan added softly, 'you will long for the city, Cousin Sara!'

'Oh no! I shall become used to the snows,' I told him airily.

Yet as I turned and went indoors I knew that he was secretly laughing at me because I was too young and silly to know the ways in which Tremannion could hold me fast.

Adam drove up in a small, open carriage drawn by two dappled grey horses. The day was hot, and I wore a pretty, summery dress, with the little gold harp brooch Grandfather had given me, pinned at the neck.

He drove carefully down the long road to

the village, and when we crossed the stream that divided Meredith's land from Adam's, I averted my eyes from the sight of the path that led away to the quarry; but I could not shut out the memory of Thaddeus standing there beside me in the moonlight.

The thought of him made my pulses leap, and a fever of longing scorched my blood; what madness, I told myself angrily! It was the heat of the day that made me feel faint, no more!

'I must call at the apothecary's in the village,' Adam said apologetically. 'It will delay us but a few moments, however.'

'Is Catherine unwell?' I asked.

He shook his head, smiling.

'Philip Evans, the apothecary, does not only dispense cures for human ills; he stocks medicines and certain preparations for the health of the animals – it is necessary in a farming community such as this.'

'Is Philip Evans related to Dr Evans?'

'I daresay they are second or third cousins! To be called "Evans" or "Jones" in this part of the world is like being called "Smith" in England, Miss Sara!'

'Please call me "Sara". May I come into the shop with you?'

'Why, yes, if you wish,' he said, after a moment's hesitation.

The village drowned in the afternoon sun; I saw a baker's shop, a tiny general store, a forge, and a saddler's; there was a sweet-shop, its window full of tempting-looking jars and, next to it, the apothecary's.

Outside the shop, there was a swinging sign with a pestle and mortar painted upon it. In the window, two great carboys filled with coloured water, glowed like jewels.

Inside the shop it was dim and cool. I had never before seen so many jars and bottles and packages, nor so many rows of little mahogany drawers, each with their crystal knob and strange, Latin label.

From the back of the shop came a tall, thin man, with a pale, intense face. A lock of dark hair drooped across his forehead, his eyes were slate-grey, and he had a weak, almost girlish mouth.

'I need some more of the new sheep vaccine,' Adam told him.

Philip Evans nodded and glanced towards me. Rather unwillingly, I thought, Adam said:

'This is Miss Sara Pryce, Mr Meredith's granddaughter.'

I inclined my head; Philip Evans murmured the briefest acknowledgement and looked quickly away. I heard a sound from the back of the shop, and a woman came forward.

She stood, resting her hands on the counter: a plump young woman, with a sullen mouth and a lot of thick black hair, very untidily dressed. Her eyes were as dark as her hair, lively, missing nothing. She eyed me with great curiosity as she pushed ineffectually at a straying strand of hair. I saw how her print dress was strained across her heavy breasts and was damp with perspiration. She looked as if she did not care much about anything, let alone her appearance.

She spoke to Philip in Welsh, low and rapid; he shook his head angrily, and she turned to me, speaking in English.

'Miss Sara Pryce, is it, then?' Her lilting voice held lazy insolence. 'Pleased we are to see you, I am sure.'

Adam looked as though he wished he had insisted on my remaining in the carriage outside.

I did not like the way the woman smiled; there was secret amusement in the curl of the full red lips. However, I nodded politely, and, with a last look over her shoulder, she went back again into the room behind the shop.

'I shall have to get the vaccine; we are out of it,' Philip said, not looking at either of us. 'It will be here tomorrow morning. I shall bring it myself.'

He gave a stiff little half-bow and bade us good day. I was glad to be out in the sun again, sitting in the carriage, for the atmosphere in the shop had been tense. Adam

130

picked up the reins and urged the horses smartly forward.

'Who was the woman who came into the shop?' I asked.

'Bronwen Evans, Philip Evans' wife,' Adam replied shortly.

'She looked very oddly at me, I thought.'

'Mrs Evans is a strange woman; they say her husband dares not say a word to her, for she has a fiery temper.'

'The other day, Aunt Anne told Grandfather that she was going to the apothecary's; he laughed about it, and she looked very cross and embarrassed. Do you know why that should be so, Adam?'

His pleasant, good-humoured face was creased with lines of worry.

'Your grandfather would not like such things discussed between us,' he said awkwardly.

'Oh, Adam, *please!*' I protested, exasperated. 'I am so tried of secrets! Does Aunt Anne have a fancy for Mr Evans?'

'It is not just a fancy,' he replied. 'Your aunt has an affection for him which he returns. They have been seen together; naturally, it angers Meredith that his daughter should be the subject of gossip.'

'But Mr Evans is much younger than Aunt Anne, and he is married!'

Adam made no reply; I was shocked, wondering if Philip was the man who came stealthily to the tower room at Tremannion; perhaps he reminded my Aunt Anne of the schoolmaster whom she had hoped to marry.

He passed a row of cottages, their doors all wide open, and the Brennion Arms where several old men sat outside drinking their ale. They paused long enough to look at us curiously, dark and silent and unmoving.

At the farthest end of the village was the small schoolhouse; a neat, white-washed building with a low roof; two little girls in pinafores strolled together in the little playground, their arms twined around one another, and I tried to imagine Anne Pryce as the schoolmistress.

We passed a few more scattered cottages, a farm or two, a number of paths leading away up the mountainsides, and then the church, as neat and white as the school; I looked at the tombstones, the weeping angels, the broken columns, the trailing ivy wrought in marble. Some of the graves were only grassy mounds on which stood wreaths of white flowers under glass domes. The sun glittered in the glass, making each rounded dome shine like an evil eye; and by the wall, the foxgloves blew, the pink bells on the long stems swinging as though they rang silent carillons on the sweet summer air. *They grow best in the cemetery,* Thaddeus had said. I did not look over my shoulder as we turned a bend in the road and headed towards Brecon.

I enjoyed Brecon very much; Adam was an excellent guide. I thought the cathedral was most impressive and Adam proudly told me its tremendous history. He pointed out a little chapel to me.

'Capel-y-Cochiaid,' he explained. 'The Chapel of the Red-Haired. I *thought* you would look surprised, Sara, when I told you! There are many red-haired people in Wales; some say it is because when the Danes and Vikings plundered our coast, they took the dark-haired Celtic women, and for generations their children have had red hair!'

I thought of Thaddeus with his great tawny mane of hair; it would not be hard to imagine that *he* had some marauding Viking for an ancestor, I thought.

Side by side, we walked the long cathedral aisles; I looked up at Adam, thinking what strength and gentleness there were in him. He was a man that a woman could lean upon, and he would never be cruel or arrogant.

Impulsively I whispered:

'I am so glad I came with you today, Adam!'

He looked pleased and answered:

'Your grandfather is anxious that you shall see as much as possible of our countryside whilst there are still many summer days left.'

I felt vaguely disappointed, as though Adam had escorted me only in deference to Meredith's wishes; but when I looked at him again and saw the obvious pleasure in his face, I told myself I was being foolish.

From Brecon, we drove to Llangorse Lake.

'It is the largest stretch of water in this part of Wales,' Adam told me. 'There are so many tales and legends woven around it that I cannot remember one half of them!'

'I should like to hear some of them, Adam!'

'We have books at Brennion that would be of interest to you. Thaddeus is making his own collection of the lesser known lake legends. He is an authority on the subject.'

I looked at the quiet water, smooth as a mirror, touched with a sheen of gold by the afternoon sun; carefully I composed my face and voice.

'I had no idea that Mr Flynn was a writer, Adam.'

'Yes; one of some talent. He has composed stories and books of strange, adventurous tales. He paints also. Ah, he is as free as air to come and go as he wishes,' Adam said half-enviously. 'He is like an eagle in his lonely eyrie; and that is how he will always be: unfettered.'

'Until he marries, that is all!' I retorted lightly.

'Thaddeus has no use for women,' Adam told me.

Save for his pleasure, to fill an evening of loneliness, I thought; but I did not pursue the subject. I sat quietly beside Adam, whilst we made our way back, eventually turning off to join the road that would bring us to Brennion. This road to Adam's house sloped much more gently than the steep one to Tremannion.

Catherine came to meet us, as we drew up at the entrance. As she had said, this was a much smaller and less impressive house than Tremannion; but it also looked less forbidding. It was long and low and rambling, with many outbuildings at the back. From near the house, a road forked away over the Beacons towards Tremannion; at this point, the boundary line between the two properties came near to the house – near enough for me to see a trim white cottage, half-hidden in a green hollow, I knew, without being told, that Thaddeus lived there.

'Did you enjoy your drive?' Cathy asked, smiling.

'Yes,' I told her eagerly. 'This is such splendid countryside.'

'Wild enough at times, though,' she said, as we walked towards the house. 'When the wind blows up here, it seems as though it would lift Brennion into the air and carry it

135

away! And sometimes the mists creep down stealthily, like ghosts of rain, cutting us off completely from the world. Brennion has always been my home; my parents were missionaries in China, and they were killed when I was a baby. Adam's mother and father brought me here, and I have lived here ever since. I do not want to leave it!'

She spoke with sudden quiet vehemence that surprised me; she saw my astonished look and added more calmly:

'Of course I shall leave here one day. When Adam marries, there cannot be two mistresses.'

'What will you do?' I asked.

Her pretty, gentle face looked withdrawn for a moment; there was a blank look in her eyes reminiscent of Rachel. Then she recovered herself, smiled brightly and said:

'I will not think about it! After all, Adam seems in no hurry to wed; there is Rowan – and Thad – all of them bachelors still! Perhaps they have decided that they will remain unwed!'

She took me upstairs, where I washed my hands and tidied my hair in a cosy, feminine room, very different from my grand, austere one at Tremannion; then she took me to the drawing-room; with her fingertips on the crystal doorknob, she smiled brilliantly at me and murmured:

'We have a visitor; Thaddeus is here. He

sometimes takes afternoon tea with us.'

My heart thudded wildly in my breast; had he known we were coming, I wondered? I tried to feel angry; what right had he to make a mockery of the fact that I had sworn not to see him again? Well, at least we would not be alone together.

Thaddeus stood by the open window; as he came to greet me, his eyes met mine with a devilry in them that told me clearly how much he was enjoying the memory of our previous meeting. My cheeks burned, for I could feel once more the insistence of his mouth upon mine, the touch of his hands upon me; I wanted, passionately, to blot out that memory and think only of Adam and myself walking in the cool cathedral aisles together.

'Miss Pryce,' Thaddeus bowed, with a slightly exaggerated air. 'I believe you have spent a most pleasant afternoon, exploring our countryside. Adam tells me that you are interested in the legends of Llangorse Lake. I have made a collection of such tales, which you may borrow, if you wish.'

And how, I thought despairingly, would I explain THAT away to Meredith Pryce?

With his uncanny insight into the workings of my mind, Thaddeus added ruefully:

'Though I fear your grandfather will disapprove of the loan as much as he disapproves of me, Miss Pryce.'

137

'If he disapproves of you, then no doubt he has cause,' I said sharply.

Cathy laughed a trifle nervously and rang for tea.

'Thad also paints, Sara, as I told you. How clever to be able to write, as well!'

'Many people might consider them frivolous pursuits!' Thaddeus murmured sardonically.

'Some of your paintings are so wild and strange that they quite frighten me!' Catherine declared, with a shiver.

Thaddeus smiled at me and said softly:

'The paintings are at my cottage; I am sure that Adam will be quite happy to escort you there if you would like to see them.'

I looked into the proud, laughing face, hating him; he was deliberately taunting me, knowing how much I longed to defy Meredith and flout convention by going to the cottage – alone, unchaperoned by Adam or anyone else.

I knew all too well the utter folly of my desires. This was the man with whom I was never going to be alone! My vow seemed a feeble thing; I was a helpless moth at a bright candle-flame.

No, I reminded myself fiercely! I am like Meredith Pryce – strong, singleminded, knowing and taking what I want from life. I need a man like Adam, kind and gentle-mannered, not THIS man.

To my relief, Adam came into the room, carrying a book.

'Sara, I have found this for you to read! *Legends of the Lake*. Keep it for as long as you wish.' I gave Adam my most dazzling smile and thanked him warmly, aware that Thaddeus was watching me.

Adam turned to speak to Cathy; Thaddeus spoke to me softly, his eyes dancing with mischief.

'I have a small hideaway, Miss Pryce. Few people know of it. I use it when I need to escape from the world, when I must be completely alone; there, I write or paint and do my best work. I don't think you know of it – a tumbledown cottage, overlooking a small quarry, a gloomy place and said to be haunted. However, I find the place exciting – and strangely peaceful at the same time. Last night, returning from Brecon, I passed the place. The moon was an unforgettable sight, a great flood of silver washing everything in its light.'

I looked steadily into the bright green eyes.

'You make it sound most attractive,' I agreed.

'I was alone,' he declared wickedly. 'One should enjoy such pleasures as moonlight in congenial company.'

'I do not find your company congenial!' I retorted. 'Now – or at any time, Mr Flynn!'

He shook his head reproachfully.

'You are a kitten with tiger's claws!' he told me. 'Well-sharpened claws, too, it seems!'

'Of necessity!' I assured him gaily. 'You are a fraud! You think if you flatter a woman, she will hang on your every word!'

At that moment the maid brought a tray of tea, and the talk turned to the coming sheep-shearing.

'It is hard work for everyone,' Cathy told me. 'At Tremannion, the sheep are brought into the big pens and sheds, near the Home Farm, and there is such a noise all the day, with the sheep bleating and the men talking! Mrs Pugh has to feed the men and I have never seen such great stacks of food in my life. She takes them gallons of tea. "Very thirsty work is shearing, miss," Daniel Pugh once said to me.'

'I should like to see it,' I said.

'Perhaps Meredith will take you,' Adam said. 'He is always there, and the men say he has a dozen pairs of eyes, another gift from the Devil! Rowan will be with him, of course.'

'No doubt,' said Thaddeus pleasantly, 'the master of Tremannion feels that the shears will move faster for his presence!'

'There will be the Harvest Supper, soon afterwards,' Cathy said quickly. 'All the tenants and servants and the shearers will attend; it is quite the biggest event until Christmas.'

'The days will grow shorter and colder,' Adam said. 'How swiftly time flies away from us!'

'It is not something that you can catch in a net, as though it was a butterfly,' Thaddeus said, looking at me. 'We should enjoy every moment that we have, round it out with our pleasures. Do you not agree, Miss Pryce?'

I would not be drawn; I smiled non-committally, all too well aware of the eyes that scarcely left my face.

'You must visit us again soon,' Cathy urged when it was time for me to go.

'We may meet again, perhaps, Miss Pryce,' Thaddeus said, with deceptive gentleness. 'Who knows?'

My eyes flicked away from his scrutiny, and I shrugged, as though the matter was of no interest to me.

'I will walk you back to Tremannion,' Adam told me. 'It is not far from here, and there is a pleasant road.'

'You have a lovely home; and you are well looked after, Adam,' I said, as we walked from Brennion.

'Cathy runs the house excellently; she has done so since my parents died, soon after my coming of age.' He stopped and pointed to a flock of sheep below us, fanned out like cottonwool tufts over the green slope. 'Those are Brennion sheep, Sara; I know my own, and each flock has its distinctive brand

141

mark on every animal. Brennion sheep will never match Tremannion sheep, but they are fine animals, for all that.'

The route home took us within a few yards of the white cottage in the hollow; the door was shut, and the shutters covered the windows. I wondered where Thaddeus would go when he left Brennion – perhaps to his secret eyrie in the quarry.

'May I take you out again?' Adam asked.

'Would you like to do so?' I asked, glancing up at him.

'Most certainly. Today has been very agreeable; Meredith declares that I am too much occupied with Brennion and should shed my responsibilities.'

My heart stirred uneasily; there it was again – the feeling that Meredith was gently persuading Adam, as well as myself, into the way he wanted us to go.

'I daresay Grandfather will be annoyed to know that I have seen and talked with Mr Flynn today,' I said casually.

Adam's face was unexpectedly stubborn.

'Meredith and I have never been in agreement where Thad is concerned. Thad has been my friend since we were children, and he will remain so.'

'I believe Mr Thaddeus Flynn has quite a reputation with women!' I murmured gaily.

'That is no concern of mine,' Adam pointed out.

When we reached Tremannion, I thought how forbidding the place looked, even on such a golden evening as this. When we went indoors, there was no one about except a servant who told me that Aunt Jessie was very unwell and had gone to bed.

'I must see what I can do for her,' I told Adam.

'We shall meet again soon,' he promised. 'You and Meredith are coming to dinner at Brennion next week.'

When he had gone, the house seemed as silent as a tomb; I did not like the deep soundlessness as though nothing lived or breathed within these thick walls. It seemed impossible to believe that, outside Tremannion, the sun shone brightly.

I went to Aunt Jessie's room.

Jessie lay on her bed, her arms folded tightly across her waist as though she was in pain. The curtains were drawn, but I could see how white and pinched she looked.

'What is it, Aunt Jessie?' I asked. 'Are you overcome by the heat?'

She smiled faintly.

'In this house that no sun can warm? No, Sara, I think I have eaten something disagreeable, though I cannot imagine what it could be. I have some pain, and my head aches. I have been feeling faint and overcome with nausea.'

'Shall I send for Dr Evans?'

'No; I shall probably be well enough to-morrow.'

'Is there something I can bring you?'

She sighed.

'I need a draught; but the medicine cupboard is in Anne's room and she has not yet returned. I keep some remedies here of my own, but I do not have the one I need now.'

'Why does Aunt Anne have charge of the medicines?' I asked.

'Because she is entrusted with the sedatives and medicines that Rachel needs; Anne keeps the key. The only other medicines in the house are for the animals and Rowan has charge of those. However, I should like a little weak tea.'

'I will see that you have it,' I promised.

She smiled wanly at me.

'You will have to eat your evening meal alone, Sara; Rowan is dining with Mr Williams and it will be very late before Meredith returns.'

I touched her hand gently; she gave me an odd, unhappy look, and her eyes seemed to be full of tears. After serving Jessie her tea, I went to my room; Olwen brought me hot water and helped me to change.

'The house seems very quiet,' I said. 'Are all the servants out, too?'

'Nearly every one, yes, miss. To the Fair at Llanmor. Mrs Pryce said they could go; except me and someone to wait at table.'

144

I heard the faint resentment in her voice and felt sorry for her; it was a fine evening, and all her friends would probably be at the Fair.

'Will it be too late for you to go when you have finished here?' I asked.

'No, indeed, miss!' she said hopefully.

'Then hurry along, Olwen; I can manage.'

The pleasure in her face made me feel happier, as I went downstairs to the table, laid for one, in the vast dining-room. The place seemed enormous, shrouded in a silence broken only by the sombre voice of the great clock in the hall.

As soon as I had finished my meal, I told the servant who had waited upon me, to go along to the Fair; Llanmor was only a few miles from Tremannion. Perhaps I should not have sent all the servants away, I thought; but I decided to tell Aunt Jessie, sure she would understand.

Nevertheless, the sense of complete isolation lay heavily upon me; with the sun going down, the shadows in the house seemed very deep and menacing, as though the house was shrouded in curtains of black velvet.

I had no wish to sit alone in the drawing-room, nor did I want a book from the library. I decided to see how Aunt Jessie was feeling; as I went slowly up the wide staircase, I wondered what kind of a picnic it was that could have kept Anne and her mother out so late; no doubt they were making the most of their day's freedom.

When I looked in at Aunt Jessie, I saw to my relief that she was sleeping soundly and had a better colour. I closed her door softly and glanced nervously over my shoulder along the wide corridor. I thought someone moved, near the door of my father's old room.

Well, I was Meredith Pryce's grand-daughter, not a coward, I reminded myself; I forced myself to walk slowly along, and found the door half-open. I pushed it to its fullest extent; no one was there. There were fresh flowers in a bowl, the clock ticked away, the coverlet had been turned back; I thought of Megan, bringing hot water to the room each morning, and shivered; had she gone to the Fair this evening, I wondered – and first prepared my father's room for a man who would never sleep there again?

Restless and nervous, I looked in at all the rooms; no one lurked in any of them. I went up to the old nurseries and sat on the rocking-horse; but I felt foolish riding to and fro on the broad, painted back, and climbed down again. Perhaps my mother's old room would be peaceful and not haunted by something I could not name, I reflected.

I stood inside it and thought: it is just

another ordinary room, no more; then I noticed something I had not seen on my previous visit: in the far wall, between a carved oak chest and a high-backed chair, I saw a door. It blended so well with the dark wood of the panelling that it was scarcely noticeable at first sight.

I went across and tried the handle, expecting the door to be locked; but it opened, though rather stiffly, and I found myself looking down a short flight of steps.

I had neither candle or lamp, and the dusk was deepening, like a tide that creeps in stealthily; I put my foot cautiously on the first stone step, then the next, straining my eyes to see through the gloom.

However, I was disappointed to discover, at the bottom of the steps, what appeared to be a storeroom of some kind, not much bigger than a very large cupboard. Furniture and boxes of all kinds were ranged around the walls; I lifted the lid of a chest, and my fingers encountered the stiff covers of books; the only light came through a small slit high in the wall.

I wondered if anything stored in this room had belonged to my mother; but it was growing too dark to see properly, and I decided to return again when there was more light.

The silence all around me had finely attuned my ears to the slightest sound; as I stood with one foot on the lowest step, ready to return, I heard faint movement in the room above; a steady footstep, as though someone moved in the gloom.

All my senses were alert, scenting danger.

'Who is there?' I cried; and the terrible thought flashed through my mind that if someone closed and locked the door at the top of the stairs, I could remain a prisoner for a long time before I was discovered.

Panic lent wings to my feet; I gathered up my skirts in my hands and raced up the stairs. Sobbing with relief, I thrust against the half-open door and ran into my mother's room.

No one was there; nothing stirred, there was no sound, no movement. Yet I knew, with terrifying certainty, that someone had just left the room by the other door.

The unfriendly shadows spun their dark web around me, and I could not see properly. It was only as I reached the far door, and stubbed my toe against something on the floor, that I realised my intuition had been right: there had been someone in this room, a moment ago.

I bent and groped for what lay at my feet; it was a small book with a soft leather cover. I held it close to my eyes, and in the last of the light, I could just make out the gilt lettering on the cover: 'Holy Bible.'

I held the Bible against my chest, taking

comfort from its significance. When I had entered this room, I had seen this Bible on a small table near the door, and wondered if it had been my mother's. Whoever had come into the room after me had sent it flying to the floor whilst making a swift exit.

Now I knew that my wild imaginings had not conjured up an intruder where there was none. Someone had followed me here, and whoever it was had intended to make me a prisoner in the storeroom – I was certain of that. Had I not run back so swiftly, it would have been accomplished by now; but the intruder would not risk being seen, even in the little light that was left of the dying day.

I put the Bible back on the table and went from the room, closing the door behind me; now all my fears returned to torment me – for I still had to make my way past the old nurseries, back to the main part of the house; and whoever had been in my mother's room would probably still be hiding in the shadows, waiting for me.

Every shadow held menace, for it could conceal someone who watched and waited for an opportunity to harm me; but *who,* in this house, wished me ill, I wondered.

Only Jessie was in the house at this moment; but Jessie was ill and asleep in her room. Had the illness been feigned, I wondered? She had seemed to be in great pain.

I thought of Meredith, the one person who could have taken my mother's letter, read it, and resealed the envelope; but Meredith was away. What of Rowan? He was dining with Mr Williams – or so he had told Aunt Jessie; Anne and her mother had not yet returned from their outing.

My flesh prickled coldly with the sudden realisation that my secret watcher was not necessarily a member of the household; after all, Anne had received a late-night visitor with apparent ease; there was the small staircase I had used the previous evening – Tremannion, I reminded myself, had many exits and entrances.

I strained my ears; the silence seemed to grow tremendous, as though it was a high wall, shutting me off from all help. I took a deep breath and began to walk swiftly along the way I had come a short time ago. My heart beat very fast, and a confused little prayer for safety formed itself in my brain. I knew I must keep walking, for the longer I dallied, the deeper would grow the concealing darkness that was my foe.

I reached the short flight of stairs leading down to the bedrooms, still forcing myself not to hurry too much, though I glanced fearfully over my shoulder several times, still certain that I was being followed.

I went down the stairs and walked until I came to Jessie's door; I hesitated for a moment before I turned the handle and looked in. I could just see the figure in the bed; she turned and moaned softly in her sleep as though she was restless.

I shut the door quietly and walked to my own room; I felt safer in this part of the house, though it was almost dark. Normally, the lamps would have been lighted, but all the servants had gone to the Fair, I remembered.

Once in my own room, I breathed a sigh of relief. I lit my lamp, then I went cautiously out into the corridor, and lit the others. The light made me feel safer, although I was still uneasy. I took a lamp along to Jessie's room, and she did not waken when I placed it on the table, near her bed.

Back in my own room again, I rubbed cologne on my burning forehead, wondering bitterly what kept Anne and her mother out so late. If only someone would come back, so that I was not alone in this dark, brooding house. Well, I could sit in Jessie's room, I reflected. There, at least, I should feel some measure of safety.

When I stepped out into the corridor again, I found that the lamps were out.

Now I knew the danger I was in; I felt cold with horror, realising that I was being hunted with cunning and great determination. The hunter had the darkness and possibly a great knowledge of the geography

151

of this house to make the task easy; all I had was the slender hope that someone might return soon.

I stood there, irresolute, for several seconds. I could not lock myself in my room, for there was no key to the door. I panicked; I was not even going back in there to fetch my lamp, I thought. If I was out of doors, I might have a chance to escape, but never whilst I remained in the house.

Swiftly I ran towards the stairs; I caught hold of the banister rail to give me strength and support, and did not realise, until afterwards, how close I came to death in that moment; someone moved from the shadows, and, with split-second awareness, I gripped the rail more tightly and tried to dodge away; the blow from behind caught my shoulder and sent me reeling.

I almost lost my hold but not quite. I stumbled and fell, my arm all but wrenched from its socket. I fell a couple of steps, and sat there, thinking of the long drop down those curving stairs into the hall below.

Reaction set in; I began to scream. As my screams died into hysterical weeping, a figure came stumbling to the top of the stairs, a lamp in her hand. It was Jessie, her face white and terrified; at the same time, Megan came from the door that led out of the hall below into the servants' quarters. She, too, carried a lamp.

'Sara, what is wrong?' panted Jessie, helping me to my feet.

'Someone tried to kill me!' I cried. 'I lit the lamps in the hall and then they were put out! It was dark, and someone tried to push me downstairs!'

'In Heaven's name, Sara, who would do such a thing?' Jessie whispered incredulously.

I looked suspiciously at the squat, dark figure coming slowly up the stairs, staring at me as though I was mad.

'The others have all gone to the Fair!' I cried. 'I believed the house to be empty, save for Aunt Jessie! Why are YOU not with the others?'

'To the Fair, is it, miss?' She looked outraged. 'Better things I have to do, indeed, than waste time and good money so shamelessly! I am sitting downstairs, quiet like, in the servants' sitting-room, and then I hear screaming! What in the world is wrong, miss?'

'Someone tried to push me downstairs!' I said defiantly.

She pressed her thin lips tightly together and shook her head, exchanging a significant look with Aunt Jessie.

'Megan,' Jessie said tiredly. 'Please light the lamps upstairs; and then bring hot milk to Miss Sara's room. I will stay with her.'

The old servant went away, grumbling

audibly to herself that she should not be expected to perform such tasks in her free time, Aunt Jessie took me to my room.

'It was horrible!' I cried. 'You must listen to me, Aunt Jessie! I am not imagining things!'

I told her the whole story, from the time I had gone into my mother's room until she had found me on the stairs.

'You are overwrought,' she declared. 'No wonder, wandering about by yourself in the dark. It is very easy to imagine all kinds of things in an old house like this. As to the little room leading from your mother's bedroom, it is just a place where lumber is stored. It should have been locked; your mother almost had an accident there, once.'

She sighed and said, half to herself:

'The things that are happening now are like those that happened long ago.'

'Tell me about them!' I begged.

She shook her head; the lamp-light shone on my mother's amethyst ring that I was wearing, and I saw her look at it thought- fully. There were little beads of perspiration on her forehead.

'Are you feeling better?' I asked anxiously.

'Yes. I am not in pain, though I do not feel myself.'

Megan brought the milk, her face screwed up into lines of disapproval. When she had gone, I said:

'Aunt Jessie, *please* tell me why you said these happenings are like those of long ago!'

'I should not talk about it.' She pursed her lips. 'Old scandals are best forgotten. Oh, very well, then. Years ago, Rachel and Meredith had a violent quarrel. It was worse than any I had ever heard between them, and I do not know what brought it about. I went to my room and stayed there; I was frightened, for Meredith is a violent man when he loses his temper. After a while, I heard him stride past my door, along the corridor, and then I heard Rachel running after him, screaming just as you screamed tonight. They reached the top of the stairs, still quarrelling furiously; then there was a single, dreadful scream from Rachel. I rushed out and saw Meredith standing at the top of the stairs; when I reached him, I saw Rachel lying in the hall. She could have been killed; she swore he had tried to kill her by pushing her; afterwards, he denied it, of course. She was badly bruised, two of her ribs were broken – and she lost the baby she was expecting. She was six months pregnant, and it was a boy. If it had lived it would have been Meredith's young son and heir to Tremannion when David died.'

I was shocked; no wonder this house was haunted, I thought. The storms that battered its walls in winter were less terrible than the wild storms always raging within, ever since the days of Seth Pryce, the first gypsy owner, who had turned his mistress out of doors.

'What did Grandfather do when he saw Rachel lying at the bottom of the stairs?' I asked.

She raised her head and looked at me; her eyes were wide with horror and disbelief.

'What did he DO, Sara? Shall I tell you? He strode down the stairs, right past where she lay and out of the house, without looking at her! He simply left her lying there!'

'Grandfather would not do such a thing!' I cried.

'I speak the truth, child. I have lived here many years, seen and heard many things; I am surprised at nothing now – but the memory of that night still lives in my mind! David and Anne and Rowan were children – mercifully, they were upstairs in the nursery, sleeping soundly. Anne found out what had happened, when she was older. She hated her father for what he had done.

'Meredith would be angry with me if he knew I had told you all this, Sara; for you must know that he wants you to see only what is good in him.'

Chapter Six

When I went downstairs in the morning, it was obvious that Meredith knew what had happened the previous night. He glanced sharply at me, but said nothing. I was last down to breakfast, and he motioned us all to be seated.

Anne looked at me speculatively.

'I trust you enjoyed your day,' she said.

'Very much; and you?'

'It was delightful!' She glanced triumphantly at Meredith, who did not raise his eyes from his plate. 'We visited some cousins of Mama's on our way home, and they persuaded me to stay for a while. Seldom have I enjoyed a day more.'

After breakfast, Meredith said:

'Come to my study, Sara; I want to talk to you.'

Obediently I went to the study with him. He pulled up a leather arm-chair for me, on one side of his desk, and sat down on the other side, regarding me thoughtfully.

'Sara,' he said, 'you have been under considerable strain recently, in view of your mother's death and Lily's accident. It seems you are brooding – which Dr Evans insists you must NOT do – and your imagination is playing tricks. That is a dangerous situation.'

'So Aunt Jessie told you what happened last night?' I said. 'It was NOT imagination! Someone tried to kill me!'

'*Who*, Sara? There was no one else in the house save your Aunt Jessie and an old servant. *I* am the best judge of what is good for you. You shall go to Swansea for a short holiday; it has some fine shops and you can buy whatever pleases you. Catherine shall accompany you, and Adam will escort you both. He will arrange it when we dine at Brennion next week.'

'You do not believe me!' I said bitterly. 'I KNOW what happened! Other strange things have happened to me since I came to this house!'

'Tell me about them,' he commanded.

'I was locked in my father's room, the first morning I was here. Someone also took a letter from my mother's jewel case. Perhaps it was the same person who followed me last night, and then tried to thrust me down the stairs!'

'Letter?' His clasped hands were resting on the desk, and I saw the knuckles suddenly gleam whitely; his voice was sharp.

'The letter was left to me by my mother,' I said slowly, watching his face. 'On the envelope she wrote that it was not to be opened by me until my twenty-first birthday. It was sealed with several seals, all exactly like THIS one!' I picked the seal from his desk and held it out to him; his face was expressionless.

'The letter disappeared,' I told him. 'Then it was returned. It could easily have been read and resealed!'

'There are only two such seals, to my knowledge,' he said coldly. 'One was David's – presumably he gave it to your mother. The other is mine. Do you suggest that *I* took the letter and read it, then refastened the envelope? Do you really think that, Sara?'

I shook my head helplessly.

'You obviously mislaid the letter,' he continued, 'and imagined it had been stolen. Come, child, do not look so woebegone! I am not blaming you! When the mind is disturbed, it becomes confused and plays strange tricks, as you have seen in the case of your grandmother! Bring the letter to me; *I* will lock it safely away until it is time for you to have it.'

Reluctantly I did as he asked; I fetched the letter from my room, took it into the study, and placed it in front of him. He picked it up and read the handwriting; I could not tell what he was thinking.

He looked up suddenly and smiled.

'When you have thought it over, you will realise that imagination can be a powerful force, Sara,' he said softly.

'*Someone* put out the lamps that I lit,' I retorted.

'Perhaps you truly believed that you lit them, but did not do so.'

I shook my head, knowing the folly of pursuing the matter; for a moment, I wondered if I was going mad – but no, I clearly remembered all I had done last night.

'You will enjoy a trip to Swansea,' he said.

I stood up and he escorted me to the door. I recalled the light-footed agility with which he had walked the corridor on the night I had gone out without permission. It was an extraordinary thing in so powerfully built a man, I reflected, and who but Meredith Pryce would know, intimately, ever corner of his house?

'Did you enjoy your drive with Adam?' Meredith asked, as he opened the door for me.

'Very much. Mr Flynn was at Brennion, when we returned; I found him most entertaining.'

I would never have spoken so had I not felt angry and resentful. Meredith's eyes smouldered like live coals. His mouth was like a steel trap that could crush and maim an unwary animal. When he spoke, his voice was unnaturally quiet and precise.

'Do not try to provoke me, Sara; you will

160

find it a two-edged weapon. Such men as Flynn are dangerously attractive to impressionably young women. You have never seen an eagle take a young lamb; *I* have, Sara – it is not a pretty sight.'

The doubts continued to rage in my mind, as I walked back to my room. I can trust no one, I thought. *Nothing* is too incredible to be believed, in THIS house.

The next few days passed without incident. The inquest on poor Lily was held in the village school, and Dr Evans repeated his belief that her death had been caused by a fall. She was buried in the little cemetery in the shadow of the small white church. Her funeral depressed me, adding weight to Meredith's argument that I needed a holiday.

On the Sunday following Lily's funeral, we all went to church; a state occasion, Anne called it sarcastically.

'Papa is a hypocrite,' she told me. 'For the only God he believes in is the God of Tremannion!'

'Aunt Anne, that is blasphemous!' I protested.

'No, my dear child!' she replied with a tight little smile. 'It is an assessment of a man who goes to church merely because it feeds his liking for power; he knows that nearly everyone in church owes him allegiance, for they live in his cottages, they plant his crops, tend his cattle and sheep, plough and sow and toil to make him rich!'

She made me uncomfortable when she talked like that; she reminded me of a sword, bright, sharp, and deadly.

We gathered in the hall of Tremannion to wait for Meredith; Aunt Jessie, Anne, Rowan – stiff and uncomfortable in his best clothes; Rachel, in a very elaborate outfit, her fingers plucking nervously at the air – I tried not to watch her; and me, Sara Pryce, remembering vividly the happy days when I had walked to a pretty little Kensington church with my mother.

Meredith came slowly down the stairs, a tall, magnificent figure; he looked awe-inspiring. He looked at us all and nodded, as though satisfied with what he saw; then he handed me two books.

'These were your mother's,' he said.

One book was the Bible I had picked up from the floor of my mother's room. I opened it and saw the name 'Celia Heriot' written on the fly-leaf. The other book was a prayer book, and the fly-leaf bore the same inscription. It seemed strange that my mother should have left such personal things behind when she left Tremannion, I thought.

We rode to church in the big carriage, drawn by the black horses; Meredith addressed himself to Rachel once or twice, in the briefest terms, but she did not answer him. I was conscious of his eyes on me; and I kept seeing Rachel, huddled in a heap at the foot of the stairs, the unborn child dead within her, whilst Meredith strode past her, uncaring.

Many of the Tremannion servants walked down to church. When we arrived, I stepped down nervously from the carriage, averting my eyes from the sight of Lily's grave, with my posy of flowers wilting upon it. I felt the reassuring pressure of Meredith's fingers as he helped me from the carriage and realised that he knew what I was thinking.

We were the last to arrive; the church was full and there was a hushed silence as we walked to the Pryce pew. I felt dozens of pairs of eyes upon me.

It was Meredith who found the right place in my prayer book, as we sang the first hymn; he seemed proud to have me beside him, as though I was his most prized possession, to be shown triumphantly to these people. His deep voice soared magnificently above all the others around us. I had heard that the Welsh possessed fine singing voices, but I had never before heard such singing, so rich and rounded and full of emotion.

Across the aisle, I could see Adam; beside him was Cathy, in a dove-grey bonnet, tied with blue ribbons. In a small pew nearby,

Philip and Bronwen Evans stood several inches apart from one another. He stared straight ahead and made no pretence at singing, whilst she occasionally glanced over her shoulder to give us a quick, insolent stare. It was as though she said: These may be the lords and ladies of Tremannion, with their fine retinue of servants, but I am not impressed by such a great show.

I was glad when the service was over; we came out of church, Meredith walking with me, and Rachel with Anne, which was all wrong, I thought unhappily.

The rest of the congregation lined the sides of the path as we walked by, giving us the same watchful, unsmiling look that I had seen on the faces of the old men drinking outside the Brennion Arms.

Cathy and Adam came across and spoke to us.

'I am looking forward to seeing you at Brennion again next week, Sara,' Adam told me with a smile. 'Are you enjoying the book?'

'Yes, thank you. The lake legends are fascinating. My favourite is the tale of the wicked town that was swallowed up by the waters.'

'Possibly a similar fate will befall Tremannion one of these days,' Anne murmured. 'We have no lake, but I am sure the ground will open and the house will sink

164

into a deep, dark cleft, to be lost forever. I cannot think of a better fate for such a house!'

Adam laughed and replied:

'It would need a very large cleft to swallow a house of such a size. I trust that you are not suggesting the inhabitants should be there when this calamity occurs?'

'Do not tempt me, Adam!' she retorted dryly, 'or I might well give you the reply that such a question deserves! Imagine it! Tremannion crushed in the green jaws of the Beacons, swallowed up into the darkness from which it sprang!'

I looked at her in bewilderment; she was a constant source of surprise to me. What a fine turn of phrase she had, I thought; for the first time it occurred to me that she must have been an excellent teacher.

Cathy was talking to Rowan, her small, quiet face more animated than usual. Jessie stood a little apart, watching them; she looked like a woman who had a great deal on her mind. I saw Meredith turn and speak to Rachel, as the carriage drew up outside the gates; but she turned petulantly away and walked across to the new grave where my flowers lay; she stared fixedly at it for several minutes, until Meredith took her arm, almost roughly, and drew her away towards the waiting carriage.

Philip and Bronwen stood near the church

gate; I saw the quick veiled glance that passed between Anne and Philip, and I was acutely aware that Bronwen's bold, dark eyes saw it; she knew the truth about those two, I realised.

The rest of the day passed peacefully enough; in the afternoon, Meredith took me for a walk to one of the highest points around Tremannion. I was quite out of breath when we reached the top, but he stood there like some warrior of olden days surveying a captured kingdom.

'Look at that view, Sara! To the east is Pen-y-fan, the highest peak in this part of Wales. The mountains you see in the distance are the Black Mountains. To the west lies Carmarthen; but look northwards, beyond and above us! In my younger days, I climbed to the very top of Pen-y-fan and from there, on a fine day, it is possible to see Plynlimmon and Cader Idris!'

'They are lovely names,' I said, fascinated. 'England seems a thousand miles away, and the Severn as wide as an ocean!'

'England IS a thousand miles away!' he cried. 'Are you content to be HERE instead of there? Tell me that, Sara!'

'I am content,' I said dutifully, because I knew that was the answer he wanted.

I went to dinner at Brennion with Meredith,

and it was a pleasant outing. Cathy had eagerly accepted Meredith's suggestion that she should accompany me to Swansea.

'I need a new gown for the Harvest Supper,' she told me excitedly. 'It is many years since I stayed in a hotel.' She glanced quickly at Adam. 'It is a busy time here for you, Adam; *can* you be spared to escort us?'

'Brennion can manage without me for a day or two,' he declared, looking at me.

'Excellent!' said Meredith, lifting his wine glass. 'I shall reserve a suite of rooms for you all.'

As we were leaving Brennion, Adam held my hand in his and said:

'This holiday will be great fun, Sara! To be able to spend so much time in your company is an unexpected treat!'

'You make me speechless, Adam!' I murmured, pink-cheeked.

'I assure you I speak with sincerity,' he answered quietly.

'So you are to go jaunting off to Swansea, eh?' said Rowan, when I met him next day.

I was in the stable-yard, feeding Sheba and Solomon; he came across to me wearing his working clothes and looking as though his day had been long and hard.

'It is just for a day or two, Cousin Rowan,' I replied. 'I shall enjoy choosing a new gown to wear at the Harvest Supper; Cathy will choose one as well.'

He put his hands on his hips and stared down at me.

'Adam is to accompany you; he will consent to leave Brennion NOW, when it is near time for the sheep to be brought in for the shearing, and there is so much to do!' Rowan said, shaking his head in disbelief.

'I wish YOU would come too,' I said impulsively. 'You work very hard; do you never take a holiday?'

'I do not need one. I like to be here, and I like to work. What would I do in a city?' He looked at his hands and shrugged his shoulders.

'I have seen cities,' he added indifferently. 'I am not at ease there. You know by now, Cousin, that I do not make pretty speeches nor care for fine clothes and dainty food, silver and linen. All this displeases my Uncle Meredith. I am as I am made! I prefer to be in the fields with my men and the sheep!'

His jaw had a stubborn thrust, his eyes looked bleak. Suddenly he looked at me, a long, thoughtful glance that I could not understand.

'One day, Cousin Sara, *I* shall be the richest man in Wales. I shall need fine sons to inherit the land that will be mine when Meredith is dead. You are small-boned.' He looked critically at my hips, then his gaze travelled upwards again, to my face.

'You do not look strong,' he added, with a frown. 'Nevertheless, I think you would bear healthy children; and, as my wife, you would be mistress of Tremannion. You would lack nothing, and I should treat you well; I do not think you would be a spendthrift. Yes – you would look well at the head of my table.'

I stared at him, dumbfounded. He might have been discussing the finer points of cattle in the market place, I thought indignantly. I had never received such an outrageous proposal of marriage – if it could be called such.

'Are you agreeable?' he asked calmly.

'No, I am NOT!' I choked angrily. 'I am not a ewe to be mated with a ram! Marriage is a thing of love and tenderness! Is that of no account to you?'

'Love?' He gave a short laugh, though a spark that might have been desire flickered in his eyes for a moment. 'All young girls have their heads full of giddy notions about love! I have told you that I will care for you, treat you well, as my wife.'

Unexpectedly he caught my arm and bent his head until his face was only inches from mine.

'I WANT to marry you, Sara!' he whispered, with soft compelling urgency. 'I WILL marry you. Men may phrase it how they will, they marry to take a woman to bed and get fine children for themselves.

OUR sons shall farm Tremannion!'

'Never!' I retorted.

His eyes narrowed.

'It is the only way!' he murmured.

'I don't know what you mean!' I cried.

His voice was slow, as though he had plenty of time.

'When you come back from Swansea, I will ask you again,' he told me.

'You will be wasting your time! My answer will be no different!' I assured him; gathering my skirts in my hands, I turned and ran from the stable-yard.

I went to my room and sat there, thinking about his proposal; it had horrified and dismayed me. Clearly, Rowan saw nothing wrong in it; he was of the earth, earthy, and made no secret of the fact.

I decided to walk over to Brennion, the following afternoon, and have tea with Cathy; I took the short cut, and when I came in sight of the cottage, I kept my eyes firmly fixed on the road ahead.

Thaddeus came to the door and called my name softly, enquiringly.

Reluctantly I stopped and looked towards him, my heart beating fast; he strolled across with a leisurely air, and I thought, once again, what a handsome man he was, with his lean hips and wide shoulders, his lazy grace, his tremendous air of vitality. I watched the muscles move beneath the taut silk of his shirt, enjoying the way it made me feel.

He smiled at me; his teeth were white against his tan, laughter lines crinkled the skin at the corners of his brilliant eyes.

'Are you bound for Brennion?' he asked pleasantly.

'Yes,' I said, as coolly as I could.

'Catherine and Adam are not at home; I saw them drive away half an hour ago.'

'I see. Thank you.' I looked at a patch of sky above his head, knowing he was amused that I would not meet his gaze.

'It is a long walk back to Tremannion,' he said persuasively. 'Let me offer you some refreshment. Cathy has given me a bottle of her home-made wine. I shall enjoy showing you my pictures. Forget your fears and your stupid conventions, Sara – such things are merely a hindrance to enjoyment!'

'I wonder,' I said despairingly, 'if this was the way in which the Devil once tempted the master of Tremannion?'

He threw back his head and laughed.

'Oh, you are delightful! You, with that disapproving face and prim little air, and those sudden, odd remarks! Come, forget stupid rules – I shall not *eat* you!'

He took my hand in his and led me into the cottage; I went unresistingly, for what else could I do? The very touch of those fingers upon mine, that warmth of flesh on

171

flesh, could make my blood sing in my ears.

It was cool inside the cottage; all the windows were wide open to the sun. I took off my hat, and laid it on the table, looking around me with great curiosity. The room was furnished with simple good taste; there were some carved wooden masks on the walls, there was an abundance of books everywhere, and the chairs looked comfortable. Along the far wall his paintings were displayed; I walked across and looked at them.

As Cathy had said, most of them were wild and strange; they showed the Welsh countryside in all its moods, but his pictures of the storms were the best, for he had made the gaunt rocks and twisted trees look like people, bent and crouched low, tormented, and some of them with evil faces, full of menace.

I looked from the paintings to the pile of manuscripts that covered the big desk near the window.

'You are very talented, Mr Flynn,' I said.

He put a crystal glass into my hand; it contained a liquid that shone like pale-gold sunshine.

'Mr Flynn!'

His rebuke was astringent.

'Thaddeus,' I murmured. Oh, who *was* this man to steal my will from me, snare me with his charm, I wondered wildly?

'I like the painting of the old castle falling into ruin,' I told him. 'It has a look of Tremannion about it.'

'I used Tremannion as my model; the picture was intended as an illustration to my book of legends. Sit down, Sara; you are like a bird poised for instant flight!'

I sat on the edge of a small sofa; to my consternation he sat beside me. I would have preferred him to be the length of the room from me. Cautiously I sipped the liquid and found it tasted pleasant.

'How do you gather your tales?' I asked.

'From the people of the village; they are full of tales, eager to recount old beliefs and superstitions. I have studied parish records, too, and many books of ancient customs. Wales is an enchanted country, rich in such lore. Her stories should be read aloud at the fireside, on a winter's evening.'

'What will you do when your book is finished?'

'It will be autumn then; I shall go away; to Spain, Italy, Greece – anywhere, in search of the sun.'

'Will you return to Brennion?'

'Not until the spring, if then,' he replied indifferently.

'You are a wanderer,' I murmured.

'I have always been so, since my father's death,' he retorted. 'He gave me a taste for foreign cities and showed me their treasures.

I daresay I have loved too many places too well to settle for just one of them.'

'Were you quite young when your mother died?' I asked hesitantly.

'I was at boarding school.' His face looked closed and aloof; I looked at him from beneath lowered lashes, thinking distractedly that Cathy's potent home-made wine seemed to have lit a smouldering fire in my veins.

'This is not a day for remembering old tragedies.' He added, 'Will you have some more wine, Sara?'

'I think not; it seems – very strong,' I said breathlessly.

He moved closer to me slowly as though he had all the time in the world.

'You are not pretty,' he said appraisingly. 'Not as the world sees prettiness in a woman, for you are too thin, too dark, but it seems I have lost my taste for golden curls and pink cheeks. Your face has character. You are a rebellious spirit, and I fancy Meredith will not easily subdue you.'

'I am sure he does not wish to subdue me!' I replied, annoyed.

He laughed softly, and suddenly put up a hand, pulling the pins from my hair; startled, I tried to draw away, but there was a look on his face that stayed me. I had never seen that expression of brooding tenderness before, belying the mockery in his eyes.

'No!' I whispered, trembling. I put up a

hand, but he caught my fingertips and deliberately held them prisoned in his free hand whilst he continued to remove the pins. I was bitterly angry with myself that I had not the courage to stop him as he continued the work of letting my hair tumble to my shoulders.

'There!' he said with great satisfaction. 'One day I shall paint you as you are now, and call it *The Changeling*. Perhaps that is what you are – a fairy child. Changelings had a hard time of it at the hands of the old wives; I have been told they were bathed in a solution of foxgloves which killed them.'

'How cruel!' I murmured.

'Ah, but fairy's children caused much mischief and havoc amongst ordinary people. ARE you one, Sara!'

'I have caused no havoc–' I began.

He leant forward and for one wild, blissful moment, I thought he was going to kiss me; I felt a surge of disappointment when he deliberately drew back, smiling as though he guessed my thoughts.

'It is not yet autumn,' he said lazily. 'It will be some weeks yet, before I fold the shutters over these windows and fly south, as the wild geese fly. Do you remember Adam remarking on the swiftness of time passing?'

'Yes.' I smoothed a non-existent crease in my skirt, so that I would not have to lift my head. 'I do remember; you answered that time was not captured in a net like a butterfly, but that we should take each moment, rounding it out to our pleasure.'

'Do YOU believe that, Sara? Do you not wish to round out the time we have, making it rich and splendid?'

'I do not understand you,' I replied.

'Come, you are intelligent enough – a rarity in a young woman!' he retorted impatiently. 'I might even find you more fascinating than the woman who lives in Brecon!'

'They say you have no use for *any* woman!' I replied furiously.

'They speak the truth. I am free to follow whatever road I choose to take. I need to travel alone; but I find it pleasant to stay awhile, sometimes, and enjoy what Fate has sent!' His smile was mocking. 'If Fate has sent a woman who intrigues me, then I enjoy her for a while, as one enjoys a summer afternoon. Then I am gone; another summer, another woman. That is the way my life goes, Sara!'

'How selfish!' I cried contemptuously. 'And how unjust! You are a heartless man!'

He shook his head, his eyes bright with mockery.

'I have never yet taken a woman who did not wish to be taken – as YOU do, now!'

I would have leapt to my feet, but he stayed me with one swift, fierce movement.

He put his lips against my burning cheek, and I closed my eyes; his mouth travelled down from my cheek to my lips and his kiss had a lazy confidence, a warmth like the sun, a sweetness like honey from the comb. Would I never understand the complexities of this man, I wondered, dazed? Last time we had met, the roughness of his kisses had bruised my mouth.

His hands slid around to the back of my neck, under the heavy mass of hair, as he pulled me closer to him. I felt the tingling rapture I had known when I danced alone on a bright, new morning, above the old sheep-dip; and then my heart seemed to stop beating, for Thaddeus was making soft promises with his body, his lips...

With a tremendous effort I came back to reality, knowing I trod quicksands, not mountain tops, and it was Catherine's wine that had built such a fire within me. I pulled free, trying to rearrange the pins in my hair, with unsteady hands.

His laughter was triumphant, destroying the moment of tenderness.

'I was right!' he cried. 'You are a passionate woman, not a prim miss! And, like all women, you fear that passion! So you will never know how to fulfil each moment as it was meant to be fulfilled!'

'Fine talk for a man!' I flung at him, nearly in tears. 'It is not easy to be a woman!'

'Well said, Sara; you are growing up!'

'You do not care for honour or reputation!' I said scornfully. 'YOU disregard them as you do other conventions. It is nothing to you!'

'I take my pleasures where I find them; I am the same as other men. We could have enjoyed these summer days, until the foxgloves die.'

Until the foxgloves die. The words had a sad sound, like a tolling bell. I bent my head to hide the pain in my face.

'You will come to me again,' he said softly. 'Not here; to the quarry, where no one goes. We shall be truly alone there. You will come because you must, and I will teach you how to enjoy loving…'

'You are mistaken! I shall never come to you!' I replied scornfully.

'We shall see. I shall command you silently!' he said, laughing.

'Keep your legends and tales for your books, Thaddeus Flynn! You have no magic to bind me!' I retorted.

I stood up, snatching my hat from the table, anxious to be gone from him. I glanced towards the window and thought I saw a movement, just behind the bushes and trees on the other side of the path.

I went across to the window, shielding myself behind the curtains, and looked out cautiously.

178

'What is it?' Thaddeus asked; he came up to me and put his hands on my shoulders.

'Someone is out there, watching us!' I whispered.

'Nonsense; you are imagining it!'

'I am not! Ah – LOOK!'

The figure moved away, revealing herself for a split second; she wore a dark print dress and moved clumsily because of the heavy flesh on her bones.

It was Bronwen Evans, Philip's wife.

Chapter Seven

I turned to Thaddeus.

'There! You see? She has been watching us?'

'Why should she?' His voice was dry. 'She has other things to think about. I daresay she has been to Brennion to deliver some medicines that Adam has ordered. If there had been orders to deliver to Tremannion, that would have been a different matter entirely! Philip would have brought them and made sure he handed them over to your Aunt Anne!'

I was annoyed, hearing the laughter in his voice.

'My aunt is behaving very foolishly and

wrongly!' I retorted. 'To let herself be the subject of gossip in such a fashion. There can be no future for her in such a relationship; besides, I cannot think what on earth she sees in him!'

'Love has always been blind!' he replied coolly. 'You should not presume to judge Anne. Meredith Pryce spoiled her life when she was a young girl, little older than you are today. If she takes her pleasures where she finds them, then that is her affair; she is intelligent enough to have considered the consequences.'

'It is time I was going,' I told him; the mood of tenderness between us had vanished.

'The afternoon is young yet,' he protested softly, with his hands upon my shoulders still as he stood behind me, he bent his head and lightly touched the nape of my neck with his lips. Scarlet-cheeked, I jammed my hat firmly down on my head.

'Good-bye!' I said coldly, pulling free.

His soft, amused laughter followed me out into the sunshine; that, and his farewell.

'Good-bye? No, it is au revoir, darling, for we shall meet again soon!'

The way he said the word 'darling' was a caress in itself...

Determinedly I hurried along the path, my eyes scanning the rocks and bushes until I saw the sudden flash of a print dress. As I left the path, Bronwen whisked out of sight behind a high spur of rock; I wondered at my own boldness as I followed.

When I reached her, Bronwen Evans was leaning against an outcrop of rock, her face pink and shining. She looked hot and dishevelled; her hair was awry, one button was missing from her dress, and there was dirt on her cheek. Lily would have said that this woman had all the makings of a slut.

She stared at me defiantly, with calm insolence.

'What are you doing here?' I demanded.

'Mind your own business, miss! Brennion land is this, and no part of Tremannion. Miss Pryce you may be, and a fine young lady you think you are, but I am not one of your servants, remember! All airs and graces it is at Tremannion, and underneath it all, things done that would shame respectable people!'

So she *had* seen us! Guilt put the colour in my cheeks, as I said coldly:

'Why were you spying on Mr Flynn's cottage?'

Her astonishment was genuine.

'Spying on Mr Flynn is it, now?' She gave a short, contemptuous laugh. 'No, miss! It is Miss Anne *I* am seeking; oh, very strait-laced indeed when she comes into the shop, and too good to speak to me, looking the length of her nose and giving her orders; ah, but they do not talk of it at Tremannion!' She put her hands on her hips and looked at me as though with scorn for my ignorance.

'They do not tell how she and my husband behave shamefully, alone together, and not gathering whinberries, I can tell you, miss! They are lovers, my husband and *her!* She is too old and sour to conceive, and sorry I am, for it would please me to see her belly swollen with her own guilt!'

Bronwen laughed and turned away; her coarseness appalled me. I continued on my way back to Tremannion, feeling both guilty and thankful that she had not seen me at the cottage. As I came within sight of the house, I heard the soft sound of laughter, followed by a man's voice, speaking very quietly.

I hastened towards the sound and found them after a few moments' search; they lay together in a green hollow, almost completely concealed by bushes. Their arms were entwined, and Anne's head was buried against Philip's shoulder. He held her closely, and I saw one hand move to cup itself about her breast.

'Aunt Anne!' I called urgently.

She sprang to her feet, pulling the bushes apart, glaring at me.

'Who sent you to spy on me?' she demanded fiercely. 'I am free to do as I wish outside the walls of Tremannion!'

Philip said nothing; he turned his face

away as though he wished he had not been seen. He was like a schoolboy caught out in a lie, and I could not understand what attracted my aunt to him.

'I came to warn you!' I told her. 'I have just seen Mrs Evans, and she is searching for you both!'

I left her, standing there, still glaring at me; as I walked on to Tremannion, I reflected thankfully that I would be glad to be free of it all for a few days.

The following day, I decided to return to the old lumber room that led from my mother's old room. I was extremely curious about it, hoping that I might find a clue to the strange happenings in this house, if I searched diligently enough.

I hurried past the old nurseries; there was something sinister about this part of the house, despite the fact that it had once been occupied by children. The quietness here was so intense that one had the feeling of being completely isolated from the rest of the world.

I tried to count the bedrooms and dressing-rooms below me; one of them surely adjoined the hidden lumber room. I worked out exactly *where* they would adjoin, and then I realised how many twists and turns and corners there were in the house to baffle me.

I was forced to give up; that afternoon, I

walked twice around the outside of the house, carefully scanning the walls for a narrow slit; but I could not find one.

Meredith's generosity was overwhelming; he insisted on placing a considerable sum of money at my disposal for my visit to Swansea.

'I am a rich man,' he told me proudly. 'My granddaughter is able to buy what she pleases, without regard for cost. I am anxious that you shall enjoy yourself; and Sara,' he added softly, 'remember that Adam has a great regard for you; I trust you will find yourself willing to return that regard in full measure.'

'Willing? That is a strange word!' I murmured.

His eyes were piercingly bright.

'Have I not told you I desire your happiness? I know much more of life than you do, my child! With Adam, you will find much happiness!'

'How can you say that, when we scarcely know one another?' I asked.

'Time will remedy that; you will have time together, whilst you are away. Use it well.'

He made it sound like a royal command and made me feel trapped into acceptance of his wishes by the sheer weight of his generosity to me.

My mother's voice, with its undertone of

bitterness came back down the years to me. *So he will try to buy you?*

I will never be bought in such a fashion, I thought rebelliously. Yet I allowed myself to think of Adam with a moment's tenderness; with him I would be safe; at peace with myself, no longer tormented by desire for a man who wanted me only whilst the summer days moved on towards autumn; who would leave me then, without a qualm and forget about me.

I met Meredith's bright, steely glance; he was watching me intently.

'You want me to marry Adam, but I do not love him!' I said unhappily. 'You cannot *order* love!'

'When will you learn that I know what is best for you, Sara? As for *love!*' The very word seemed to wilt under the scorn in his voice. 'Love is the sick fancy of a silly young woman! There is more than that to a marriage!'

'Did you not love Grandmother when you married her?'

'No!' he said, to my astonishment. 'Neither did she entertain such feelings for me. Ours was a contract agreeable to us both.'

Greatly daring, I retorted:

'Perhaps, because you did not love one another, you and Grandmother are not happy together.'

'You do not know what you are talking about,' he replied with cold disapproval. 'Such marriages as ours *can* bring – rewards. It is your grandmother's state of mind that puts distance between us. Remember, Sara, love is a trap from which death is often the only escape; and sometimes, even in death, there is no release.'

Something in his voice frightened me; it was intensely bitter.

'I do not understand!' I told him.

'Ask your Aunt Anne – she is trapped by an infatuation she believes to be love, and from which she cannot free herself! Ask your Aunt Jessie who married a waster, for love of him, and was left penniless, with a child to care for!'

'And my father, perhaps, was trapped by love,' I said quietly. 'For he gave up everything to marry my mother; and she loved him so much that she forgot honour, reputation, everything...'

'Who told you that?' he demanded sharply.

'I have seen my mother's marriage lines and my birth certificate,' I replied.

'Forget them both, Sara.' His voice was unexpectedly gentle. 'You will make your own way, and the past need not concern you; with all its sins and follies, it is done. What was between my son and your mother is unimportant now. Think over all I have said concerning Adam; you will have ample time to reflect during the days to come.'

'Rowan has asked me to marry him,' I said, and regretted the remark as soon as I had uttered it.

'*Rowan?*' I heard Meredith draw a sharp, incredulous breath. 'It is not possible! Are you speaking truthfully?'

'I would not speak otherwise about such a thing; he asks me to give him an answer when I return from Swansea.'

'You will tell him that you cannot marry him; do you understand, Sara?' Meredith said curtly.

'Oh yes, I shall tell him that; because HE does not love ME – he wants a wife who will bear him fine sons for Tremannion, so he says, and one who will look well at his table, when he is master.'

I looked for some reaction in Meredith's face; but it could have been carved from stone. Only the eyes glowed with a terrible fire, and I knew something was wrong.

'Why are you so angry?' I asked curiously.

His face looked grey and drawn, as though he was in pain; I saw the beads of perspiration along his forehead.

'What is it?' I whispered, alarmed. 'Are you ill?'

'No!' he said emphatically. 'I am tired, no more. This is one of the busiest times of the year for any sheep farmer. In spring, it is the lambing; in summer, it is the shearing. There is a great deal to do, and the men work the better for knowing they have a vigilant master. After it is all over, I will rest, as Evans keeps telling me to do.'

Meredith had reserved a splendid suite of rooms for us in Swansea's finest hotel. I was delighted with our surroundings, and the attentiveness of those whose job it was to look after us. Swansea was a fine city with big shops, and – to my surprise – a splendid sandy beach. When Adam pointed out to me the great docks to which cargo boats came from all over the world, nothing would content me but that we must see them. Catherine declared she was too tired for such an expedition, as the day was hot; she planned to spend the afternoon resting, in preparation for the concert we were to attend that evening; so Adam and I drove alone to visit the docks.

'I fear you may not like them,' Adam said anxiously. 'There is a great deal of noise and dirt and perhaps rather rough language, where there are docks.'

'I do not care only for pretty sights,' I told him. 'I want to understand and know about what is happening in the world.'

'You are not like other young ladies,' Adam said with a smile. 'You are as Thaddeus said – a wild, free spirit, whom

188

Tremannion would never hold.'

I made no reply, but I felt a delicious warmth tingle through my veins.

The docks fascinated me; I watched coal being loaded and thought of Meredith Pryce's mine, and all the other mines owned by such men; it seemed strange and fearful that some men should burrow deep into the veins of the earth, in darkness and danger, to search out glistening black treasure. I thought of the times I had lain in bed and watched tongues of flame flickering between the coals, grateful for the warmth. It was the first time that I had ever thought about the getting of coal from the earth, and of the men whose livelihood it was.

'The mining valleys are grim and ugly places,' Adam told me. 'There are rows of houses so small you would not think one man could live in them, let alone whole families. These houses are built in terrace on the mountainside, in thin, grey streets; then there are the pits with their slag heaps, and the gear and machinery everywhere, the lines of buckets going up to the tip, and the railway sidings with the trucks loaded with coal for the docks. When the men come up from the coal-face, they are black and filthy, so that you would scarcely recognise them as ordinary men; the mountains that were fair and green, like the Beacons, are all scarred where the coal has been worked.'

189

I looked at him in surprise.

'Adam, I have never heard you speak with such eloquence before!'

'These are not my words,' he admitted frankly. 'They were Patrick Flynn's; he was Thad's father and cared passionately about the people who get the coal and live amongst it. Because of this, he quarrelled violently with Meredith; there was a fall in the Five Valleys mine, some years ago, and many men were killed. Patrick publicly denounced Meredith, declaring he knew that the mine was unsafe and had refused to close it; worse, that he cared nothing for the widows and children left without fathers, as a result of the disaster.'

'What happened?' I asked, fascinated and shocked.

'The publicity meant that pressure was brought to bear upon your grandfather and he was forced to make changes,' Adam said uncomfortably. 'He did what had to be done, spent a great deal of money on the mine, and he made provision for those in need; but he never forgave Thad's father for the affair, nor for the things written and said about him.'

'Where did the Flynns live?' I asked.

'Over the Beacons to the north, a mile or two from Tremannion; you cannot see the house because it lies in a dip in the ground. It is much like Brennion – or was, for it was completely gutted by fire, a few years ago, and only the shell remains. Some say that gypsies were camping there and started the fire.'

'Patrick Flynn was not living there at the time, then?'

'No. He went away, soon after Nancy's death, and never returned. Thad spent his holidays with us, whilst his father roamed the world.'

'Adam, tell me about Nancy's death; why is it said that it was not an accident?'

He hesitated.

'Your grandfather would not like me to discuss these things. It is an old scandal, best forgotten. Meredith went to Flynn's house one night, just after the matter of the mine disaster was settled, and they had a violent quarrel. No one ever knew what the quarrel was about or whether it concerned the mine; but next morning, Nancy was found drowned in an old sheep-dip. Patrick was utterly distraught; he declared that Nancy had been so terrified by the quarrel that she had run from the house to seek help, and he had searched for her all night. She must have lost her way, poor soul, and stumbled into the water.'

'I suppose they did quarrel about the mine?'

'It was assumed so,' Adam said, frowning. 'What else?'

'I feel so hedged about by secrets at Tremannion,' I told him. 'So I am glad you have told me, Adam; though it is a tragic tale, and my grandfather, of course, bears much of the blame.'

'He cares a great deal for you, Sara, whatever he has done in the past. It gives him great happiness to know we are here together.'

'Is that why you came?' I asked sharply. Then I bit my lip. 'Adam, I am sorry; that was rude and ungracious. Only, it seems that Meredith Pryce decides what we shall all do, as though we were little wooden dolls and he held the strings.'

'I am sure he would not wish to be thought of like that; perhaps he seems to wield such power because he is a man of great character and strength of will; also, he is extremely wealthy.'

'Do YOU like him, Adam?'

'Yes,' he said quietly. 'If he is a hard man, then he has his reasons for hardness. I did not come to Swansea simply to please your grandfather, Sara; my greatest pleasure is in having your company.'

He put his hand over mine and I let it stay there for a moment.

However, I was surprised to discover, next day, that Meredith had insisted upon Cathy accepting a large sum of money to spend whilst we were in Swansea.

192

She told me about it when we were choosing gowns in an elegant and fashionable establishment; we had shopped lavishly that morning.

She fingered a gown of watered silk and said frankly:

'Neither Adam nor I are rich. Adam has poured a great deal of money into Brennion and suffered some severe setbacks, such as the one that wiped out much of his flock. I have but a small allowance from money left by my parents. Your grandfather insisted on making me a very handsome gift of money, and I did not want to accept it; but he declared it was little enough to do in order to show his appreciation of my accompanying you. I have not told Adam, for I know it is wrong that I should accept such a gift from a man; but the circumstances were such that a refusal would have been churlish.'

'I am sure he would not wish you to be troubled,' I assured her. 'Meredith is a most generous man.'

'I know; and I am enjoying it all so much,' she said softly.

'I am enjoying it too,' I told her, thrusting aside any lingering doubts as to Meredith's reasons for buying Cathy's gratitude.

'Do you know,' Cathy asked, 'how much affection my cousin has for you, Sara?'

She looked at me very intently from those

grey eyes of hers; I felt uneasy, not knowing how to reply. She seemed disappointed that I said nothing.

'He is not a man to give his affections lightly,' she declared with sudden vehemence, as she turned away to examine another gown.

If I married Adam, I thought, and found with him the peace that I so sorely need, there is no reason why Cathy should not remain with us at Brennion; but perhaps she would bitterly resent no longer being mistress there.

The skies were grey and overcast when we left Swansea, and the tops of the Beacons were shrouded in mist as we reached Tremannion. The house seemed to rise suddenly from the mist, like a sad, grey ghost, and I shivered, wishing I did not feel such reluctance to return.

I was glad to see Aunt Jessie; she came bustling to meet me.

'Well, child? You have enjoyed yourself?'

'Oh yes, thank you, Aunt Jessie! I have bought so many things; and there are presents for you all!' I told her.

She looked pleased and surprised; the servants took my luggage and the many parcels upstairs to my room. I changed from my travelling clothes, washed, and unpacked the tortoiseshell combs I had purchased for Jessie.

Tea was laid in the small dressing-room; there was a batch of scones, hot and freshly buttered, and a great fruit cake. I was hungry and eager to tell Jessie about Swansea.

I gave her the combs; she unwrapped them and looked at them with astonishment, her lower lip trembling.

'It is a long time since I had such a pretty gift,' she told me.

'Does no one ever buy you a present, Aunt Jessie?' I asked.

'Who is there to do so?' She laughed and shook her head rather sadly. 'Morgan was always surprising me with such things; but most men do not think of giving gifts, save on a big occasion. Thank you, Sara; the combs are beautiful. I have sent word to Meredith that you are here; he is inspecting the shearing sheds and asked to be told as soon as you returned.'

Meredith came in as we were finishing tea. He strode into the room, immediately dwarfing everything in sight as he always did, and held out his hands to me.

'Well, Sara? You look better! Come and tell me if you have enjoyed yourself.'

'I have!' I told him happily. 'I have a gift for you. We shopped and went to a concert, and Adam drove me to the docks because I wished to see the ships loading and unloading.'

He looked at me searchingly and nodded, apparently satisfied.

'So you found Adam pleasant company?'

'Yes; Cathy, also,' I replied quietly.

'I have poured tea for you, Meredith,' Jessie said; her voice sounded strained and she did not look at him as she spoke.

After tea, I went upstairs to unpack; I still had an hour to myself before it was time for Olwen to come and help me dress for dinner.

The first thing I saw, when I entered my room, was the white lace dress I had been wearing on the night Lily died; it was spread carefully over the bed, the dark, dried bloodstain clearly visible on its skirt. It brought back, with cruel clarity, the events of that dreadful evening when I had discovered the small, crumpled figure lying by the hearth.

I stared at it, drawing a deep breath, refusing to admit to a feeling of nausea. I remembered how, the day after Lily's death, Olwen had asked me if I wished her to have the dress cleaned. I had told her that I did not intend to wear it again, and she had hung it at the back of a wardrobe in the dressing-room, carefully covered with a sheet.

Someone had known the dress was there; why had it been taken from its hanger and laid out so carefully? Was it a warning? A reminder that there were people who did not welcome me at Tremannion?

So far as I knew, only Olwen was aware that the dress was in the wardrobe, for she had placed it there. It was a woman's trick, this, I thought, looking at the dress. I would not let it upset me; I would not mention it to anyone; let whoever had done this *wonder* what my reactions had been, I thought angrily!

I believed that Anne had done it; from the moment I had arrived, she had made her hatred of me so very obvious.

I folded the dress carefully, so that the stain did not show; when Olwen came in with the hot water, I glanced sharply at her, but she looked her usual pleasant, smiling self.

'You may have this dress, Olwen,' I said, watching her. 'I do not want it. I daresay you can have the stain removed.'

I held it out to her; she took it from me, looking delighted.

'Oh, *thank you*, miss!' she said. 'Pretty, it is; and it will clean, for sure.'

I wore a brand-new gown that evening; it was of palest green taffeta, its rustling skirt stiff and rich, with an overskirt of soft white muslin. The scalloped hem was fastened with true lovers' knots embroidered in pink silk, and I had slippers to match the dress.

Anne was dressed in grey; when she saw

me, she looked me over from head to toe, and murmured:

'"Consider the lilies of the field; they toil not, neither do they spin, yet even Solomon in all his glory was not arrayed like one of these."'

'Anne!' Jessie rebuked sharply, her face distressed. 'You should not speak so; it is most unfair and ill-mannered of you!'

I held out to Anne the small parcel containing the brooch I had bought for her, and I had the pleasure of seeing her look disconcerted, as she took it from me.

The Tremannion sheep were being brought in for the shearing; down they came, from the high Beacons, from the green slopes below the house, from the far corners of Tremannion land, great white flocks whose fleeces lay heavily upon their backs; all day, the droves of them went towards the big pens near the Home Farm, harried by barking dogs, running before the men who shouted orders in their own tongue. The noise went on all the time, the baa-ing and bleatings of protest, the tramp of the men's feet, the dogs; I had never seen such a sight in all my life, and my interest delighted Meredith.

'Will you take me to see the shearing?' I asked.

'Of course,' he said. 'It will be a sight you

198

will not easily forget, Sara. We have been fortunate, for the expected rains have not come; wet fleeces cannot be shorn. I have long told myself that the day would come when you would stand by my side and see the finest sight in the world: the great flock of Tremannion sheep brought down to be shorn of their fleeces!'

Even the house hummed with activity. I heard scraps of talk; Mrs Pugh and her hired helpers were busy all day in the farm kitchen, baking; the men were putting up trestle tables at the end of one of the sheds, for the mountains of food and drink to be brought to the shearers. Over at Brennion, Adam was working all hours helping to bring in *his* sheep, for his flock, though much smaller than Meredith's, was quite a big one; and so I saw nothing of him during the days before the shearing.

I hoped that Rowan would be too busy to seek me out and demand an answer to his question; I was not looking forward to having to tell him I could not marry him. However, I was unable to elude him for very long; he knew that I went to the stables every day, even when I did not ride, in order to feed the horses; and it was there that he came upon me, one afternoon.

'Sara?' He stood squarely in front of me, so that I could not escape. 'What is your answer?'

'I have given you my answer,' I said firmly, with no wish to hurt him by my rejection of his proposal.

'I suppose I am too rough for you?' His face was dark with suppressed anger, as he spoke. 'You want fancy manners and fine ways, is that it? You are like Uncle Meredith, thinking that I am good enough to look after sheep and make others rich. It is *my* care, *my* skill with the flocks, *my* hands that have made Tremannion rich!'

'I am sure that your Uncle Meredith appreciates that fact, as I do,' I pointed out. 'It does not mean I can change my mind and marry you. I would marry only for love, not admiration of all you have done here. Besides, you have not worked in vain; Tremannion and its flocks will one day be yours!'

'Yes!' he agreed vehemently. 'I shall not be cheated of what is mine!'

He moved closer to me; his face looked tired, he breathed heavily. I could smell the sweat on his body, as I looked at the torn shirt and dusty breeches.

'No one else can make you mistress of Tremannion!' he added. 'Think on that! I have taken a fancy to you and so I will put you at the head of my table.'

'I don't want to be there!' I reiterated wearily.

His eyes narrowed; they were full of secrets.

'I think you will change your mind!' he said softly.

'No! You must look for the mistress of Tremannion elsewhere, Rowan,' I told him.

I saw the stubborn disbelief in his face. He was as stupid as the sheep he tended, I thought. It was unkind of me to think of him like that, I realised; but I had an uneasy feeling that he had not given up his pursuit of me.

Meredith kept his promise and took me to see the shearing; it was a hot day, when we went into the sheds, with a cloying heat that was brooding for a thunderstorm.

The men had been hard at work for several hours when we arrived; the air smelled of grease and sweat, and was full of the complaints of the sheep. They bleated continually as they were driven in from the pens to be dealt with by the men who sat at the long benches. These men eyed me curiously; they spoke to one another in Welsh, their voices rising and falling musically above the clip-clop of their shears.

Their skill fascinated me; each man held a sheep expertly, shearing so that the heavy fleece from the animal fell away cleanly, like a discarded cloak. I thought the poor sheep looked very pathetic and naked after such treatment, but, in view of the heat, perhaps

201

they were glad to shed such a burden of wool. Meredith assured me that their fleeces would be as thick as ever again when the winter came.

After the shearing, each animal was branded with the Tremannion pitchmark, before being set free; then the whole business began again.

'Rowan shears the rams,' Meredith told me. 'He will entrust no one else with the task. Look at him – he looks like the farm labourer he is at heart!'

Rowan, at the far end of the shed, was stripped to the waist, his sturdy body gleaming as he worked. He looked up and his eyes met mine briefly, a curious expression in them.

Mrs Pugh and her helpers – a bevy of giggling young village girls – brought jugs of tea and plates of food to the men; and when they had set the food down on the tables, they gathered up the great piles of fleeces for sorting.

'Will you and Miss Pryce take some refreshment in the parlour, sir?' Mrs Pugh asked diffidently.

'Yes.' Meredith turned to me and looked 'at me searchingly.

'Have you enjoyed what you have seen this morning?' he asked.

'Yes!' I answered truthfully. 'I have enjoyed it all!'

He gave a smile of deep satisfaction.

'You and I think alike,' he declared enigmatically. 'We know what is important – and what is unimportant.'

Chapter Eight

After the shearing was done, Meredith and Rowan and Adam were busy making arrangements for the big Wool Auction; and in the house the women made plans for the Supper and festivities that would begin soon. As for me, I felt flat and very restless, now that the excitement was over. With so much else to think about, it had been easy to put memories of Thaddeus from my mind, but now they crept back as stealthily as the shadows crept into Tremannion. I could not deny them, hard though I tried to do so; and so the pull of that tremendous fascination he had for me drew me to the quarry one afternoon when Aunt Jessie had gone to Brennion to discuss the Supper arrangements with Cathy.

It was an afternoon of overcast skies, the air heavy and robbed of its freshness; Olwen's prediction concerning the coming storm seemed about to be realised, and I hoped it would not rain before I reached the quarry.

He will not be there, I told myself; I shall be glad about that, for then I can return to Tremannion without feelings of guilt; but I knew I merely made excuses to myself and hoped that Thaddeus WOULD be there.

My excitement mounted to an unbearable tension as I drew near; my pulses leapt when I saw the open window and half-open door. I rapped on the door and went in.

The place was clean and sparsely furnished; in one corner stood an easel with a half-finished canvas upon it. I saw that it was a painting of a girl's head; she looked like me, and the dark hair tumbled about her shoulders.

Thaddeus was seated at a small table, writing vigorously; beside him, lay a pile of papers. When he saw me, he rose to his feet and came towards me, smiling with the lazy warmth that promised so much and made me so helpless.

'I knew that you would come today!' he said softly.

'How CAN you have known such a thing? I did not decide to come until a little while ago!' I retorted.

'My sixth sense told me you were coming!'

'I do not believe in such nonsense!' I replied, with a shiver.

'I think you do; I called, Sara, and you came. One person can call silently to another and be answered as you have answered me!'

He cupped his hands around the back of my neck and tilted my face to meet his; I waited, but he did not kiss me. Instead, he looked down at me with grave intentness.

'WHY did you call me?' I whispered.

The white teeth flashed in a wicked smile.

'I was lonely!' he murmured. 'And Brecon is a long step on such a stifling day as this!'

I pulled sharply away, tears of rage and disappointment in my eyes.

'I hate you, Thaddeus! I wish I had not come!'

'That is the first time you have called me Thaddeus; so we are making progress; and you do not hate me, as you well know. What other answer did you imagine I would give? We made a bargain, you and I – a little summer-time of loving, and then no more.'

'*I* made no such bargain!' I cried.

'In that case, why are you here?' he asked reasonably.

'WHY do we always quarrel when we meet?' I asked despairingly.

'I have no wish to quarrel with you, my love. We have much better things to do. Perhaps I will make love to you.'

I knew he was testing me, to see if he could shock me; and he succeeded, for I felt my cheeks grow warm.

'Poor little Sara!' he said gently. 'You have been sheltered all your life by your mama

205

and know nothing of the appetites and lusts of men! Nothing has prepared you for this; but I have told you, I will do nothing you do not wish me to do; your heart cries out for me, and your reason tries to stifle the cry.'

He pulled me close to him and kissed me, slowly and lingeringly. I could feel the tautness of every muscle in his body through the thin shirt; I opened my eyes as he kissed me, and saw that his eyes were open too, brilliant with a strange emerald fire. Deliberately he put up a hand, and, with his fingertips, gently stroked the lids down over my eyes.

Thaddeus let me go reluctantly; I knew that if he had not done so, had his hands sought permission to love me as he desired, then I could not have denied him; the knowledge that Thaddeus did not love me, but merely found me desirable, made no difference to my feelings; and, with the realisation of my own weakness, came compassion and understanding for my Aunt Anne.

Love is a trap, Meredith had said bitterly; I was truly caught in its snare and even doubted my longing to be free.

'You are young and inexperienced in the ways of love, Sara,' Thaddeus said lightly. 'It would be sweet to teach you and you would be a most responsive pupil.'

'You should not talk to me like this!' I

protested, blushing.

'Your ardour invites me to say such things. It would be so easy to take you; but it seems I have some vestige of conscience left!' he said ruefully.

'I suppose your mistress in Brecon is – experienced?' I said bitterly.

'In the ways of love, yes; *I* was not her teacher,' he replied, unperturbed.

I leant against him, wanting his arms around me again; but he made no movement towards me. Instead he said consideringly:

'In truth, I think you need teaching such a lesson, Sara; for you behave like a wanton, not a well-reared young lady!' He was laughing at me, and I hated him, again. 'I would not be rough or cruel with you! Oh, there is no cause to retreat behind alarm, though you go too far, sometimes; I am in no mood for love-making. It is too hot, too airless. I am going to finish your portrait, and you shall sit for me.'

Without another word, he removed the pins from my hair and arranged it about my shoulders; then he sat me on a chair, turning me this way and that, until he was satisfied. Then he went to his easel and picked up his brushes.

'Something troubles you,' he said, after he had been working for a while. 'What is it?'

'Tremannion,' I said, with a sigh.

'Tremannion is a house; a house is no more than a pile of stones. Is it rather not the people within those walls who trouble you?'

'Yes. Strange things have happened since I have come to live there.'

'Tell me about them,' he said, still working at his canvas.

I recounted all that had happened from the moment that the stone had been flung at the coach on my journey to Meredith Pryce's house. He made no comment and I could not tell if he found my tale foolish or not. When I had finished, he still said nothing, but went on painting with great concentration.

'You have not believed one word I have said!' I told him angrily.

'I did not say that,' he retorted.

'You think, as Grandfather does, that I imagine these things!'

'That is not so. I need time to think on what you have said.' He glanced towards me, and a slow smile touched the corners of his mouth, as he added:

'Sara, do not look at me so, with your eyes so bright and your mouth so prim that I must stop my work to come and kiss away its primness, until it grows soft and yielding beneath mine.'

When at last he let me go, I had no breath left. I looked up into his face, feeling blissfully happy, and when I would have opened my mouth, he put a finger to my lips, his eyes dancing.

'Hush! You are going to say that you did not want to be kissed, and that you will never come here again! Why waste your breath, my darling? We both know it is not true!'

'Thaddeus, I think you are a magician, like Merlin, only not old and grey as he appears in Adam's book!' I said.

'And you, I swear, are a changeling, Sara Pryce.'

I put out my hand and touched the thick tawny hair caressingly. I did not care about tomorrow; I was not yet betrothed to any man, I reminded myself.

'I should like to read YOUR tales!' I murmured.

'Better still, you shall hear them, whilst I finish your portrait,' he told me gaily. 'What shall it be? The *toili*, with their eerie phantom funerals? The warriors of the days of King Arthur, who lie sleeping in a mysterious cave guarding a great pile of treasure? Or shall I tell you of the fairy mothers and the maidens who were good and virtuous – not like YOU, Sara Pryce – and whose skin was buttermilk, their hair golden, not dark as a gypsy's!'

I tossed my head at him and laughed; he began to tell me the tales he had gathered, and I listened, enthralled; I was sorry when finally he laid down his brush and declared:

'It is time you returned to Tremannion; I have other work to do and you distract me.'

'I do not want to go!' I protested.

'I know that; you want to stay, to tempt me, see if I will tease and touch you, so that you may wonder if, this time, it may not stop at kisses! You are like all women, desiring power over a man. No woman has power over me.'

I looked at him, unable to trust myself to speak; he read the truth in my eyes, for he shook his head and added, in a hard voice:

'You do not love me, Sara! I am different from any other man you have ever known, and so you are curious; you want to explore every nook and cranny of my mind and my heart. That you cannot do! You need a husband, a man who is kind and faithful; did I not tell you that you have a passionate nature? Tempt me too much, and you may regret what forces you unleash in me!'

How could love and hate for this man be so closely linked within me that they were inseparable, I wondered? I stood up and rearranged my hair, without glancing at the portrait.

'Good-bye, Thaddeus!'

'Au revoir, have you forgotten already? Do not pout; it is unbecoming. Children and silly young misses pout, and you are neither.

Go home, there's a good girl; you can come again soon!'

'Thank you!' I said bitterly; but he seemed to have forgotten I was there, as he stood carefully examining his afternoon's work.

I found the walk back to Tremannion exhausting; in my room, I bathed my face repeatedly in cold water, as though I tried to wash away guilt. When I went downstairs, Jessie had just returned from Brennion; I wondered what she would have said if she had known how my afternoon had been spent.

The heat was unbearable that evening; we dined with all the windows open, but there was not a breath of air to refresh us.

Rachel joined us for dinner; her eyes were very bright and restless, her manner excited.

'So you have decided to give us the pleasure of your company?' Meredith remarked sardonically.

'My room is stifling,' she declared. 'Anne has gone to Carmarthen. There is going to be a storm, Meredith! Such a storm as may well split this house asunder!' Her eyes glittered. 'How I should enjoy that!'

'No doubt! It would take more than a summer storm to bring this house down!' he retorted. 'You are over-excited, Rachel.'

'On such a night as this, Anne was born!' she answered softly. 'Have you forgotten?'

I saw the white ring of anger around

211

Meredith's mouth and wondered why her remark should so infuriate him. Across the table, Rowan's eyes met mine, with scarcely a vestige of expression in them; he had spoken little to me since the day we had met in the stable yard. Jessie ate her food without lifting her eyes from her plate, as though she feared being involved in an angry scene between Meredith and his wife. Rachel paid no attention to me at all; she went on talking in a high, excited voice about the things Anne and David had done when they were children.

'Do you remember the day they were lost, Meredith? It was just before Nancy Flynn was drowned.'

There was something evil in the way her eyes glittered; she seemed to be goading him and was thoroughly enjoying herself. I realised that she knew exactly what she was saying; her words were not the vague ramblings I had been accustomed to hearing from Rachel.

'They had walked over to visit Patrick and got lost. You punished them, I remember, for going out without your permission, and Patrick was angry...'

'Go to your room, Rachel,' Meredith said quietly.

After all these years, I can still remember the icy menace in his voice; Meredith's eyes were fixed on his wife's in a cold, unwinking stare – so might a snake look at a rabbit. In spite of the heat, the gooseflesh prickled on my arms.

Rachel glared at him and laughed; then she began to cry, and sprang to her feet, running from the room; Jessie half rose from her chair, but Meredith motioned to her to sit down.

'She does not require attention, Jessie,' he said curtly.

I was afraid of him at that moment; I considered what vengeance he would exact from those who angered him; and I knew, as surely as though I had been told, that the quarrel between Patrick Flynn and Meredith Pryce, on that dreadful night of Nancy's death, had not concerned the Five Valleys coal mine.

After dinner, I played the piano, at Meredith's request, but I did it half-heartedly, and begged to be excused after a short time.

'What is it, Sara?' he asked.

'The heat,' I replied.

'This weather will soon break and it will be cooler. Tomorrow, I am going to the Wool Auction; you are going to drive to Talgarth with Adam; it is a pretty little village at the foot of the Black Mountains.'

'Did *you* arrange this outing with Adam?' I asked.

'Certainly; why do you ask?'

'Should you not let him decide such

things? It must seem obvious to him what you are trying to do!' I retorted.

'Nonsense! My suggestion was eagerly accepted.'

'What if *I* do not wish to go?'

'Then, no doubt, you will find excellent reasons for not doing so,' he replied, with sudden weariness.

I saw how the colour had gone from his face, leaving it grey and drawn; I went across to him and knelt by his chair.

'You are ill! You have been working too hard!' I told him.

'It is nothing,' he retorted impatiently. 'There is always a great deal to be done at this time of the year. Evans insists upon concocting some ridiculous brew for me and constantly reminds me that I am not a young man; does the fool think that *I* do not mark the passing of the years? Consider your position, Sara, when I am no longer master of Tremannion; you might well find life intolerable. Therefore, I have tried to ensure that you are protected and your future is safeguarded. My thoughts are all for you; why then, this wilful desire to destroy what I have tried to accomplish?'

To my astonishment, he touched my bent head briefly with his hand; such a demonstrative act from so reserved a man moved me profoundly. I had ample proof of the fact that he loved me dearly. If there were traits in his nature that I found difficult to accept, and if I could not bend my will to his, at least I could learn compassion for him, I reflected; for he was closer to me, by blood ties, than anyone else in my life.

'Go to bed, child,' he said absently.

I kissed his forehead.

'Good night, Grandfather,' I whispered. 'And – please DO take care.'

The first flash of lightning came as I reached my room; it lit the sky vividly, clothing the dark mass of the Beacons in an unearthly blue light. It was still airless, with no sign of rain, so I left my windows open.

It was Olwen's free evening, and I undressed, lying with only a sheet to cover me, watching the flashes of lightning. When I heard the owl's twice-repeated cry, I knew that Anne must have returned from Carmarthen, and that Philip Evans waited for her in the shadows outside the house.

From afar off, I heard the first, deep-throated growl of thunder; the lightning flickered more brightly, and little fingers of flame seemed to run down the sky; the storm was worsening and coming nearer. Soon, I heard the quick patter of raindrops and jumped down from my bed, breathing the cooler air gratefully; the rain fell with steady insistence and I closed the windows before I returned to bed.

Worn out by the day's events, I drifted into sleep, in spite of the approaching thunder; storms had never frightened me – my greatest fear was that of being shut in a small space and kept a prisoner there.

I dreamed that I was locked in a tiny room, at the bottom of a flight of steps. There was no way out and no light, save that from a slit high in the wall. When I tried to cry out, my voice had no sound. I beat vainly on the walls and, somewhere in the distance, I heard the sound of Thaddeus Flynn's mocking laughter.

I awoke, damp with perspiration, to hear a particularly loud crash of thunder; the rain still hissed at the windows, yet I could see no lightning, which puzzled me. The darkness around me was like a thick curtain of black velvet.

There was a momentary lull in the storm; I thought I heard a faint movement close to my bed and the sound of someone breathing heavily.

Instinctively I reached for the matches to light my lamp; but my groping fingers encountered only soft, heavy folds of material.

The curtains had been drawn around my bed.

Frantically I groped for an opening; up and down, from side to side, went my trembling hands; furiously I fought down rising hysteria – all I had to do was find an opening in the curtains and make my escape from this soft, clinging prison.

As my fingers sought an opening, they came into contact with something solid on the other side of the curtain; something that moved away instantly, with an angry jerk.

I screamed out wildly, but my scream was drowned by another crash of thunder. Terrified, I inched across to the far side of the bed; then I leant down and desperately searched for the small gap where the curtains brushed the floor.

I found it and lifted the curtains, sliding out beneath them to the floor; I crawled to the farthest corner of the room, and a little of my terror receded, now that I was free. I crouched against a heavy chest, on top of which were several volumes of Shakespeare's plays, bound in calf and very heavy. Carefully, I reached up and took down a book.

The lulls in the storm were brief, for it seemed as though all the wrath of Heaven was concentrated on Tremannion; but, in a few seconds of calm, I heard again the sound of faint movement and the heavy breathing, coming closer to me.

When I judged the time to be right, I scrambled to my feet and hurled the book in the direction of the sound; I could not see, still, for the curtains had been drawn across the windows.

I did not wait to see if my missile had found its target; foolishly, I raced across the room, determined to escape into the corridor; and then came disaster, for I stumbled over the bed hangings and fell.

Someone wrenched the hangings violently from their rods; no nightmare was ever so dreadful as the reality that faced me as the curtains were flung over my head. This would be slow death by suffocation, I thought, horrified, muffled in fold upon fold of thick material, blinding me, smothering me in a soft darkness from which there was no escape.

I could not breathe; I was pinioned by a strong pair of arms so that I could not move to free myself, though I struggled desperately. The blood drummed in my ears, and I felt myself beginning to lose consciousness. With the last of my strength, I tried to claw the cloth from my nose and mouth, but the vicious grip on my arms made it impossible, and I thought my lungs would burst.

Suddenly, the arms that had held me slackened; I was vaguely aware of two things: someone running from the room, and a commotion coming from the room next door to mine.

Weakly I pushed away the bed-coverings from my head, and lay on the floor, gasping in agony for breath. After a little while, I was able to get to my feet and stumble across to the window; it was an effort to pull back the curtains and open the window enough to let in the sweet, cool air; I thought I would never get enough of fresh air. I stood there, trembling, the tears running down my cheeks.

The storm was rolling away, the thunder becoming muted, and the lightning flashes more intermittent; but still there was a noise in the room next to mine.

I did not want to go into my father's old room, to see what was causing the noise; I had tasted enough of adventure for one night. Someone else would have to deal with this situation, I thought wearily, as I pulled a wrapper about my shoulders. It sounded as though a wild animal raged in the next room, creating some terrible havoc.

I found my way to the bedside table and lit the lamp; I searched for clues that might lead me to my attacker, but found none. I considered the strength in the arms that had held mine. Rowan? But no man seeks to murder the woman he hopes to marry, and I believed that he had not yet given up the idea of making me mistress of Tremannion. It was unthinkable that Meredith should want to harm me, and plump little Aunt Jessie certainly did not possess steely strength such as I had encountered; that left only Rachel and Anne, both of whom hated me.

The noises from the next room had ceased; but I thought I heard the faint sound of someone crying. Cautiously I opened my door, and stepped out into the corridor; light came through the open door of my father's room, and, as I approached, I saw that the lamp which always stood by his bed had been lighted.

The lamp lit a scene of utter chaos. Books had been scattered everywhere, china smashed, the vase of flowers overturned, and every flower shredded into minute particles, the little clock lay on the floor with its glass broken. In the midst of it all, Rachel sat on the disordered bed, weeping bitterly.

I realised, then, that my grandmother had saved my life; for the intruder in my room had heard the noises coming from the next door bedroom, and fled. I shuddered, thinking what might have happened to me had my attacker not been disturbed.

I sat down and put an arm about Grandmother's shoulders.

'What is it?' I asked. 'Who has done this?'

She lifted her head from her hands and stared at me; her face looked terribly old, her eyes were bright. She wore her night-clothes and her hair hung loose, almost to her waist, making her look like a grotesque caricature of the young girl she had once been.

'*Grandmother?*' she repeated slowly. 'No

one calls me that! Who are you?'

'I am Sara, your granddaughter,' I replied firmly. 'Your son, David, was my father.'

'Sara.' Her thin hand clung to mine with astonishing strength, crushing my fingers in a grip that hurt. 'I am sure I have never before seen you, nor heard of you.'

I looked into the blank, bright eyes and said gently:

'You HAVE seen me, but I expect you have forgotten that fact. Tell me why this room has been wrecked; it was my father's, you told me, and was always kept in readiness for his return.'

The bitter, desolate crying began again. She crossed her arms over her breast and rocked herself to and fro.

'*I* have done it!' she cried. 'For he will never come back! *Never!* He is dead, *dead!* Meredith came to me, tonight, and told me so, over and over again, driving his words like nails into my brain. He made me look and listen, as he spoke; he told me that Davey's body was brought from the sea, many years ago! He saw it, he declared! Tonight he said that I am *mad,* a stupid, witless old woman!'

Helplessly, I stroked the bowed head, wondering why Meredith had felt the need to drive home the truth to his wife so cruelly. He knew that she wavered precariously between sanity and madness, and the dividing line was very thin, although at this moment, Rachel's mind was clear and lucid.

'Listen,' I said, 'it is true that David is dead; but whilst he lived, he was happy; you must remember that; and you have Anne to care for you.'

She stared at me, clutching fiercely at my hand.

'He wanted to punish me,' she declared passionately. 'He was angry because I reminded him of the night that Anne was born. He prefers to forget his old sins and follies! That night was just like this one; the Beacons shook with the violence of terrible thunder, and the lightning seemed to set the sky on fire. I was alone in this house, save for the servants. Meredith returned next morning and would not look at my child. He had spent the night with another woman; I cannot remember her name, now ... but there were always women to comfort Meredith. Jessie declared it was because I turned from him, after Anne's birth. I hated him to touch me. David was not conceived in love, neither was the child that died within me the night he tried to kill me. Do YOU know of the appetites of men or their cruelties?'

'Hush!' I murmured, trembling. 'You must not say such things!'

'They are true. There are other, strange things, of which I have spoken to no one,'

Rachel whispered. 'Did you but know the truth, why, then...'

She bit her lip and stared hard at me; I had a feeling that she was about to tell me something that was vitally important, impart some knowledge she had kept to herself through long, bitter years; but she changed her mind and shook her head.

'I shall never come into this room again!' she declared.

'Perhaps that is for the best. I will tidy it for you and have the door locked, so that no one comes here. Would you like that?'

She nodded and sighed deeply, as though she was very tired.

'You must not grieve over what happened long ago,' I told her. 'David loved you, and you loved him; he would not wish you to grieve so.'

'Yes,' she agreed, like an obedient child. 'I must not grieve. The door shall be locked.' She bent forward suddenly, peering hard at me, her face only inches from mine.

'Celia's child!' she murmured. 'How strange! You are kind, yet I should hate you, for your mother stole Davey! SHE says I should hate you for that!'

'Who does?' I asked sharply.

'Megan,' Grandmother answered listlessly, as though she had suddenly grown weary of the subject.

'It is wrong of her to say these things; you

223

must not allow her to do so!' I declared.

'This house is full of evil and bitterness!' Rachel said vehemently. 'You should not stay! If you do not go, you will become part of the hatred, the evil!'

'Grandmother,' I said, 'did you come to my room tonight and pull the curtains around my bed? Will you try hard to remember if you did so? Mine is the room next to this one and has a four-poster bed.'

She frowned, and her eyes were so blank that I realised her brief moments of sanity were vanishing into the mists of madness again.

'*I* did not go into that room!' she replied wildly. 'Jessie used to sleep there, but she did not like the place, for she swore it was haunted by the ghost of Seth Pryce's mistress, who slept in that bed when she lived here.'

'It was no ghost that came to me tonight!' I retorted.

Rachel shook her head vaguely, her lips moving soundlessly; she allowed me to lead her back to her room and was as docile as a child until I tried to persuade her to go to bed. She refused and sat in a chair, rocking herself to and fro, shivering and crying.

'I want Anne!' she declared piteously. 'SHE is kind to me! SHE has never hurt me as *you* all have! Anne knows how to make me sleep!'

Loath though I was to summon Anne, I knew there was nothing else I could do; I looked around the room and saw two doors, at opposite ends of the big room. I went towards the door that was on the inner side of the house, but as I tugged at the handle, Rachel turned her head sharply.

'Come away!' she cried. 'Davey is asleep upstairs in the old nursery, and you will only disturb him if you go to him! *I* am the only one who uses that stairway!'

I went over to the other door, on the outside wall; beyond it, a flight of steps, thickly carpeted, led down to another door, beneath which I saw a thin finger of light.

I went down the stairs and tapped reluctantly; Anne answered my knock. She did not open the door wide, but it was sufficient for me to glimpse, fleetingly, a room that was luxuriously furnished and full of light.

She was obviously not alone; she wore a loose; pretty wrapper, her hair flowed about a face from which all the lines of bitterness had been smoothed away. She had a soft, fulfilled look, and I reflected that it was a pity she should waste herself upon a weak man who was another woman's husband.

'What do you want?' she demanded in a surprised, hostile voice.

Briefly I explained to her what had happened.

'I will tidy my father's old room,' I concluded. 'The door can be locked. Perhaps it will be less upsetting for your mother not to go there again.'

She closed the door behind her and walked past me, up the stairs. At the top, she turned, and said to me, with a cool mockery that reminded me of Thaddeus:

'Who are YOU to say what shall be done here? You are not yet mistress of Tremannion!'

'Yet, Aunt Anne?'

She laughed scornfully and did not reply.

When I reached Rachel's room, Anne was kneeling with her arms about her mother, gentleness in her voice; Anne Pryce had as many facets as a diamond, and each new one surprised me as it caught the light.

I returned to my father's room and set about restoring it to order, moving as quietly as I could, and reflecting that the inhabitants of this house slept as soundly as only people with good consciences were reputed to do. Surely the noise of the storm must have awakened some of them? Was there someone still waiting for me in the shadows, I wondered uneasily?

When I had completed my task, I went to my own room; I placed the lighted lamp upon the table and dragged a heavy chair across the room, so that its back was against the door. I tucked a rug around me, and there I dozed fitfully for the rest of the

226

night. When daylight came, I was stiff and cold; I gathered up the hangings that had been wrenched from their runners, and went across to the window.

It was going to be a sparkling day; the rain seemed to have washed away all the dust and staleness of the past days, and the world looked as though it had been rinsed clean and laid out to dry in the sun.

On an impulse, I opened the door of the little dressing-room and looked inside; it was tidy and empty, except for my clothes. No one would hide in there, I reasoned, for the only exit was into my bedroom.

At six o'clock, I went into my father's room; I looked at the heap of broken china, the smashed clock, and felt no emotion; the events of the previous night had left me drained of all feeling.

At precisely five minutes past six, Megan appeared with the jug of hot water; she looked taken aback and none too pleased to see me.

'Megan,' I said, 'in future this room will be locked and no one will come here.'

The sloe-coloured eyes stared defiantly into mine.

'Not for you to give orders, miss; for the rest of the house, it is Mrs Jessie who says what will be done. For this room, it is the master's wife. If SHE tells me not to, then I will bring no more hot water.'

She took malicious delight in putting me in my place; I watched her place the can of water on the wash-stand with slow deliberation. When she turned to leave the room, I said quietly:

'You told my grandmother, many times, that she would hate me. You knew that was wrong and mischievous of you; why did you do it?'

Dull colour ran into the sallow cheeks.

'Going to tell the master, are you, miss?' she asked angrily.

In spite of the air of defiance, I heard a note of uncertainty in her voice; I knew that Meredith would have no compunction about dismissing even an old servant; I realised, also, that Megan was genuinely attached to her mistress.

'I shall not tell him,' I replied, 'unless you continue to upset my grandmother by saying such things. Why do you wish me harm?'

She glanced at me sharply, but her hands trembled as they moved over her apron.

'Harm, is it? Not from ME, miss! Others, perhaps; that is THEIR business. Davey was the light of Mrs Rachel's eyes. She lived for the day when HE would be master here, and not Mr Meredith. Then your mother came and took him from her.'

'All this nonsense!' I retorted. 'It is the way of life for people to marry!'

'He need not have gone from here; even

though he needed to marry HER in haste.'

'I am aware of that, Megan,' I replied coolly.

She looked taken aback and slightly shame-faced.

'It would have been forgotten!' she muttered. 'They could have stayed, not run off to England. She coaxed him away, and if she had not, then he would have been alive today to comfort his mother; and if his mother tells me these things, when Miss Anne is about her business, and there is no one else to listen, should I not agree with what is true? And there is the master, behaving as though it was royalty coming to this house, when you came, miss. A shame it is, then, that he has no thought to spare for HER.'

'I know,' I said wearily. 'Miss Anne feels the same way. I understand that; but you have no right to tell my grandmother she should hate me, for all that. It can only confuse and disturb her.'

She folded her lips tightly together and went away, without another word.

Before I went down to breakfast, I glanced at myself searchingly in the mirror; I was older than the girl who had lived such a carefree life, so happily sheltered from all things violent and ugly; THAT girl would not have known how to deal with the events of the past few days, I thought wryly; but I was rapidly learning that to face such situations is to mature, not by years, but by experience.

For a moment, I allowed myself to think of Thaddeus, to remember the ecstasy of his kisses, the message in the touch of his hands; it was like finding warmth in a cold and barren place.

Grandfather and Rowan had left early for the Wool Auction; Anne did not put in an appearance, and only Aunt Jessie was seated at breakfast.

'I am not hungry,' I told her. 'I would like some coffee, that is all. Aunt Jessie, may I please have a key to my room? Last night, at the height of the storm, I was attacked. Someone came into my room, pulled the curtains around my bed, and attempted to smother me with them. The curtains have been torn down; I should like them to be taken away.'

I saw the astonishment and doubt in her face.

'Yes,' I added resignedly, *'you* will say it was a nightmare, as will my grandfather if I tell him what happened. I am so confused by all that happens here that I wonder if perhaps it *is* true, and I dream these things. Certainly I cannot prove what I say; but last night, someone moved on the other side of the curtains as I tried to grope my way through them. I was held by the arms and the curtains drawn tightly over my head; THAT was no nightmare! Why did you give me that room, Aunt Jessie? YOU slept there, and did not like it!'

'The choice was Meredith's,' she replied calmly. 'He wished you to have it because it is the biggest and finest in the house, and has an excellent view of the Beacons. He scoffs at talk of ghosts; but, remember, he suggested to you, after Lily's death, that you might like another room.'

I shook my head.

'I will not be frightened away by whoever wishes me such ill in this house! However, I SHOULD like a key, for then I would feel safe at night.'

'Very well; you shall have one, Sara,' she promised.

Then I told her what had happened to my father's old room, and how I had spoken to Megan about it.

'I will see that Megan has her instructions for it to be locked,' Aunt Jessie told me. 'She is difficult, I know, but she serves Rachel faithfully.'

'I *do* understand,' I sighed. 'Everyone, it seems, resents my presence here; except you, and, of course, my grandfather.'

'I have no cause to resent you,' Jessie pointed out. 'Meredith is a very wealthy man and has no doubt ensured that, after his

231

death, you will enjoy much of that wealth; but it is MY son who is heir, and nothing can change that fact. As I have told you, it is my one desire to see him take his rightful place here, the place his father would have had before him. No doubt by the time Rowan attains his inheritance you will have married and left this house. Whilst you live here, it is my duty to do all I can for your comfort, and it is a duty I have never found irksome. I am quite fond of you, Sara.'

There was no mistaking the sincerity in her words; she seemed to me to be the one person in this house without bitterness or hatred in her heart.

'I wish that you could have looked kindly upon Rowan,' she added regretfully. 'He would have been a good husband to you.'

I looked up sharply, and she nodded.

'Oh yes, he told me what passed between you! We are very close, my son and I; it went deep with him that you rejected him!'

'But, Aunt Jessie, he made no mention of – of – *feelings!* He spoke of me as someone to bear his children and grace his table!' I protested indignantly.

'What more does any man ask but that?' she pointed out crisply. 'It does not mean he would be an inconsiderate husband; because he speaks little and perhaps clumsily, it does not mean that he has no feelings. Perhaps, when he asks you again – as he will

– you answer will be different. *I* would not resent your being mistress here.'

'Grandfather wishes me to marry Adam,' I said, exasperated. 'And YOU would be happy to see me wed Rowan; but I do not care deeply for either of them, and truly, I have not yet had time to discover whether I could ever do so!'

'Perhaps there is someone else you love?' she suggested.

'No one!' I lied.

'If you marry Adam,' Jessie said, 'then Cathy will leave Brennion, for she could not endure seeing another woman there; she has loved Adam deeply for years, though he treats her as a favourite sister.'

'How do you know this?' I asked, astonished.

'I have eyes, child,' she retorted dryly. 'I have seen how she looks at Adam, and I have heard the tone of her voice when she speaks of him. He is unaware of her love and always has been; men are blind!'

'I have thought that Cathy cared for Cousin Rowan,' I faltered, bewildered.

She laughed at my folly and shook her head emphatically.

'Cathy and Rowan have always been friends; she understands him as few people do, but there is no more to it than that; and it will be a black day for Catherine Grey when Adam takes a bride to Brennion!'

Chapter Nine

I did not enjoy the outing to Talgarth, for I was weary from lack of sleep, and my mind still too much occupied with the events of the previous night.

Adam commented, with some concern, on the shadows beneath my eyes.

'You are not yourself, Sara; did last night's storm keep you awake?'

'Not the storm.' The need to talk to someone was overwhelming. I told him all that had happened, watching him closely. I saw the doubt in his face.

'You do not believe my story,' I said resignedly. 'Had I told Grandfather, he, too, would have doubted me.'

'It is a strange enough tale,' he pointed out frankly. 'But the explanation may be simple. You have spoken of Rachel's violence; she denies entering your room to harm you, but it may be that she does such things and has no memory of them afterwards. She wrought havoc in David's room, you say. *There* is your attacker, I am sure; you know she resents your presence at Tremannion.'

I was silent; I knew it seemed the most feasible explanation. It was pointless to tell him of my suspicion that someone entering Tremannion by one of its many doors or windows could have attacked me. I had no proof, nor could I name anyone outside the house who would wish to harm me.

Adam took my hands between his and said earnestly:

'Dear Sara, it distresses me to see you so unhappy. I have a deep regard for you, as you must know; I want the right to care for you, for the rest of your life; as my wife, you would be safe at Brennion – and happy.'

There was tenderness and concern in his face; I bent my head, not knowing how to answer him, remembering clearly the sense of peace and safety I had known when we stood together in Brecon Cathedral. Adam represented a sure refuge from the storms that raged about me; he was a man I could lean upon, trust implicitly, offering me a love that would never falter. Perhaps Meredith was wise and far-seeing, after all, in his desire to see me married to this man.

A small traitorous voice within me whispered that love should not be peace and contentment and safety; it must be a wild rage within the heart, a storm in the senses.

'Sara?' Adam said softly. 'You are silent. Perhaps I have spoken too soon and startled you; but I have known affection for you since the moment we met, and it grows daily. Though we have known one another only a little while, I feel that we could achieve great happiness in marriage.'

'Meredith wishes us to wed, as you know,' I said, looking at him thoughtfully.

'Do you believe that his wishes have influenced me and reinforced lukewarm feelings? If so, you are mistaken, Sara,' he replied firmly.

'Give me time,' I pleaded. 'I am – deeply fond of you, Adam; but I am unsure of myself.'

'I understand,' he said gently. 'I promise you I shall not be impatient, nor expect an answer before you feel ready to give it.'

He lifted one of my hands to his lips and kissed my fingertips. He would be a considerate husband, though not one capable of great passion, I thought; perhaps that was a good thing. Passionate love could wreck a life and destroy happiness.

I felt safer, now that I was able to lock my bedroom door at nights; but, by day, I was wary, feeling that I could trust no one.

I thought a great deal about Adam's proposal, sorely tempted to give my happiness into his keeping; Meredith noticed my preoccupation.

'You are quiet, Sara,' he said.

'I have much to occupy my thoughts.'

'I believe that Adam has asked you to marry him,' he replied.

'Has he consulted you then, Grandfather?' I asked.

'I am your guardian; naturally he asked my permission to approach you; would you have expected him to do otherwise? What was your answer?'

'I have asked for time to consider the matter.'

He looked disappointed.

'I wish to announce your betrothal on the night of the Harvest Supper,' he declared firmly.

'That is too soon; the Supper takes place next week!' I protested.

'Come, you do not need time; you know that Adam will be good to you; it will be an excellent match!'

I did not reply; the urgency in his voice troubled me.

I walked to the little stone house in the quarry the following afternoon; no, I did not walk. I flew on winged feet! But Thaddeus was not there. The door was locked, and though I waited impatiently for some time, he did not put in an appearance. I went slowly homeward, my heart heavy, my feet no longer winged, but slow and dragging.

That night, Adam and Cathy dined with us; Cathy wore one of her new gowns.

'It looks delightful on you,' I told her.

'Yes,' she agreed, without enthusiasm. 'It

is more costly and beautiful than any *I* could have purchased; but I confess to a feeling of shame for allowing your grandfather to pay for my new wardrobe.'

'Why, Cathy!' I exclaimed, surprised. 'You knew it was a gift that he was happy to make, in view of the fact that you accompanied me.'

Her smile was tight, her face aloof.

'We both know that was not the reason for the gift; Meredith wishes you to marry Adam. When a man of wealth and position desires a thing greatly, then he is able to use everything in his power to achieve his ends.'

'You talk as though he could wave a magic wand and compel two people to care for one another; but this is not possible,' I pointed out.

'Adam cares for you. I can read the truth in his face. Do not hurt him, Sara, nor treat him lightly, for *I* care deeply for Adam, and if you do this, there can be no friendship between us!'

The serene little face was no longer quiet; Cathy's cheeks were flushed, her eyes bright. The dove had become a tigress.

'You love Adam, do you not, Cathy?' I said frankly.

She drew a long, shuddering breath.

'Yes,' she admitted. 'His happiness is my one concern. Brennion is my life.'

'When Adam marries, there will be room for you, still, at Brennion,' I pointed out, troubled by the intensity of her expression and her obvious distress.

'I am not sure that I could remain to see Adam there with a wife,' she replied quietly. Then she smiled at me, the tension gone from her face, her eyes serene again.

'I own I *should* feel great jealousy towards you,' she told me gently. 'I do not; but, be warned, Sara, Adam's happiness will always be of the greatest importance to me! He is loyal and generous and has great goodness of heart.'

'That is obvious; Mr Flynn must have cause to be grateful for Adam's kindness,' I agreed.

'Thad is a wanderer; the cottage is his only home. He has gone off on his travels again; for how long, no one can say.'

Perhaps he has gone no further than Brecon, I thought bitterly.

At breakfast next morning, Jessie complained to me of a severe headache.

'My headaches are becoming more frequent of late,' she said. 'I need a supply of the powders that Philip Evans makes up for me. I shall walk to the village and call upon him this afternoon.'

'Let me go, Aunt Jessie,' I begged. 'Grandfather is away today and I am so tired of having nothing to do.'

She pursed her lips doubtfully.

'Meredith would not approve. He would insist that you go in the small carriage, with Roberts or one of the grooms.'

'I know; but there is no need to tell him, Aunt Jessie,' I coaxed. 'A walk in the air will refresh me.'

She agreed that I might walk down to the village after lunch. I was troubled about Aunt Jessie; she seemed preoccupied, as though something weighed heavily upon her mind. Perhaps this fact accounted for the increasing severity of her headaches, I decided.

I was glad of a definite objective to fill some part of the long day. Adam and Cathy had driven to Llandovery to visit old friends who were staying at the inn there, and Meredith was in Carmarthen. Rowan was somewhere out on the Beacons, I had no idea where Anne was, and I had not seen Rachel since the night of the storm.

By the time I left the house, the weather had changed with its usual capriciousness, and mists were wreathing and curling about the Beacons like the smoke from a great camp fire in the sky. The air was so damp that I was glad to wear a cloak and pull the hood about my face. In places the road was quite slippery, for it had rained very heavily during the night. The little brook that foamed under the bridge was swollen with the rains and hissed angrily as it raced over the stones. It was a sad day, reminiscent of autumn, serving to remind me sharply that summer would soon be ending.

I was glad of the solitude and freedom, as well as the exercise of the walk; though my thoughts were poor company. As usual, the village seemed to be deserted, like a place long since abandoned by its inhabitants. I thought I saw movements behind curtains; somewhere a child cried, and a dog barked. A man's voice shouted to the dog to be silent, and the silence crept back again, giving me the eerie impression of being watched by unseen eyes, from the small, deep-set windows. It seemed as though every step I took was noted. I shivered, reflecting that the apprehension I felt so keenly at Tremannion had reached down to this place, to touch me with cold fingers.

The baker's shop was closed, and there was no sign of life at the forge. I walked towards the Evans' shop; but as I approached, I was halted by the sound of a woman's voice, low and fierce.

'No better than a woman of the streets she is, the fine Miss Pryce of Tremannion, telling my husband that he is a great clever man and too good for ME! I know what passes between them, and one of these days I will find them together, taken in adultery, like in the Bible!'

'It is a shameful business,' murmured a sympathetic female voice in reply. 'No better than anyone else, the Pryces, with their airs and graces!'

'I will tell you this!' Bronwen cried with passionate fury. 'She will be sorry for what she has done! I will give her cause to repent it! Mind, I am not saying *how*.' The voice became mysterious. 'But tears and regret there will be.'

'God will punish her, Bron,' the other woman said righteously.

'I shall not wait for HIS vengeance,' Bronwen said vindictively. 'For why have the Pryces flourished and grown rich on greed and wickedness all these years, their sins unchecked, unless He is asleep?'

The conversation fascinated me, though I was faintly disturbed by the triumphant viciousness in Bronwen's voice when she spoke of revenge. There were sounds of impending departure from within the shop; the voice of Bronwen's companion murmured something to the effect that no doubt He had duly noted all things concerning the Pryces of Tremannion and the time for punishment could not be far off…

I was in no frame of mind to face Bronwen for a while; I walked quickly past the shop, with bent head, and did not stop until I reached the gate of the little white church.

Thankfully I went into the tiny cemetery; it had the unearthly stillness that such places possess on mournful days. The grasses were all beaded with drops of moisture, and the foxglove bells hung dispiritedly on their stems. I walked past poor Lily's grave to the big, iron-railed enclosure where the marble angel stood sentinel over the Pryce tombs. Even in death, it seemed, the Pryces of Tremannion must be separated from their fellowmen and women, as though they were far above them.

I walked towards the church door, reflecting how different it all was on Sundays, with servants and tenants lining the path between the graves, the splendid isolation of the Pryce pew, the rich sound of singing, and the fiery energy of the preacher as he measured the enormity of our sins by the thump of his fist on the Bible.

Gently I lifted the latch, and the door swung inwards without a sound. I thought I would sit inside awhile and compose my thoughts, but I saw that I was not alone. A figure knelt, head bowed, at the altar rails, quite unaware of my entrance.

I did not want to disturb the woman who prayed so earnestly; cautiously I tiptoed away, closing the door behind me. I was puzzled, having recognised the cloak slipping from the smooth brown head. Cathy knelt there, and I had believed her to be in Llandovery with Adam. She must be greatly troubled in spirit to have foregone the outing in order to visit the church in the village.

I reasoned that I had given Bronwen's temper time enough to cool. The bell jangled loudly and unmusically, as I opened the shop door. Bronwen came from the back room immediately. Her face was sullen, her eyelids puffy as though she had been crying, and I felt a stab of pity for her.

Her look was hostile, her voice surly.

'Yes?' she said.

'My aunt, Mrs Jessie Pryce, is troubled by headaches and is anxious to have a prescription that Mr Evans recommends for her,' I said. 'I would be grateful if I might have a supply to take to her.'

Without a word she went to the back of the shop, I heard her voice, hard and indifferent, as she spoke to Philip. I sat down on a small chair and waited.

Philip Evans brought me several small paper packets a few moments later; his face and voice had no expression in them.

'I have written the dose on the packet; they are to be taken with caution, Miss Pryce,' he said. 'Be so good as to remind Mrs Pryce of that, will you?'

'Yes, Mr Evans, thank you,' I said.

I was glad to escape, for the very air seemed to snarl and bristle with the antagonism between husband and wife.

During the next few days, I noticed that Anne seemed to have an air of suppressed excitement about her; it was nothing to do with the coming festivities, I felt, though I had never before seen her so animated.

Tremannion was full of activity; Aunt Jessie explained to me that it was customary to set sheaves of corn on either side of the massive front door; boughs and trails of greenery would decorate the house, and two of the finest fleeces, from a ram and one of the ewes would be hung at the foot of the stairs, in the hall, where they could be seen and admired by the visitors.

'It will be quite a party at dinner,' Jessie declared. 'All of us here, even Rachel, then Adam and Catherine, Dr Evans and Mr Williams, the veterinary surgeon, and some distant cousins of Meredith's from Tenby.'

'Let us have foxgloves in the house,' I pleaded. 'They will make a pretty decoration!'

'They are little more than weeds, Sara! However, if it pleases you, then you may put some about the house. They will die quickly. The medical men make better use of the foxgloves than we do!'

'What do you mean?' I asked.

She frowned, as though trying to remember something.

'Digitalis – that is the word! It is an old remedy!'

'That is the Latin name for the flower, Aunt Jessie.'

'Well, there is something they make from the plant, then, a drug to stimulate the heart when it is too slow. Anne would know; she has studied such things.' There was a note of respect in Jessie's voice.

'Dr Evans has warned Meredith not to overtax himself,' she added. 'It will place a strain on his heart, so he says. Meredith will have none of it, of course; but I am not easy in my mind about him.'

'Is he ill?' I asked, greatly alarmed.

'He says he is not. If he takes care, he will live to be master of Tremannion for many years yet,' Jessie prophesied.

Three days before the Harvest Supper, I rode out of Tremannion in the small carriage, with Roberts driving. It was Lily's birthday, and I wished to place some flowers on her grave. Meredith thought the idea morbid and absurdly sentimental, but gave me permission to go.

The day was warm, though overcast; we reached the bridge that spanned the stream and were halfway across when I heard the sharp sound of a stone whistling through the air. In the split second before disaster overtook us, I thought: *this is how it was on the day I came here!*

The carriage rocked violently from side to side; I clung on desperately, hearing the frightened neighing of the horses as they reared up on their hind legs, there was a loud shout from Roberts, followed by a wild scream of fear. The rocking, swaying coach miraculously righted itself, although the terrified animals still snorted furiously, their hooves clattering on the stones of the bridge.

With a mighty effort, I wrenched open the door and climbed down; the box where Roberts had sat was empty. He lay face down in the stream.

Sobbing, I scrambled down the bank, slithering in the mud. I knelt at the water's edge and clawed frantically at Roberts' coat; though he was a small man, I had great difficulty in pulling him from the water; and when, panting; I heaved him over on to his back, I realised that he was dead; blood ran from a huge wound in his forehead where it had struck against a boulder.

I was violently sick, reflecting bitterly that my insistence on visiting Lily's grave had been responsible for Roberts' death; the stone had been meant to kill us both by overturning the coach, and it was only the fact that the horses had not bolted which had saved my life.

How long I knelt there I do not know; my

face was wet with tears, as well as with spray from the water where it struck the stones. I scrambled to my feet and ran all the way back to Tremannion, my lungs and heart feeling as though they would explode, for it was uphill all the way.

Near the house, I stumbled on a loose stone and fell; I lay there, with scarcely the strength left to rise to my feet, as Rowan came running from the house.

He lifted me to my feet as though I was a child.

'What is wrong?' he demanded.

'Roberts has been killed!' I sobbed. 'Someone threw a stone at the coach!'

He half-led, half-carried me indoors; Cathy stood in the hall, removing her bonnet, and I remember that she had come to see Aunt Jessie, to discuss the final arrangements for the festivities.

She looked at me, round-eyed with surprise and dismay; she took me to the library and laid me on a couch, whilst Rowan was despatched for sal volatile and hot tea; Aunt Jessie sat beside me, twisting her hands in her lap, her face frightened.

'What is happening here?' she asked despairingly. 'There seems to be some malign influence hanging over the house.'

'The evil from the old days,' Cathy said softly. 'Seth Pryce's mistress is said to have hidden near the bridge, after she was turned out of this house, and to have flung a stone at the carriage, that was taking his wife down to the village, one day. They say the accident left her lame for the rest of her life. This house is cursed!'

Jessie glanced at her and frowned; I said shortly:

'It was a human hand that threw the stone; I heard it whistling through the air.'

She coloured slightly and stood up.

'I will tell Adam what has happened,' she said. 'He will be most concerned for you. I hope you will soon be recovered from your experience.'

Cathy had walked from Brennion; she had been going to stay to tea, yet now she was making her departure. How easily she could have detoured and come by way of the bridge, I thought. Yet my own thoughts made me ashamed; Cathy was quiet and gentle and kind. The danger that closed like concealing mists about me, making it impossible to see my way in safety, did not come from HER.

'Adam is with Thad at this moment,' Cathy added.

'He has returned, then?' I said casually.

'Yes; quite unexpectedly, only a short time ago. I believe he plans to leave Wales soon, to go abroad.'

Meredith was perturbed about the accident and its effects upon me, though he insisted that the Harvest Supper should not be postponed on account of Roberts' death.

'A stone was flung,' I insisted. 'I heard it; that is what happened on the day I came here. Can you not believe there is someone near me who wishes me ill?'

He stared down at me, a strange, brooding expression on his face.

'Sara,' he said quietly, 'you gave a letter into my keeping for safety; you told me it had been taken from your room and then returned. I want you to think carefully; are you certain that you did not simply mislay this letter?'

'I am certain,' I replied calmly.

'My study is not locked,' he said, as though to himself. 'Servants clean it; anyone in this house has access to it. An easy matter, undoubtedly, to break open a letter and then find the seal to fasten the envelope afterwards.'

'But *who?*' I whispered.

He shrugged.

'That I do not know – as yet. It would be wise to announce your betrothal, as I suggested; it would be wise for you to be married and in Adam's care without delay!'

I looked at him in astonishment.

'Am I no longer safe in YOUR care, then?'

'It is not the same thing,' he retorted, with an evasiveness that surprised me. 'Well, Sara?'

I drew a deep breath; the decision I had made had been shaping itself in my mind all day.

'You have been kind to me, Grandfather, and given me a home here; you treated me generously and have been concerned for my well-being; but I cannot remain here nor marry Adam. I believe my life to be in danger whilst I am under this roof. I shall return to London. I am certain that there is work of some kind I can do.'

His face was livid with fury.

'You talk wildly, Sara! If there are such threats as you claim, I will deal with them! *You* – go to London?' There was a world of contempt in his voice. 'To work – at *what*? Become a servant or a governess, a mere servant at the beck and call of everyone! Your mother fled from here when she had no need to do so! If she had stayed, her life would have followed a very different course.'

'One that was shaped by YOU!' I cried.

He brushed aside my words.

'You shall not repeat her folly, Sara! You will stay here, and your betrothal will be announced, as I have said.'

Had I been less overwrought, I might not have found the courage to defy him; but my words were blurred with tears because I cared for this strange, overbearing man who was my grandfather.

251

'I will not marry Adam!' I said stubbornly. 'I have thought much about it, and, although I have an affection for him, it is not strong enough for me to consent to be his wife. You cannot MAKE me marry him! You must not order my life in such a fashion. People are not puppet dolls to be manipulated by the strings that YOU hold! I give you deepest affection, my trust, I will do all I can to please you and repay you as best I may, but you must not ask the impossible of me!'

He stared at me in silence; his mouth was a hard, tight line, his face looked gaunt; then he turned on his heel and went from the room.

I did not come down to dinner that evening; Olwen brought a tray to my room. Jessie fussed anxiously, offering me a sedative, but I refused; worn out by the day's events I slept soundly, and awoke to a grey morning, the clouds over the Beacons heavy with rain.

I felt a strange, unnatural calm. I decided that when Grandfather left the house that afternoon, I would go to Brennion and tell Adam of my decision. After I had seen Adam, I would call upon Thaddeus.

Breakfast was a silent meal; Meredith addressed only one remark to me.

'I have ordered the horses to be saddled for us, Sara; a ride will do us both good.'

'Very well,' I said obediently.

We rode silently together in the crisp air that already had the coolness of autumn on its breath; I sensed the depths of Meredith's anger and disappointment and the gulf between us made me sad. In spite of our differences of opinion, I knew there was a thin, but unbreakable link between us; such bonds exist only between certain people and are not broken, even by death, I reflected.

I vowed I would go straight to Brennion, for I owed Adam that courtesy; but my promises melted like mists in the morning sun, as soon as I saw the half-open door of Thaddeus Flynn's cottage. I had no power to pass the door, but as my feet led me towards it, I despised myself for my weakness.

I knocked and entered; Thaddeus stood in the centre of the room, his arms folded, his face thoughtful. He looked for all the world as though he was about to pass judgment on me, and never moved when he saw me there.

'Go to Brennion, Sara,' he said, 'or back to Tremannion; you have no place here.'

'Have you no better welcome for me than that?' I asked. 'You did not greet me so last time I came! When did you return, Thaddeus?'

'Yesterday afternoon,' he replied.

'There was an accident, then, by the

bridge. A stone was thrown at the coach. Perhaps YOU did it?'

'Perhaps I did!' he agreed mockingly.

'Did you come straight from Brecon?' I asked angrily.

'I have not been to Brecon. I have been in search of solitude, such as I expected to find here.'

The inference was so obvious that I hated him. He stood motionless, as though he was carved from granite. His green eyes, clear and cold as an emerald sea, were narrowed as he gazed at me; I looked at the tanned skin stretched tautly over the high cheekbones, and the unyielding line of his mouth. Impossible to believe the eyes had once been full of laughter, the mouth tender with kisses and soft words.

'Why are you so angry?' I asked.

'It is YOU who are in a strange mood!' he retorted. 'You appear like an avenging angel! What do you want of me?'

'Nothing!' I retorted contemptuously.

'That is not true! If I let you, you would twine yourself about my life like tendrils of ivy that can tear down the strongest walls, in time! That I cannot permit! I shall go from here, as I came – free!'

'Take me with you!' I pleaded. 'I will ask nothing of you!'

He laughed scornfully.

'Are you mad? Why, you would be

254

dishonoured in everyone's eyes as surely as though you were my mistress!'

'I do not care what people think! I cannot marry Adam!'

'You *should* marry him; he will take excellent care of you!' Thaddeus answered dryly.

'I do not love him!' I replied passionately. 'Nor ever will! Neither can I remain at Tremannion for I believe my life to be in danger, and my grandfather will never rest in his efforts to bring about a marriage with Adam. So I shall go away; to London, perhaps. I shall work. I am not afraid of being alone, nor poor!'

'Fine words!' he applauded cynically. 'And what will Meredith's petted and indulged little granddaughter do, alone in a city that is fierce and cruel to the poor and defenceless? He can compel you to return, of course, and he will certainly do so; no doubt you will be glad to come back here, having made your bid for independence and shown him that you possess a fiery spirit!'

His cool assessment hurt me bitterly; I had never in my life struck anyone; but I lifted my hand to strike the mocking smile from Thaddeus Flynn's face.

He caught my hand in flight and held it fast; and that contact of flesh against flesh aroused sleeping fires within him; he bent his head and kissed me, as though to mend the quarrel between us.

His kiss became more compelling, and I struggled against him; he put his hand against the back of my head, cradling me, his smile amused and light-hearted. He would always be master of himself; no passion would ever overwhelm HIM, I thought.

'Have I not told you to be careful what fires you stoke so assiduously?' he asked softly. His eyes glowed, as he touched my forehead, my cheeks, my lips, and my throat with his kisses; then he put me from him, with a sigh of regret.

'Ah, Sara, what pleasure it would be to teach you the arts of love!' he murmured.

'I have no intention of accepting your invitation!' I retorted.

'It was no invitation; I am mindful of your youth and position!' he teased. 'It gives me some pleasure to know that Meredith Pryce will not find it easy to subdue your spirit. One day, you will be a most enchanting woman, Sara. A pity I shall not be here to see it!'

'Are you not coming back to Brennion?' I asked fearfully.

His face was cold and forbidding; it was as though the sun had suddenly gone behind a bank of storm clouds.

'No. It is time I was gone.'

'You said – when the foxgloves die,' I whispered. 'A summer-time of loving – those were your words. The summer is not over.'

'We have had that summer-time; it is almost autumn.'

'The foxgloves still bloom!' I reminded him, feeling as cold as though a snow wind blew over my heart.

'I cannot stay longer,' he replied irritably, as though I wearied him.

'Where will you go, Thaddeus? And when will you return?'

'I cannot answer either question! Perhaps I shall go to Greece; to Italy, where I can paint. I shall go soon. My book is finished.' He smiled coldly. 'No doubt, it is a good thing I shall not return here; for it might be to find that you have become a well-padded matron, with a dignified air, and a brood of Adam's children!'

'I have never hated anyone as I hate you!' I choked.

With my head held high, I turned and walked away; no word of farewell passed between us. I was in no mood, now, to go to Brennion, so I turned back along the way I had come.

Meredith had called Thaddeus a waster and a scoundrel; a fair enough description, I assured myself. Let anger against this man sustain me until I had truly learned to forget him! I had made myself foolish in front of him, cheapened myself by revealing my feelings for him; everything I had done shamed my mother's careful upbringing, as well as my own deepest instincts of modesty and reticence.

So it was over; all loving done, between us two; but it would not be easy to forget this man who was so strange, so compelling. I would leave Tremannion and return to London. It might be that one day I would come face to face with Thaddeus Flynn again, and discover that he meant nothing to me.

Chapter Ten

I had scarcely left the cottage when I heard the sound of horses' hooves, and my heart almost stopped beating when I saw the tall, commanding figure riding towards me, mounted on Solomon.

Meredith reined to a standstill, only a few yards from the cottage door; he glared down at me, every line of his taut body expressing savage anger.

'Well, Sara?' he said coldly. 'I thought to find you at Brennion, although instinct has whispered, of late, that your reasons for not wishing to marry Adam are less innocent than you would have me believe. Did I not tell you that you were to have nothing to do with Flynn? How dare you disobey me so flagrantly and make such a mockery of my concern for your reputation!'

The hand holding the riding crop quivered; behind me, I heard the cottage door open, and as I turned my head, I saw Thaddeus step out. He leant negligently against the door lintel and eyed Meredith unconcernedly.

Meredith looked at me as though I was fit only to be trampled under Solomon's hooves.

'So you are his mistress?' he said, vitriolic scorn in his voice.

Tears sprang to my eyes.

'I am NOT!' I cried fiercely. 'Whatever deceit I have practised, I have not brought dishonour upon myself nor shamed you!'

The cold disbelief in his face hurt me sorely; he looked past me towards Thaddeus, and his hand tightened on the whip as though he yearned to use it.

'May I point out, sir,' Thaddeus said sarcastically, 'that this is Brennion land? You are not the lord of Tremannion *here!* In fact, you are a trespasser!'

'I have a mind to give you a thrashing you will remember all your days!' Meredith snarled.

'Idle threats, Meredith Pryce! You would regret your rashness, for I have no respect

259

either for your age or your position!'

I thought my grandfather would choke; then a cold, cruel smile touched the angry mouth.

'If my granddaughter is not your mistress, then have you suddenly become impotent? YOU, who boast of your conquests of women? Or does she lie to me? Perhaps you *have* seduced her, as your father once seduced my wife!'

There was a silence so terrible it seemed as though the world had ceased to spin on its axis for a moment, holding us all fast in an emptiness that seemed to stretch into eternity. The blood surged in drum beats in my head; even Thaddeus was startled into immobility.

'You are out of your mind!' Thaddeus said incredulously, at last.

Meredith threw back his head and laughed.

'No doubt you would like to believe that!' he declared.

Both men seemed to have forgotten my presence; the grasses shivered softly beneath my feet in the breeze, and Solomon pawed the ground restively, rolling his eyes until the whites showed, his ears twitching.

Slowly Thaddeus walked up to Meredith, until he stood beside him as though he would tear him down from the saddle; his face blazed with fury.

'You are a liar!' he said contemptuously.

'It will be a joy to enlighten you, Flynn!' Meredith retorted. 'Rachel Hughes was pregnant when I married her; she was a plain, stupid creature, little more than a child, extravagantly indulged by elderly parents who had no other child. Her father, Owen, was very rich and respected, and had urgent need to find a husband for his daughter, who refused to name her seducer! The prospect of such disgrace in his family all but turned Owen's brain, so we struck a bargain; he made me a very handsome settlement in return for my name and a home for Rachel's bastard! The child she bore was a girl; the sour, shrivelled creature with a nettlebed for a tongue, who has lived beneath my roof all these years, is your half-sister Anne!'

I stared, horrified, at Thaddeus; a muscle quivered in his cheek; his self-control seemed to be superhuman.

'If it was true,' Thaddeus sneered, 'you could not have kept it to yourself for so many years!'

'*I* did not know the name of the man who fathered Rachel's child for many years! I did not ask to know!' Meredith retorted. 'She cried it aloud, in anger, one night – some years after we were married. She stood at the top of the great staircase at Tremannion, and whispered it savagely to me. *Patrick*

261

Flynn! If she had died that night, I would not have grieved, though it was no action of mine that sent her hurtling to the hall below; she missed her footing.'

'Do you expect me to believe that?' Thaddeus cried.

'As you will; it is the truth.' Meredith's voice held a scalding bitterness, as he continued:

'Rachel had chosen her time well. She told me the truth only a short time after your father had caused me to be publicly censured for the way I ran the Five Valleys mine and managed my affairs. The self-righteous Patrick Flynn, who dared to point his finger at ME, had given Rachel a child, *after* he was married to your mother! When I heard that, from Rachel's own lips, I rode over to his house, intending to kill him!'

'Instead you killed my mother,' Thaddeus said very quietly; and I saw his intense struggle to control his anger.

'I did not kill her, I told her the truth. Your father was like a man demented, and the violence of our quarrel so frightened her that she ran from the house, seeking help. In the darkness, she lost her way and fell into the old sheep-dip; unless you prefer to think she took her life deliberately!'

'YOU killed her, Meredith Pryce!' Thaddeus repeated softly. 'As surely as though you held her head under those waters!

Damn you, why did my father not proclaim your guilt to the whole world?'

'And reveal his own?' Meredith said scornfully. 'Patrick Flynn was the upright man whom everyone praised for his fine principles, and his courageous stand against the wickedness of the master of Tremannion! He told me he kept silent only for the sakes of Rachel and Nancy, for his illegitimate daughter, and for his beloved only son! He even said that if I tried to reveal the truth, he would brand me as Nancy's murderer on whatever evidence he saw fit to invent! When Rachel knew what had happened, she declared that she would add her testimony to your father's and swear I had also attempted to kill *her!*'

'Checkmate!' Thaddeus said with cold fury. 'So, for the only time in your life, Meredith Pryce, you could not manipulate events and people to your advantage! In all this sorry tale, that is my one cause for rejoicing!'

I saw him spring, like a tiger, at the man on horseback, as though to drag him down and beat him senseless; I tried to cry out, but no sound came from my lips; as though he anticipated the action, Meredith touched Solomon's flanks and wheeled away, with split-second timing.

He rode away towards Brennion without another word to either of us; I glanced warily at Thaddeus; the sun made tawny fire of his hair, but his eyes glittered, and he looked like a man carved from stone as he stood there, staring ahead of him.

'Thaddeus,' I whispered unhappily.

Slowly his head turned in my direction; his face and voice were expressionless, as he said:

'It is as well that we shall never meet again, for the very name of Pryce sickens me! I am glad that Anne is my half-sister, for although she carries the name, there is none of THAT blood in her veins, thank God!'

'You forget your father's part in the matter!' I said despairingly.

'I do not, Sara. No doubt he lived with remorse, as men do, and tried to make amends! I shall think of my mother often – dazed by shock and grief, stumbling into those icy waters, crying out for help! It was Meredith who drove her there – never forget that! YOU condone his action, because you see him as a kindly, benevolent figure, fool that you are!'

I knew that it was hopeless to argue with him, to tell him that I was not blind to my grandfather's true nature; he had, after all, suffered a great shock.

I walked slowly back to Tremannion, my eyes so hazed with tears that the fair green countryside was blurred and unreal. I thought how Meredith had reached out and touched the lives of others, changing their course for ever; Nancy would have been alive today but for him, Anne would not have been the embittered woman that I knew.

Yet the truth, strange and terrible though it was, could make no difference to me now, I reasoned; it served to strengthen my resolve to leave Tremannion, and I would see to it that Meredith never found me; poverty and hardship would be more willingly endured if I had peace of mind; and such peace could never be mine until the wide waters of the Severn divided me from the strange, unhappy Pryce family.

Yet I had a feeling that the story was not yet done; that Meredith's revelations were but a prelude to a mightier drama that was soon to be played out at Tremannion; and, though the day was bright, a chill sense of foreboding closed about me, like the mists that so often hovered over the Beacons, ghosts walking on the roof of the world.

When I reached my room, I bathed my forehead with cologne and lay down, reliving the dreadful scene at the cottage. I was beginning to understand the complexities of Meredith's nature; though Rachel and Patrick Flynn had both defeated him, he had enjoyed knowing that Anne hated him and would have welcomed the truth that he was not her real father. It was a satisfaction he would never give her, I reflected; doubtless he felt that neither Thaddeus nor I would ever tell her who she was.

When Olwen came to dress me that evening, I made her search out the most splendid gown in my wardrobe. I passed over the jewels that Meredith had given me in favour of my mother's ring and a pair of handsome earrings that had been a gift from my father to my mother. Olwen looked curiously at me when I asked her to take special pains with my hair; but when at last I was ready, I knew that I had never looked better. Such attention to feminine detail might seem absurd, under the circumstances, but only another woman could understand how they served to help me in facing the ordeal that lay ahead; no one knew how my hands shook, nor how I dreaded facing the assembled Pryce family at dinner.

Though I was punctual, they were all assembled. Meredith inspected me from head to toe, his face inscrutable. Rowan's dark, brooding eyes held an admiration for which I was grateful; Aunt Jessie was her usual, slightly flustered self, and Anne's glance held frank curiosity.

I had little appetite; conversation was purely formal. Meredith did not address any remark directly to me. Anne seemed in unusually high spirits, but I was too concerned with my own affairs to give that fact much thought.

When the meal was over, Meredith said coldly:

'Come to my study, Sara.'

'Why, Father!' Anne said gaily. 'By your voice and countenance, Sara has disgraced us all by committing some dreadful crime, for which she is about to be tried and judged. What HAS she done?'

Such flippancy from Anne was rare indeed. I resisted a wild impulse to laugh hysterically at the word springing so easily to her lips: *father*.

Meredith said nothing to her; without a word, I followed him from the room, holding my head high. There was a fire burning in his study; with studied courtesy he placed a chair in front of his desk and sat down behind the desk, opposite me.

He did not beat about the bush; he said coldly:

'You will swear to me that you will never see Thaddeus Flynn again!'

'How can I do that?' I retorted. 'You desire me to marry Adam and live at Brennion! Thaddeus Flynn is Adam's friend!'

'Adam will see reason,' Meredith replied smoothly. 'He will recognise the folly of continuing the friendship!'

'I am not sure that you can manipulate

Adam so easily!' I retorted. 'He is loyal and has a stubborn streak!'

'That is a matter you must leave to me; will you swear never to see Flynn again?'

'I shall not see him; for *he* has decreed it so and is leaving Wales, in any case!'

'He tires easily of his women, I am told. I am prepared to accept that you have not been his mistress, but I dare say that is but a matter of time. You have cheapened yourself by your behaviour!' Suddenly he crashed his fist down on the leather blotter on his desk. 'I am very angry with you, Sara! You sit there, looking so cool, so proud! You have lied and deceived me and behaved like a trollop! Were you a son of mine, I would soundly thrash you!'

'If I were your son!' I retorted, 'the occasion would not have arisen! I am sorry that I have lied to you and deceived you, but as to my feelings where Thaddeus Flynn is concerned, I cannot feel regret!'

'A man like that will have his way with you, and when he has made sport of you, will toss you aside, crush you under his heel like an insect!'

'As YOU have crushed people?' I whispered.

After all these years, I can still remember every word that he spoke in answer to my taunt.

He rose to his feet, towering above me,

terrible and splendid, full of a strange fire that seemed to burn at white heat like a mighty furnace at the heart of him.

'Who are YOU to sit in judgment on me!' he demanded. 'When I inherited Tremannion, it was neglected and impoverished! My father squeezed every penny from the estate to pay for his obsession with gambling; Morgan squandered what was left of his inheritance, and was too lazy to farm the place. I wanted to see Tremannion proud and splendid and prosperous, as it should have been, and I needed money to realise my dream. I made a fair bargain with Owen Hughes; many such bargains are struck, Sara, in homes both rich and poor! For all that she was a plain, stupid, childlike creature, I felt a certain concern and responsibility for her that would have become affection – *if* she had let it! Ah, that surprises you! It is true; but Rachel made no secret of her contempt for me, on her wedding night and forever after. She could not forget that her father had coerced her into marriage – but it was I who bore that burden, aye, and the burden of Flynn's guilt, in her attitude to me!'

I felt his anguish; and I wept silently for him. It was wrong, I thought, to make so many excuses for the weak and foolish, and condemn those who were strong, calling them cruel and ruthless.

'When David was born,' Meredith continued, 'Rachel had a plaything; Anne was always too stubborn, too independent to please her. On David, my wife lavished an affection that was unhealthy in its intensity; how strange, considering that he was unwillingly conceived by her and fathered by a man she detested! David was all hers; she would not let me make a man of him, until I over-rode her and had my way! So, beneath my roof, there was Anne, whose mother encouraged her to hate me! Davey, made soft and spoiled, and unwilling to farm Tremannion, finally escaping from her over-protective love. There was Jessie, who needed nothing from me save a home, and her son who waits for the day when HE will be master here. I made Anne stay here and care for her mother – it was a payment I had a right to exact! Yes, I have been a hard man – to all who have worked for me, to those who live under my roof! I have taken my pound of flesh and more; how else would I have made Tremannion great? How else acquired the wealth that has made me the most powerful man in the county! Women seek love, Sara; they crave it. Men know that love is, at best, a frail thing, and so they seek power, which is more lasting and a more comfortable thing to live with!'

He paused for breath; I bowed my head, like a tree in a mighty wind, letting the storm pass over me.

'And YOU, Sara!' he said accusingly. 'You, for whom I have cared more deeply than for any of them, I have desired to make your future safe, make you more powerful than any woman, and you shall not wreck those plans! Sit in judgment on me, then! Believe that your heart has been torn asunder! I tell you that you can forget Flynn, if you but put your mind to it; can you not see that it gave him great pleasure to entice you, knowing how angry I would be when the truth was discovered? Now *I* have given HIM something more to ponder on, when he is far from here! It is all at an end, as you have said; tomorrow night, I shall announce that you are to marry Adam; be thankful that he knows nothing of your folly with Thaddeus Flynn!'

'I do not see how this marriage you wish to bring about can make me so all-powerful,' I told him.

'There are things I have not told you; they must wait until I think the moment is right. I am aware that all is not as it should be in this house; trust me, Sara. Be patient.'

Wearily I rose to my feet.

'When tomorrow's festivities are over, I shall return to London,' I said.

'Do you think you can escape me so easily?' he said gently. 'No, Sara. Even if you succeed in reaching London, be sure I shall

271

find you and bring you back here, where you belong. I am your legal guardian until you come of age; and I will not lose YOU, Sara, stubborn though you are!'

'Announce the betrothal, if you wish,' I replied indifferently. 'You will merely look foolish when I leave Tremannion unwed, and I have too much affection for you to wish to see you made the subject of ridicule. However, I cannot prevent you from doing as you please.'

I turned and left the room, not trusting myself to speak further, because I loved him dearly.

I felt drained of all emotion; dry, tearless, moving in a state of unnatural calm. I even slept soundly that night, for youth is resilient, and there comes a time when heart and mind must bar their doors to all feeling and emotion, retreating into a fastness of their own.

The day of the Harvest Supper dawned clear and warm; there was great excitement amongst the servants, as they put the finishing touches to the decorations, under Aunt Jessie's directions. I had never seen Tremannion look so magnificent; it seemed to proclaim its wealth and importance to the whole world. The two fleeces were placed in the hall, with great ceremony, the corn sheaves stood like twin golden sentinels on either side of the front door. I went out and gathered an armful of fox-gloves, turning my back towards the cottage near Brennion and avoiding the old sheep-dip; but my heart was heavy, and every road along which my thoughts wandered led me back to one man. Though I might dull the pain of memory with time, I knew that, just as there was a fine, unbelievably strong bond between Meredith and myself, so I was irrevocably bound to Thaddeus, in a strange mating that was only of the heart and mind.

I arranged a great fan of the flowers in the hall, and Jessie praised them, expressing surprise that they looked so well. On an impulse, I took some to Rachel. She was wandering about her room, restless, eyes bright.

'No one brings me flowers!' she declared, astonished.

'I have brought you some, Grandmother.' I looked closely at her, wanting to discover if I felt pity for her.

I could not feel other than pity; she had been foolish and had been punished by Owen Hughes's fear of disgrace and Meredith Pryce's longing for power. Neither these men, nor life had dealt kindly with her.

She put a hand on my arm.

'I remember you! It was you who brought

me a gift from Swansea! You are a good girl, Sara.' She sighed. 'Perhaps, one day, I may find it in my heart to forgive your mother for taking my son from me. Well, I must not be sad, Anne says. Tonight is the great event of the year at Tremannion; as to that, I care nothing for it, but *this* night will be different!' Her chuckle was sly, making me uneasy. 'You will see! You will see!'

Her head was nodding up and down like a mandarin's, the familiar vacant look had come back into her eyes; I left her sitting there, and felt uneasy, as I shut the door behind me.

Philip Evans came to the house, just before lunch; he was in the hall with Jessie, when I came to put the finishing touches to my flowers. He looked swiftly at me and then looked away again; I saw that he carried a basket of medicines.

As I worked, I heard Jessie carefully checking the contents of the basket with him.

'The medicine for the sick ewe – and the vaccine; yes, that is for Rowan. A *tonic* for Anne? By whose order is this?'

'Dr Evans,' Philip said shortly.

'I see. There are my headache powders, the sedatives are for Rachel. As to this medicine for Meredith, he will not take it, as you well know. He says there is nothing wrong with his heart.'

'I am obeying instructions, that is all,' Philip replied; he sounded nervous and ill-at-ease. 'Dr Evans left the prescription with me, instructing me to make it up and bring it to Tremannion.'

'He will toss it away, as he did before. Thank you, Mr Evans; will you take a glass of wine before you leave?'

'No, thank you,' he said.

He seemed most anxious to be gone; I watched him walk quickly away; his figure was slight, his gait was almost girlish in its affectation.

Lunch was an impromptu affair; Meredith was absent, having gone over to the Home Farm to check the preparations that had been made for the servants, tenants, and shearers to be accommodated in the two big barns.

I was thankful that I did not have to sit at lunch with him; it was not excitement that raced in my veins, but dread. I longed for the evening's festivities to be over; this time tomorrow, I told myself calmly, my belongings will be packed. I shall order the coach as soon as Meredith is absent from the house, and ask to be driven to Brecon. From there, I will find my way to London as best I can. I had a little money, plus my mother's jewellery; it would be sufficient to keep me whilst I looked for a suitable situation.

To my great surprise, Anne invited me to

come to her room, just before teatime.

'Come, Sara!' she said gaily. 'I have something to tell you! I have told no one else, save Mama, but it concerns you, also.'

Mystified, I entered the luxuriously appointed room. On a small table near the hearth stood a bottle with a chemist's label upon it, two crystal glasses, and a small key.

Anne was plainly dressed, as usual, her hair fastened back in its customary tight knot; but, for the first time since I had known her, she looked quite attractive; there was colour in her cheeks, a sparkle in her eyes, a softness about her mouth.

'You and I will drink a toast!' she cried.

'To what?' I asked, astonished, watching her pour the bright red liquid into the glasses.

'To the future; MY future; and what better to drink it in than this ridiculous tonic that has been prescribed for me and tastes like sugar syrup! *I* have a better tonic than THIS, to sustain me!'

She handed me a glass and picked up the second one, lifting it high, so that the liquid glowed blood-red.

I watched her drink and barely put my lips to the rim of the glass, taking the smallest sip of the sticky liquid. For all I knew, Anne was as mad as her mother.

Anne drained her glass and laughed at my confusion.

276

'I have no mind to poison you!' she said gaily; and, picking up the bottle, she tossed it into the grate. The glass shattered into fragments and the liquid oozed everywhere; somehow, it reminded me of blood, and I shuddered.

'I shall never need a tonic again!' She laughed. 'Sara, this key is yours now; you have charge of it, as from this moment!'

With a great show of mock courtesy, she placed it in my hand.

'It is the key of the medicine chest,' she explained. 'There!' She pointed to an ornately carved wall-cupboard.

I stared at her in dismay and disbelief.

'What good will that do you, Aunt Anne?' I stammered. 'He has a wife!'

'Yes, indeed!' she replied carelessly. 'A dull, stupid woman, a slut!'

'She is still his wife; he can't marry you,' I pointed out unhappily.

I could see her infatuation for Philip written clearly on her austere face. The ways of the heart may be strange, but what else *could* it be save infatuation, born of loneliness? Philip Evans was a weak man, without the strength of character that my aunt needed in a permanent relationship, but he loved her – or professed to do so. That fact was an oasis in the desert of her life – I saw the hunger in her face and felt a pity for her that I could not put into words.

'You can have no idea what it has been like here, all these years,' she said wearily. 'Caring for my mother, hating my father for what he is; only Aunt Jessie and Rowan for company – a dull enough pair! If Philip finds me desirable and will leave his wife to be with ME, why should I reckon with the consequences? I don't care what happens, Sara!'

'There can be no happiness–' I began; but she brushed my words aside.

'Oh, I have heard such warnings of doom before! It is not always true! I am answerable to no one, Sara. My mother sends me with her blessing! My father has spoiled enough of my life! Before Philip came, I had no reason to leave here – now I shall take what happiness I can find before it is too late! You will remember my words when you have grown old and unhappy here!'

'Why do you say such things? You have never liked me,' I said frankly.

'Meredith Pryce planned to set you up over us all!' she retorted, with equal frankness. 'It is true that Tremannion and its flocks cannot be willed to anyone save Rowan, but Meredith possesses a vast fortune in money; also, which he can leave to whom he pleases. Rowan will be quite content to inherit the sheep and this house; he is a man without ambition. Meredith has ambition enough for two men and plans to marry you to Adam; you will become mistress of Brennion and a powerful woman. My mother and I will be dependent on your charity! Would you care to be in that position?'

'No,' I admitted. 'But how can you be so sure of Grandfather's plans for me?'

'I know him very well. You are his ewe lamb!' She laughed at the appropriateness of her words. 'You are also the sacrificial lamb. A pretty little child to be petted and indulged and spoiled and cosseted! Do you think I have enjoyed watching him make much of you, knowing how very differently he has treated my mother and myself, how he would strip us of everything to make YOU rich? But you won't escape the sacrifice, Sara; marriage to the man he chooses, obedience to Meredith's will in all things!'

'Oh, nonsense!' I said impatiently. I looked at her closely, struck by a sudden thought. 'I believe it WAS you who locked me in my father's room the first morning I was here!'

'All right!' she said defiantly. 'So it was! I was bitter that Meredith had ordered so much fuss to be made of your arrival in this house! I spread your blood-stained dress on the bed for the same reason – you were returning from a holiday in Swansea. A holiday that had my father's blessing, on which you were to be indulged to the hilt as far as money was concerned!'

'I understand how you felt,' I admitted. 'Though it was unkind of you, Aunt Anne. I was very frightened. Someone in this house has tried to kill me, more than once!'

'I'm not to blame for that!' she replied. 'Aunt Jessie believes you have imagined it all!'

'What about the stones that have been thrown at the coach?' I retorted.

'The village children,' she said calmly. 'They hate the master of Tremannion. There is Aylwin, whose crippled father was evicted from one of Meredith's cottages for some slight misdemeanour. Gwenny, whose grandfather died of his injuries in the Five Valleys mining disaster. I have seen them hiding, with stones in their hands, waiting for the Tremannion coach to pass by.'

'Roberts was KILLED!' I cried, outraged at her lack of concern.

'My father brings his sorrows upon himself, Sara.'

I could find no answer to that remark. I looked at Aunt Anne, so happy, so confident suddenly; and I said:

'I won't be here to look after your mother. I am going back to London. So much for my grandfather's schemes and ambitions, which you so despise. He cannot fulfil them if I don't stay here.'

'I doubt if you will get to London,' Anne retorted dryly. 'Meredith is your guardian. He will bring you back. Besides, there is always Aunt Jessie.'

I was leaving the room when I remembered something.

'There is a second door from your mother's room, isn't there? When I went to open it, she said it led up to the old nurseries. Is that true?'

'Yes. Why, is it important?' she asked, frowning.

'I'm not sure, yet. Is there a similar door in Meredith's room, and, if so, where does it lead?'

'I haven't any idea,' she said indifferently. 'I have never been to his study or his bedroom above it – except when, as a child, I presented myself to him to be punished soundly for some misdeed!'

'There is another door; it leads from my mother's old bedroom down to the lumber room,' I said thoughtfully.

'Oh, well, Tremannion is riddled with odd corners, hiding places, rooms that aren't used any more. I used to hide in that little lumber room when I was a child, wanting to hide from my father's wrath. He found out, eventually, of course. He was angry and forbade me to go there ever again!'

There was a touch of the old bitterness in her voice; but the subject was not really of any more interest to her, I realised. She moved about the room, happily making her preparations for the evening ahead.

Reluctantly I picked up the key of the medicine chest. I did not want the responsibility of it – but, after all, it was a responsibility that I would not have for very long, I reminded myself.

Chapter Eleven

Olwen was so excited that she was in no fit state to help me prepare for the coming festivities; so I sent her away and completed my toilette myself.

I wore the splendid gown that I had bought in Swansea for this occasion; how happy I had been, then, I thought with a sigh! The shadows had not seemed to close so thickly around me, nor had I felt this tremendous fear of disaster about to overtake me.

When I was ready, I looked at myself in the long mirror; I was thinner, and there were shadows beneath my eyes that had not been there when I first came to Tremannion. The dress I wore was exquisitely flounced and ruffled, and I had chosen it because it was the same soft pink colour as the foxgloves that grew everywhere on the Beacons. I fastened a silver filigree butterfly in my hair and wore no other jewellery, except the string of creamy pearls that had been one of Meredith's gifts to me.

All day, the house had hummed with activity; I went downstairs to greet Meredith's cousins from Tenby; a middle-aged couple, the woman florid and sharp-eyed, the man small and balding, together with their daughter, a tall, gangling girl of about seventeen. Dr Evans was in the drawing-room, together with Mr Williams; Jessie was with them, dressed in black lace, which became her remarkably well, and Rachel, in an elaborate gown of pale blue, jewels flashing at her throat and in her ears. Anne, in bright red, looked remarkably handsome; as she turned her head to look at me, I saw the tawny highlights in her hair and wondered why I had never before noticed her resemblance to Thaddeus.

Cathy looked as cool as a snowdrop in the white dress embroidered with green that she had chosen when we shopped together; Adam left her side to come and speak to me.

I saw how closely Cathy watched us and remembered what Anne had said: that, as heiress to Meredith's fortune, I would hold everyone, save Rowan, in the palm of my hand; even Adam and Cathy, I realised, for Cathy had frankly admitted that the Brennions were not rich. The thought of such power was intolerable to me, for great power was as corrosive as great passion. Adam and Cathy might well come to hate me for my power; well, it would not happen, after all, I thought, for Meredith would not leave his fortune to a granddaughter who turned her back on him.

'You look beautiful, Sara,' Adam said approvingly. His eyes searched my face, as he added:

'Meredith has made no secret of the fact, to me, that he wishes to announce our betrothal; but you have not yet given me your answer. Indeed, I have scarcely seen you these last few days, so occupied have I been at Brennion.'

'Adam,' I said haltingly, 'I wish, with all my heart, that I could give you the answer you desire; but I cannot do so.'

'I understand; it is too soon,' he said quietly. 'You shall not be hurried, Sara, no matter what Meredith desires so ardently.'

At that moment, Rowan came across to us; I thought how much he resembled his uncle, with his dark, brooding face and powerful build.

Mr Williams claimed Adam's attention, and the two of them moved out of earshot; Rowan smiled at me with narrowed eyes and said softly:

'How becoming you look, little Cousin!'

'Thank you,' I said; there was an intensity about him that made me wonder, uneasily, if he was going to pursue the subject of marriage once more.

However, he said:

'We shall follow the ritual; after we have all dined, we shall be taken to the big shed, where the shearers with their wives and families, and all Uncle Meredith's other tenants, will have gathered for the feasting and drinking. Daniel Pugh will thank the master for his presence, Meredith will reply to the speech, and when we have danced dutifully, once, with one of the assembled company, we shall return here. What a great deal of nonsense it is! When I am master of Tremannion I shall abolish the custom!'

'Why?' I said. 'It seems a pleasant enough one, to me!'

'It is unnecessary. The men have been well paid for their work of shearing. If they wish to make merry, let them do so in their own way, as they please.'

'I expect your uncle enjoys the occasion,' I said placatingly, for he was looking sullen and angry.

'It feeds his vanity!' Rowan retorted. 'He likes to be *seen* as master, just as he likes the grand occasion, and all the pomp and show that attends upon it. Such things are not for me, Cousin!'

'*I* enjoy them, also,' I told him stubbornly.

'You asked me to marry you, Rowan, and said that I would look well at the head of your table. Of what use would that be if others did not share that table at times? It would be a dull life without such occasions as this. So you see, Cousin Rowan, you and I are ill-matched!'

'When we are married,' he replied with calm arrogance, 'you will not need such frivolous diversions.'

With relief, I saw Adam coming towards me...

After dinner, we left the house, pausing to touch the flowers and corn sheaves for luck – apparently, it was another Tremannion custom. We must have made a splendid picture as we crossed the turf – the men in their evening clothes, the women in pretty dresses, with wraps across their shoulders. The sun had gone down behind the great dark mass of the Beacons, and the sky was flushed with rose and gold, making the crags look more forbidding by contrast. A soft breeze touched the treetops far below us; it was an evening lovely enough to break one's heart, I thought. On a clear day, one might see the wide, silver waters of the Severn from the highest crags; I thought of those waters, flowing away to the sea. Already, they seemed to divide me forever from Thaddeus. *Forever;* one word that was as desolate as the tolling of a bell.

Because it was too far for us to walk to the sheds, we were taken there in carriages; I sat with Adam, grateful that he understood my disinclination to talk. Cathy and Rowan chatted animatedly together; the splendour of the afterglow made Rachel's jewels scintillate with their own fire, and I heard Anne's laughter, unexpectedly carefree, as she teased Mr Williams. Only Jessie and Meredith seemed preoccupied with their own thoughts.

When we reached the largest of the two big barns, it was a very different story; here was a great crowd of people, making a lot of noise, shouting and laughing together. The rafters were hung with bunting and strings of small, coloured flags; at one end of the barn was a long trestle table covered with plates of food, and I saw casks of ale being opened. Paper chains were looped along the walls, and oil lamps hung from the beams, making a soft yellow glow in the dusk.

I recognised most of the servants from Tremannion amongst the crowd of people assembled there; the girls, in their best dresses, tossing their heads, flirting with the men; many of those men were handsome, dark-haired fellows with a gay impudence about them: descendants, surely, of Seth Pryce and his gypsy mistress.

'Make way for the master of Tremannion!' cried Daniel Pugh, and everyone moved back from the floor to line the walls, as Meredith stepped up on to a small dais, where the local band awaited the signal to begin playing for the dancing.

He made a splendid figure, towering above them: Meredith Pryce, the lord of Tremannion. His words came back to haunt me, as they always would, for the rest of my life: *women crave love; men know that ... love is frail ... and seek power ... a more comfortable and lasting thing.*

My heart was full of my pride in him; when he spoke, his voice had an air of command, as he thanked the men for their labours on his behalf and the women for their support of the men. He spoke of the magnitude of the great harvest and the flocks of sheep that roamed the Beacons; there was dead silence, until he had finished, and then Daniel Pugh cried dutifully:

'A toast to the master!'

I heard the roar from their throats as they lifted their mugs to him; it was like the sound of a great sea breaking on the shore. At such times as this, I reflected, it must all seem worthwhile to Meredith: the driving ambition that breeds a ruthlessness capable of sweeping every obstacle from its path.

Meredith acknowledged the ovation with a smile and an inclination of his head; then he signalled to the band and stepped down from the dais.

Daniel Pugh warily took Rachel as his partner, and Meredith led Mrs Pugh on to the floor. I saw Anne and Jessie clasped by two hefty-looking men, and Cathy partnered by a shy-looking boy who had been relentlessly nudged forward by his friends. Adam led the eldest of Daniel Pugh's buxom daughters, and Rowan planted himself in front of me.

'Dance with me, Cousin,' he commanded.

'We should not be dancing together,' I answered uncertainly, 'surely you should escort one of the village or farm girls?'

'I claim YOU!' he said; his eyes were bright and his hold upon me was firm. The music was lively and I quite enjoyed it, after all, though Rowan said no word to me as we circled the floor. When he released me at the end of the dance, he murmured:

'It will be something to remember, Cousin!'

So he knew I was planning to leave Tremannion; I was surprised that it seemed to matter so much to him.

Our duty was done; nothing remained but for us to make our farewells graciously and return to the house. There was a brief lull in the laugher and conversation as the band ceased to play; then as Daniel stepped forward to escort us back to our carriages, there was a sudden disturbance at the far end of the barn where the great doors stood wide open.

I recognised the shrill voice; the crowd gathered near the doors, stood aside to let Bronwen Evans through; her hair was in its usual state of disarray, and she looked as though she had thrown on her crumpled clothes in a great hurry. Her flushed face was contorted with fury, as she walked across to Anne and stood in front of her, hands on hips.

'Left me, he has!' she shouted, so that everyone could hear. 'Where does he wait for you, eh? You parade yourself here, in front of decent people, in your fine clothes and with your fancy airs, but you are a whore! Nothing else, indeed, to be expected from a Pryce; adultery is nothing to THEM, who will lie with any fancy woman or willing man! Think you are clever, do you, plain old maid that you are? There's no man would look at you, except my husband, and soft in the head he must be! So you are going to go away with him and live with him as his mistress? Sorry for it you will be, the shameless pair that you are–!'

She reached out a hand with lightning speed and would have ripped Anne's gown from her shoulders, but two of the men darted forward and held her firmly; there was a murmur of horrified delight from the assembled crowd as the two men half-led, half-carried her away, struggling and screaming out that she would see them both dead before she had done.

Anne, with remarkable composure, walked from the barn, looking neither to right nor left, her head held high, and the crowd parted to let her through.

I was angry that Anne's behaviour with Philip had shamed her in front of Meredith; I looked at him and saw that his face was as dark and forbidding as a spur of granite; but I was near enough to him to observe the fine beads of moisture along his upper lip and forehead.

Involuntarily his hand went to his chest and a spasm of pain crossed his face; then his hand dropped back to his side, he squared his shoulders, and with a curt good night to the red-faced Daniel Pugh, he left the hall, the rest of us following him and trying to look unconcerned.

Anne sat alone in the first carriage, hands in her lap, her face quite composed. Meredith walked up to her.

'Is it true?' he demanded.

'It is true, I am going away, with Philip, tonight, and I am *happy!*'

Her face was almost radiant; I knew that she was going to tell Meredith that she was overjoyed to be free of Tremannion and his tyranny; but he forestalled her. His quiet voice carried clearly on the still air.

'If you leave Tremannion with him to-night, then you shall never return there,' he told her. '*Never*, do you hear, Anne? I will not have you under my roof ever again!'

She smiled at him.

'Not in your lifetime,' she agreed. 'When you are no longer master, I *shall* return if I please!'

Whether she meant to be cruel or whether there was another meaning to her remark, I could not tell.

Rachel was laughing softly to herself and nodding approval at Anne; we were ushered into our seats in the carriage, and we chatted brightly, as though to pretend that nothing was amiss.

I was uneasy about my grandfather; I spoke to him as we entered Tremannion.

'Is there something I can do?' I asked.

'Yes, Sara. Will you play for us?'

I glanced warily at my grandmother, remembering the last time I had played the piano in front of her; but she was hurrying away in Anne's wake, and the rest of us foregathered in the drawing-room.

I played automatically; my eyes, my thoughts, roved around the room. Meredith looked tired, his shoulders bowed; for the first time in my life I thought of him, with a sense of shock, as an old man.

Anne did not return. I thought of her speeding to meet Philip, and I was glad when the evening was done. Rachel returned to say good night to the guests, and Megan fussed, grumbling, in her wake, waiting to see her to bed. The old servant had taken no part in the festivities, declaring such things to be a lot of nonsense and a waste of time that could be put to better use. I looked at the small, dark, secretive-looking woman who had served Tremannion for so long; she looked very much like Rowan, at times, I reflected.

Jessie fluttered about nervously, saying that we must all have night-caps.

'We are all tired,' Meredith said shortly. 'I will instruct Megan that they shall be brought to our rooms. Good night.'

Mr Williams and Dr Evans took their departure; everyone else was staying over-night; as he was leaving Dr Evans drew me aside.

'Your grandfather is a sick man, Miss Pryce,' he said bluntly, 'though he refuses to concede the fact. I confess I am uneasy about him. Mrs Jessie has her hands full—' he paused and looked at me expectantly.

'I will look after him,' I said, thoroughly alarmed.

But Meredith waved me away impatiently when I expressed concern for him.

'Go along to bed, Sara. I shall be well enough to ride with you in the morning,' he assured me, somewhat irritably.

Reluctantly I went to my room; Cathy was sleeping in David's old room, next to mine, though Rachel had not been told this, for fear it might distress her. I knew that Cathy wanted to come and talk over the evening's events with me, but I felt too tired for conversation. Megan made the rounds with hot milk; she put the cup on my table without a word and gave me a strange, sly look as she left the room. I sat watching the curls of steam rising from the thin, fluted cup and slowly drew the pins from my hair, trying to forget how once Thaddeus had tumbled my dark hair about my shoulders, taking out every pin with slow deliberation.

I undressed and put on my wrapper; I lifted the cup of milk and even as I put it to my lips, I heard an agitated rapping at my door; Aunt Jessie entered, her face alarmed.

'Meredith has had a heart attack!' she whispered urgently. 'And before she left the house tonight, Anne told me she had given you the key of the medicine cupboard!'

The thought crossed my mind, fleetingly, that Jessie would have been the obvious choice as custodian of the cupboard. I had left the key on my dressing-table, rather foolishly, perhaps, in view of all that had happened in this house. However, it was still there; relieved, I snatched it up and hurried after Jessie.

We found the medicine that Dr Evans had

prescribed, and took it hastily to Meredith's room; he lay propped against high pillows, in the vast bed with its carved oak headboard; his face and lips had no colour, and only his eyes glowed like live coals. Yet, in this sombre room where he had always slept alone, he was still a giant of a man, head and shoulders above us all, as lonely as an eagle in its eyrie.

I read the label and measured a dose into the glass that Jessie held ready; when I took it to him, he would have pushed it away, but I held it firmly to his lips, until he drank as though he was too tired to resist any longer. In a little while, colour crept back into his cheeks; he turned his head towards Jessie, and said:

'Leave us now.'

I sat by his bedside and held his hand; he was silent for a long time, staring into the distance.

'I do not care what Anne has done!' he said suddenly.

'No, Grandfather; only for the way it was done and the consequences,' I murmured.

'Exactly. How well you and I understand one another, Sara! That is as it should be! I have decided that the time has come when you must read your mother's letter, even though she instructed that you should not do so until you came of age. Events make it necessary for you to know, now, what that letter has to say.'

'Have YOU read it?' I asked challengingly.

'Yes,' he replied, his glance unfaltering.

'Was it you who took it from my room?'

'It was not. I read that letter tonight, for the first time, when I was ready to go down to dinner.' A strange look of mingled pain and happiness crossed his face.

'I am tired,' he added abruptly. 'It can wait until the morning. I will give it to you, after breakfast, and you shall read it then. Good night.'

I rose to my feet; leaning forward, I kissed his cheek.

'Good night, Grandfather,' I whispered.

His eyes were closed by the time I reached the door; as I neared my room, I was surprised to see Rowan waiting for me, a look of strain on his face.

'How is he?' he demanded.

'A little better. He has taken some medicine, and when I left him, he was almost asleep.'

'I will tell my mother,' he said. 'We are anxious about him.'

I went into my room and turned the key in the lock, from force of habit. I was not tired now and had no desire to sleep. I thought about my mother's letter and felt a cold chill of fear in my heart, in spite of the warmth of the summer night.

The milk in the cup was cold; but I sipped

some of it, thinking it might do me good. I thought I detected a certain bitterness in the flavour; or perhaps, I thought sadly, the taste was unpalatable because the tears that were running down my cheeks had mingled with it.

I did not finish the milk; I drank only half of it and then sat there thinking; but I found I was tired, after all, and a great weariness engulfed me as I dragged myself over to the dressing-table. The silver-backed hairbrush was an intolerable weight in my hands; it slipped from my fingers and crashed to the floor.

Some small part of my brain that was not yet drowned in that great tide of weariness sent out small, warning signals: I remembered that, in my haste and anxiety to take the medicine to Meredith, I had not relocked the medicine cupboard, but left the key in the door; what if Rachel should discover that the door was open?

The tide would soon carry me away, I thought confusedly; with a supreme effort I dragged myself to the door, unlocked it, and stepped outside. I beat loudly on Cathy's door, and she opened it at once, still fully clothed in her evening finery.

'Sara!' she whispered, horrified. 'Whatever is wrong with you?'

'Key,' I murmured thickly, 'left it in the cupboard door ... stupid ... Rachel could ...

always locked, Aunt Jessie said ... I ... am ... so ... very, very tired.'

What followed after that is still a confused jumble of events, like scenes from a half-forgotten nightmare. Cathy jerked me roughly back to my room, where she left me to slip further down into unconsciousness for what seemed an eternity, but was, in reality, only moments; when she came back, Adam was with her.

One of them put a glass to my lips and forced me to swallow a nauseating concoction of salt which made me vomit violently; but the vomiting seemed to clear my brain a little. They stood one on either side of me and held my arms, walking me methodically up and down, ignoring my pleas to be allowed to sleep. I seemed to be crawling down a long, dark tunnel with a mere pinprick of light at its far end until, gradually, the pinpoint became bigger and brighter and my brain quite clear, although I felt wretchedly ill and weak.

Adam went away and returned with scalding coffee, which he made me drink. I knew that he and Cathy had saved my life.

'The milk,' I whispered, 'it tasted strange. Someone could have taken poison from the medicine cupboard, for I left the key in it, when I took out the medicine for Meredith.'

'How long ago was that?' Adam demanded; and I told him how Aunt Jessie had come to me.

'You were not absent very long,' he pointed out, frowning. 'It would be a risky thing for anyone to do.' Cautiously he sniffed the milk. His face was stern and angry.

'I will give this to Dr Evans in the morning,' he said. 'He will have it analysed; and I will lock the cupboard without delay, Sara.'

It occurred to me, after he had gone, that he knew his way very well about this house; I said so to Cathy, and she smiled wanly.

'We have always known our way about Tremannion as surely as though it was Brennion,' she replied, 'for Meredith has welcomed us here since we were children. Whatever you may be thinking, Sara, neither Adam nor I would do you harm. Certainly there is someone who hates you and wishes you dead; but it is not either of us. We are your friends.'

Her smile was stiff and her voice held reproach.

Much to my relief, the ill effects of the night's mischief were less than I had expected they would be; I felt listless and had no appetite, that was all, and Olwen, bringing my hot water, said:

'Why you are not looking yourself, at all, miss! A great shock it was to us all, with Mrs

Evans behaving so...'

'Thank you, Olwen,' I said briefly. 'I do not think Mr Meredith would wish it discussed.'

In spite of the previous fine evening, it had rained very heavily during the night, and the morning was dull. Meredith took breakfast in his room, and Jessie, myself, and Rowan joined the other guests in the dining-room, together with Adam and Cathy. Adam spoke little throughout the meal.

The people from Tenby left immediately afterwards; Adam and Cathy followed. As he was leaving, Adam took my hands in his and looked searchingly into my face.

'Promise me,' he said earnestly, 'that, if you need me, you will send one of the servants at once. I am very concerned for your safety.'

'There is something you must know, Adam; I am leaving Tremannion as soon as I can.'

I saw the pain in his face.

'Then I have been wrong, Sara; it is not a question of needing time in order to be sure of your feelings for me. There is someone else whom you love; it will always be difficult for you to hide your thoughts; I can read the truth.'

There was silence between us. Then he added:

'There is something Meredith Pryce does

not know, and that Thaddeus forbade me to tell him. It was Thaddeus Flynn's money that saved Brennion at the time of the great disaster, which almost wiped out the flocks. Very generously, he lent me a great deal of money, insisting that there was no time limit as to repayment. In return, he asked only to be allowed to use the cottage, from time to time, for he has no other home. Thaddeus is my friend, and he has been a good one to me; but I do know, Sara, that he will never bring happiness to any woman, for he sees women as pretty baubles, toys to give him a few moments' pleasure, before he seeks a new face, another love.'

The tell-tale flush spread through my cheeks; I bent my head, thinking, for the first time, that the person who was hunting me down so relentlessly might well be someone who cared greatly for Thaddeus.

'Remember, Sara, whilst you are still here, take great care; do not forget that I am at hand should you need me. Today, I will take the sample of milk to Dr Evans,' Adam said.

At last everyone had left, and I was free to go to Meredith; I was impatient, eager to read my mother's letter.

He was sitting by the fire in his study, in an arm-chair instead of at his desk; but he was as upright as ever, he looked refreshed, and his eyes had not lost their fire; he greeted me, and indicated that I should sit in the chair on the opposite side of the fireplace. I saw that he held my mother's letter in his hand.

'You slept well?' he asked.

'Well enough,' I answered. 'And you? Are you feeling better?'

'Last night was nothing to be alarmed about, Sara. Well, so I am tired. I think we will leave Tremannion for a time and travel, wherever you like. Perhaps you would like to go aboard; when we return you will feel differently about many things.'

I did not wish to distress him by a refusal; so I remained silent, whilst he handed me the envelope with the broken seals.

As I took the thick sheets of notepaper from the envelope, my hands felt like ice; I felt the same intense stillness at the centre of my being that I had known when Meredith revealed the secret of Anne's birth.

I looked at the firm, clear handwriting, and it seemed that my mother stood by my side, calm and lovely, with the smile I remembered so well on her lovely mouth. I have often thought, since, that seeing the handwriting of someone who has died can bring them back to life more vividly than anything else, for handwriting is a very individual expression of personality.

'My dearest child,' my mother had written, 'what I have to say cannot be other than a great shock to you, and it is something that has been a distressing burden upon my conscience of many years. There have been times when I have felt you should know the truth concerning your birth; times when I vowed never to tell you; but I fear that you may hear it, incorrectly and incompletely, from other lips; and I have little time left to me. I shall not be with you when you read this.

'My husband, David Pryce, was not your real father. You are not Meredith Pryce's granddaughter.

'I became pregnant when I was housekeeper at Tremannion, and when I discovered this fact, I was desperate, knowing Rachel would dismiss me as soon as she knew; I had no home, nor any relatives to help me, and I was nineteen years old.

'David loved me very dearly; he had asked me to marry him several times, and though I was fond of him, I refused. Eventually, however, he realised from my behaviour that something was dreadfully wrong. I was distraught; I told him I was expecting a child because I had been assaulted and raped, near the old quarry, whilst returning from the village one night. There were a number of gypsies encamped near the quarry at that time, and I had been warned of the folly of coming that way, alone.

'David at once insisted that he would

marry me; so that my shame should not be made known to everyone, he would let it be thought that he was the father of my expected child. He was terribly concerned that I had been the unhappy victim of dreadful circumstances; he also told me, frankly, that he wished to be free of the obligations of Tremannion and from his mother's obsessive love for him. He suggested that we should go at once to London, be married, and live there; I accepted his suggestions with gratitude and relief.

'I swear to you, Sara, that throughout our brief married life I did all I could to make David happy, and I believe I succeeded. I never forgot that, except for his generosity, my life would have been a grim, poverty-ridden struggle to live and provide for you. Neither did I ever cease to feel bitter shame for the fact that our marriage was founded on a lie.

'Meredith Pryce, David's father, followed us to London, and forced me to name the father of the child I carried. I could not lie to HIM; for he suspected the truth. I made him promise me that he would never divulge the true facts to his son, and he gave me that promise, angry and bitter though he was that I had married David.

'He made several more visits to see us; they were always an ordeal. When you were born, he stayed away until the day he visited us when we were staying at the seaside. You were then four years old.

'Meredith and I argued fiercely over my consistent refusals to return to Tremannion; David added the weight of his arguments to mine. In sudden fury, Meredith turned on David and told him the truth about your birth. David was terribly shocked, although he forgave me more readily than I had any right to expect. I have never been *sure* that his death, soon afterwards, *was* an accident, and that, too, has caused me much anguish.

'I never forgave Meredith Pryce for causing such agony to a man who had been a kind and thoughtful husband; as David had protected me, so did I wish to protect David from unhappiness, but Meredith had decreed otherwise. When he demanded that you should go to Tremannion, I would not let him have his way; he has tried for many years to have his way on this matter; in vain.

'Now I know the time is not far distant when Tremannion will be your only home. I pray to God that you will be happy there, in that strange, cold house whose shadow still seems to fall chill upon me, though I am so many miles away.

'Judge me how you will, my child; think of me as a shameless woman who gave herself lightly to a man, for a few moments of pleasure. I became your father's mistress

305

only because I loved him as I have never loved another human being, and that great love has been passed on to you. No other man ever touched the depths of my heart and soul as your father did; it was a strange, fierce, passionate love that we had for one another, doomed from the start, though I did not care. Such a great and powerful love can bring great happiness, great disaster – or both. It breaks all the bonds of reason and convention, the love that is stronger than life – or death. Some people never know it; others say its price is too high. I do not think it is, and I do not regret that we had a brief, golden time together, your father and I. It may be difficult for you to understand that such love is never completely severed between two people, even when there is anger and bitterness between them, afterwards. I know your father to be a hard and ruthless man; I alone knew that such was not the sum total of his nature.

'You know, by now, of whom I speak: Meredith Pryce is your father, and I have often thought you are like him, in many ways. He will be kind to you, though he will seek to buy you, to govern, and direct your life, and you will need strength to resist him. When you marry, Sara, be sure that you love deeply and irrevocably and for all time.'

The letter was signed, simply: 'Your loving mother, Celia Pryce.'

I was acutely aware of the motionless figure opposite me; I lifted my head from the letter and looked at him as though I was seeing him for the first time. He never moved, and his eyes never left my face.

'Well, Sara!' he said quietly.

I shook my head mutely, unable to speak; I thought of the bitter irony of the situation: Anne had used the word 'father' to this man all her life and had not known she had no right to call him that; I, who could truly call him my father, could not utter the word, though I knew how much he wanted to hear it on my lips.

'It has been a shock to you,' he said, 'as your mother prophesied it would be. You are my *daughter.*' His voice was triumphant. 'The child of the one woman I have ever loved, Sara!'

'I do not know which causes greater havoc,' I said bitterly. 'Great love or great hatred.'

'The two are very close, Sara!' There was sudden anger in his voice, as he added:

'She should never have married David! It was wrong of her, knowing she carried MY child! It was a source of great anger and bitterness to me that she kept the truth from me and went away, without a word!'

'What else could she have done?' I asked. 'Her life here would have been intolerable, if Rachel had known the truth; you surely would not expect your wife to condone the presence of your mistress and her child?'

'*I* am the master here,' he replied arrogantly. 'I do as I please. Rachel would not have dared to oppose me for I sheltered *her* illegitimate child! I could not forgive Celia for what she did!'

'So you deliberately destroyed her marriage?'

'*Not* deliberately, Sara! She refused all I would have done, then, when David was alive; she turned her back on me. Anger took the brakes from my tongue; do you think I did not regret the suffering I caused my son? None of this would have happened if your mother had told me the truth and stayed here, in her rightful place!'

'Did no one suspect that I was YOUR daughter, not David's?' I asked incredulously.

He shook his head, his eyes full of old memories.

'We rarely met outside the house; within its walls we were well able to keep our secret. I do now know who unlocked the door that led into the small lumber room leading from your mother's room. It has been locked, now, for years. Had you been able to move the boxes and chests stacked there, you would have discovered another, cleverly concealed door. That door leads directly to my bedroom; but, even though you looked carefully, you would not see the door in my room, for it is part of the panelling and the mechanism of its hidden catch is known only to me. Its presence is one of Tremannion's best-kept secrets, handed down from father to son, a convenient means of communication between the master and those on whom he wishes to bestow favours! My father showed it to Morgan and myself when we were young. By tradition – and for the sake of domestic harmony – the secret is never told to Tremannion wives!'

'So that is how you and my mother were able to meet?' I said.

'Yes,' he replied proudly. 'We loved, your mother and I, as few have loved.'

Ah! I know the terrifying strength of a great passion! Had *I* been in her place, and Thaddeus the master of this house, I would have gone eagerly, without thought of the consequences. Perhaps I was like Meredith in that I felt no shame for such thoughts; I could not find it in my heart to condemn my mother, keeping her secret rendezvous, surrendering herself to Meredith Pryce.

Yet, Meredith Pryce was not blameless, I thought; I felt a moment's anger, remembering what he had done to her marriage. Because of him, she had lived through long years of guilt and loneliness.

'You are MY daughter, Sara!' he said

proudly. 'Stubborn, headstrong, full of fire!'

'My mother writes, in her letter, of the strength of a great love,' I told him. 'She married for less only because of her unhappy position. *I* do not need to marry for less – and I never will!'

'Your mother recognised, also, that such love can bring disaster!' he retorted. 'That is why I have chosen for you a man whose love will never bring disaster in its wake!'

'I cannot marry Adam,' I replied, as calmly as I could. 'I have already chosen elsewhere.'

'*Flynn!*' He almost choked on the word, and I thought he would have a stroke. 'Is that the man? God forbid, Sara!'

'It is Thaddeus Flynn,' I confirmed.

'He will never marry you!' Meredith cried triumphantly. 'He will not tie himself to one woman! Oh, you think it is a fine thing, now, to renounce Adam because you cannot have the man you desire! In time, you will see the folly of such reasoning! It is one thing to feel strengthened in your decision by the force of what *you* think is a great and overmastering love! It is quite another to waste your life because you cannot have what you want!'

I was silent, knowing there was truth in what he said.

'Sara, Sara!' he whispered, 'you are my only child. Listen to what I have to say. Everyone believes Rowan to be heir to

Tremannion. It was true – until some time ago. You know how I regard my nephew; as a man unfitted for the role of master. When I knew you were at last coming to this house, I studied all the old deeds, every document, record, and paper concerning this estate. I read the wills of the previous masters of Tremannion. Do you know what I discovered? That *nowhere* is it decreed that Tremannion must pass to a male heir! You are my daughter, my rightful heiress! Though you will lose the name of Pryce when you marry Adam, it will be MY child who is mistress here in her own right, MY grandsons who will count their flocks and watch them increase! With your wealth and position, you *need* a man of Adam's stature, not an adventurer like Flynn! Brennion and Tremannion lands will be one, my last and greatest dream will be realised!'

I stared at him in horrified dismay.

'Does Rowan know this?' I whispered.

'Of course not! Do you think I am a fool! My new will is safely lodged with my lawyer, a man of complete integrity! What has passed between us in his office is known to no one else, and Rowan will not discover the truth until my death. Perhaps, now, you understand why I am anxious that you shall be married before that time!'

'You cannot treat him so cruelly, after all his years of service to you!' I said, distressed.

Meredith made an impatient gesture of dismissal.

'I have made a very handsome settlement on Rowan and his mother. Enough to keep them in comfort wherever they wish to live. I do not owe either of them more than that.'

'The sheep, the land; these things are his whole life!' I pleaded.

'And Sara Pryce is my daughter; no one else has the right to own those things!' he declared passionately.

I was silent; how does one answer a mighty wind that blows around one's head with such terrifying force?

'There is still time left to teach you many things,' he told me. 'To show you, Sara, how the business of Tremannion is conducted, so that you will know what must be done when I am no longer here.'

The black hair that curled thick and strong above his face was touched with silver at the temples; his profile looked as though it had been carved from stone. A mighty man, the Master of Tremannion; in his middle years he had fathered a child to the one woman he had truly loved: a golden girl of nineteen called Celia Heriot. I marvelled very much at the strangeness of life.

'I do not think I shall ride this morning,' he added abruptly. 'I have much to occupy me here. I shall not join you at lunch – I am going to visit Daniel Pugh. Later, we shall have much to talk about.'

'As you wish,' I said dutifully.

I knew that he waited for me to give him his rightful name; but I could not say it.

I took my mother's letter to my room and read it until I knew it by heart. I could not find it in my heart to condemn her for what she had done; but now it was more than ever necessary for me to leave this house as soon as I could; I would take no part in Meredith's plans to dispossess Rowan.

Aunt Jessie and I lunched alone; my thoughts were in a turmoil. I tried to imagine what her reactions would be if she knew the truth.

Fate had not yet done with me in this day of surprises. I decided to ride after lunch. It had rained heavily again during the morning, but the clouds were rolling away across the Beacons, showing patches of blue, and there was a freshening wind.

I asked for Sheba to be saddled; I knew that Meredith would have insisted on my being accompanied by a groom, but he was still absent from Tremannion and I was in no mood for any kind of company.

Rowan rode into the stable-yard as I was leaving it; I felt distinctly uncomfortable in his presence, but I smiled at him and wished him good day.

He did not give me an answering smile; he

merely said briefly:

'I am instructed to give you a message from Thaddeus Flynn.'

'*Thaddeus?*' I cried, my heart leaping. 'Surely he has left Brennion?'

'He cannot have done so; for I spoke to him, not an hour ago, outside the Brennion Arms. He says it is a matter of great urgency that you should meet him at the quarry tonight, as soon as it is dusk. I confess I dislike being the bearer of such a message – your grandfather would forbid the meeting if he knew of it!' Rowan added scornfully. 'However, what you do is your affair; I shall say nothing!'

He clattered past me, into the stable-yard.

I rode with the wind on my face, and, in spite of all that had happened, my heart was so full of joy that I seemed to fly over the very tops of the Beacons, instead of riding on Sheba's back. I did not even care that my next meeting with Thaddeus must surely be our final farewell. He wanted to see me again! The sun dazzled my eyes and I laughed aloud. To see him once more, feel lips and hands touch, know the exquisite delight and torment of being close to him.

All my mother's words came back to me, singing on the wind, like a great shout of happiness; he was here, close to me still, he had not gone without a word! I could not wait for evening to come; oh, the foolish innocence of my happiness as I thought only of our meeting, never questioning why he wanted to see me!

Chapter Twelve

I was glad to be alone with my thoughts, out in the fresh air; I rode for some time before I turned back towards Tremannion, along one of the many paths that criss-crossed the Beacons; I was almost in sight of the house when I saw Cathy, leaning against a stone wall.

She waved and seemed pleased to see me. I dismounted and walked across to her, leading Sheba, who was glad enough to rest and crop the turf.

'Adam has not yet returned,' she told me. 'He went to see Dr Evans immediately after lunch, taking the milk with him. Sara, I am extremely concerned about you; it seems incredible that such a thing should have been done to you! Who would wish you such harm?'

I shook my head.

'I do not know; it is someone who is persistent and determined.'

'Have you mentioned it to Meredith?'

'No; I do not wish him to be troubled. I think he is more sick than he realises.'

'You are very brave, Sara!' She looked at me, wide-eyed. '*I* would be afraid to stay at Tremannion, after all that has happened!'

'I am not brave at all,' I told her wryly. 'I have been very much afraid; but it is almost over. I shall leave here soon and not return.'

'It IS true, then? Adam said that you were going away!' She coloured, her glance faltering, as she added:

'I shall miss you. I trust that we may remain friends, and perhaps meet again one day. I know there have been times when my feelings for you have not been friendly, and I am ashamed of that fact; I have prayed earnestly for forgiveness for my uncharitableness.'

I smiled, remembering the kneeling figure in the little church.

'You were unhappy because you love Adam, and you thought I was going to marry him. He does not really see you, Cathy, because you have always been close to him; but one day he will know how much he needs you as a wife, not a companion.'

She looked at me in surprise.

'You ARE in a strange mood, Sara! You speak as though you could read the future!'

'It is as well that I cannot!' I told her ruefully.

Her glance was thoughtful and speculative.

'For all that has befallen you, Sara, you look happy today! It cannot be because you have decided to leave Tremannion; I would swear you are deeply in love! Why, you are, blushing! Is it Rowan who holds your thoughts and your heart?'

'Rowan? No, indeed! Once, I believed *you* cared deeply for him!'

'I have pity for him; he does not fit the image of the heir to Tremannion, Sara. If not Rowan, who, then?' she pressed.

I bent my head to hide my confusion; I knew a desperate need to confide in another woman; Cathy would understand and sympathise. Telling her the truth would do no harm, for soon I would have left Tremannion for ever.

'Can you not guess?' I asked, glancing towards the little cottage, from whose squat chimneys no smoke arose on the air.

'Not *Thaddeus?*' she asked, dismayed. 'Yes, it is – I can read it in your face! He is a strange man, and I do not understand him. His tongue is mocking and unkind, and he walks as though all the earth was his. It is said no woman will ever hold him! He is going away soon; he wanders where he pleases, and often we do not see him for long periods; he is packed and ready, and staying at the Brennion Arms.'

'I know!' I answered recklessly and impulsively. 'I shall see him once more, for he

317

sent a message by Rowan to tell me he would meet me at the quarry tonight, at dusk. Oh, foolish and shameless I may be to obey when he crooks his little finger, nevertheless I feel drawn to him by a force stronger than my own will!'

She sighed and shook her head.

'In time you will forget him, Sara; and it will be for the best.'

I was concerned as to how I could leave the house that evening without arousing Meredith's suspicions; I was loth to deceive him by pretending a headache and absenting myself as soon as dinner was over, but I knew he would expect me to talk to him or play to him.

However, Fate was unexpectedly kind; Dr Evans dined with us and challenged Meredith to a game of chess, which he accepted eagerly, for he rarely had an opportunity to play.

'One day I will teach you chess, Sara,' Meredith told me. 'What will you do with yourself this evening? You will not be lonely?'

'No; I shall not be lonely,' I told him.

It should have been a fine, clear summer evening; but the wind had dropped and a misty, mournful rain was falling. The Beacons looked dour and unfriendly; I knew that night would close in early.

Dr Evans and Meredith retired to the study; I went to my room, and changed from my evening gown into my warmest clothes, taking a heavy cloak from the wardrobe. As I fastened it about my shoulders, I heard a tap on the door.

With pounding heart, I turned the key; Aunt Jessie stood there. She had seemed pale and quiet during the meal, and now she looked at me in great surprise.

'You are surely not planning to go out, Sara?' she said.

'Just for a walk,' I answered guiltily.

'It is no fit evening for such an excursion; and Meredith would forbid you to go alone, if he knew!'

'I MUST go, Aunt Jessie!' I assured her.

She looked gravely disturbed.

'There is something amiss tonight. I feel it, in my bones! This house has an air of menace that it always possesses before some great disaster strikes. I feel as though evil lies in wait in the shadows!'

'You imagine it!' I told her.

'I am not an imaginative woman, Sara! Something is wrong. Rowan is missing; he should have returned long since, and no one has seen him since this afternoon. I know that something has happened to him!'

'He knows every inch of the countryside around here,' I pointed out. 'He will return soon.'

She shivered, unconvinced, and looked at me with a melancholy expression.

'Whom do you go to meet, Sara? Is it, by chance, my son?'

'No. It cannot matter if you know the truth, for I am soon leaving Tremannion. I am going to meet Thaddeus Flynn at the quarry; do not look so distressed, and please say nothing to Meredith!'

She stared after me dubiously, as I hurried away. Outside the house, the air smelt cold, and the heavy clouds, swollen with rain, seemed to press down upon me. I made my way to the bridge, and then took the path that climbed to the quarry. I was alarmed to see that there had been several falls of stone during the recent spate of wet weather, and at times I had to leave the path, skirting small piles of boulders; I had almost reached the tiny building when I heard a strange rumbling sound, as though the earth grumbled to itself. I came to an abrupt standstill as a shower of small stones and fist-sized boulders tumbled from just above me, to bounce on the path and go sliding down the face of the quarry.

The dusk was beginning to deepen and I saw no sign of Thaddeus. Perhaps he had changed his mind about our meeting, or remained hidden, to tease me, I thought.

There was scarcely room to walk along the last part of the muddy, treacherous path, for the rains and falls of stone had eroded it, bringing it perilously near the quarry's edge. I looked at the long drop beneath me and shuddered.

The door of the little building that Thaddeus used was half-open.

'Thaddeus!' I called softly, stepping inside.

It was gloomy inside the cottage; the easel at which he worked was gone, only the chair and table remaining. I had arrived first at the rendezvous, that was all; yet I felt an ominous sense of impending disaster, as the flesh prickled coldly along my arms. I knew I must leave this place, and it was all I could do not to run.

Even as I turned towards the door, the light was blocked by a figure who stood there for a second, before entering.

The man leant negligently against the wall; there was only the width of the table between us. He stared coldly at me, as I stammered:

'You have been absent a long time, Cousin! Your mother is worried for your safety.'

'When my work is done,' he said shortly, 'I shall return to Tremannion. Thaddeus will not come here; there WAS no message. *I* wanted you to come here, because there is something I have to ask you. Will you marry me, Cousin Sara?'

I let out a breath of relief; I was annoyed

and bitterly disappointed. It was a stupid trick of Rowan's, but I held on to my temper, as I said quietly:

'You have had my answer, Cousin. I will marry only a man I love. I do not love you, nor do you love me; we have spoken of all this before today, and I thought you understood that. In any case, I am leaving Tremannion and returning to London.'

He laughed derisively.

'Meredith will soon bring you back. He is as soft as a girl where you are concerned! The money he squanders on you is mine by right! I haven't sweated in the fields just so that others might give themselves airs and graces and live in fine style!' His voice was very soft. 'I don't intend to be cheated, Sara. No bastard daughter of Uncle Meredith's shall take what is mine!'

'How do you know who I am?' I stammered, a frightened little pulse beginning to beat in my throat.

'Old men became careless!' He sounded contemptuous. 'He left his desk drawer unlocked, and it contained a draft of his new will, plus a statement as to your parentage! I would have killed him then, but the will was made. Marriage to you will ensure that justice is done!'

'Was THAT your reason for asking me?' I demanded scornfully.

'I found you attractive.' His eyes smouldered, whether with anger or desire I could not tell. 'I told you, I thought you would bear healthy children; how better to revenge myself on a man who for years has thought of me as dull, stupid, an animal amongst the animals!'

I could not help but feel a momentary pity for him; he was embittered and frustrated, as Anne had been. Both of them had been Meredith's prisoners. Now all the damned-up resentment and frustration was erupting like a volcano...

'*I* knew who you were soon after you came to Tremannion!' he boasted. 'I read the letter your mother left you; I was in Uncle Meredith's study, looking for his gold seal to refasten the envelope, when I saw the draft of the will! Don't you find that amusing, Sara?'

My mouth went dry; I backed away from him.

'If you took the envelope from my room, then did you also kill Lily?' I whispered.

'No. It was an accident. When you first came here, my mother noticed the amethyst ring you wore and remembered that Uncle Meredith had bought it soon after David left Tremannion. What man gives a costly gift to a new daughter-in-law, she asked me? I, too, was curious as to the answer, and I told her to search your room. Lily surprised her there and tried to take the letter from her, threatening to tell you and Meredith that she had found my mother there. My mother was frightened and tried to push Lily away. Your maid fell and her skull was fractured. My mother was in a fine state! Women are weak creatures, at best! I told her I had read the letter and found it unimportant; women are not to be trusted with such secrets!'

In one swift movement he toppled the table between us, and caught my shoulders in a fierce grip.

'I wanted to kill you then!' he told me bitterly. 'You think you can come here and take what is mine, and think yourself too good for me!'

'You said you found me attractive!' I gasped.

'Aye. Against my will!' he agreed sullenly. 'I would have turned that to good account had you promised to marry me and let me revenge myself on Meredith. I would have been SURE of my inheritance, as your husband. I could have killed you many times. *I* have a key to the lumber room of which my uncle knows nothing! I almost had you that night, when I would have sent you hurtling down the stairs! And on the night of the storm; but for Rachel, you would be dead now and no longer a threat to what is mine! You are as careless as Uncle Meredith, you know.' His smile was cold.

'You left the medicine cupboard unlocked; Anne would never have done such a foolish thing.'

'The milk?' I whispered. *'You—?'*

'Yes,' he said. 'You cheated me then! Not this time!'

'Adam has given a sample of the milk to Dr Evans!' I cried.

He shrugged.

'So? It will be easy to convince people that Rachel tried to poison you; my mother will bear witness to that fact, if it is necessary. No, Sara, I have too much to lose, if you live! When your body is found at the bottom of the quarry, your death will be accounted an accident!'

I could not move, I could not breathe, so frightened was I; Thaddeus would not come, no one would come. Rowan intended to kill me, cold-bloodedly, and there was no way of escaping him; but at least I could try, if only fear would release her terrible hold on me.

Rowan shook me as though I was a rag doll; when I screamed, he lifted one hand and struck me again and again across the face, until my screams died to sobs. I tried to fight him off, but I was as puny as a child against his muscular strength. He pulled me hard against him, twisting my arms behind my back.

'I WILL have one kiss, Sara!' he told me.

He forced my face against his, until our lips met, and he kissed me with a ferocious strength that made blood ooze from my throbbing mouth. When he had done with me, he began to drag me towards the door of the little cottage.

I was battered, defeated, exhausted; for an instant I thought I saw the face of Thaddeus through a red haze of pain, but I knew myself to be deluded. From behind us, came the unexpected sound of a deep rumbling, as though the earth protested at such violence being done. A heavy shower of stones spattered the roof of the cottage. Rowan looked up sharply, and, for a second, his hold slackened sufficiently to let me pull myself free.

We were at the door; somehow, I found enough strength to fling myself past him. Outside, the path was slippery, and I fought to keep my balance; but at the end of the path was the bridge – and safety, I thought.

Rowan swore and lunged at me. I clung frantically to a boulder, my fingers slipping helplessly from the wet, smooth sides. Another rumble, like a warning growl, halted him again. I thought the cottage seemed to be moving; but it was an illusion, I told myself, part of my fear and confusion.

Rowan caught my shoulder with a cry of triumph; now the long drop to the foot of the quarry was only inches away; and then, as I made one last, frantic attempt to pull free, I heard a shout, lower down the path that led up from the bridge.

A figure ran towards me; a man who was lithe, muscular, sure-footed. I recognised him, crying out his name, as my life hung by seconds.

The running figure reached me, thrusting Rowan aside, and flinging me backwards on the turf; I fell, striking my head against a boulder.

The only reality I knew before my tired senses released me into oblivion was the fact that I was held in strong, gentle arms, being comforted like a child awakening from a nightmare.

I lay on the sofa in the drawing-room at Tremannion, covered by a rug. I felt stiff and sore and my right arm seemed to have been wrenched almost from its socket. There was a lump on the back of my head, and I opened my eyes cautiously; somewhere a clock struck eleven.

Cathy was sitting beside me; gently, she laid a hand on my forehead.

'What has happened?' I asked.

'Hush! You must rest!' she whispered. 'Dr Evans says you seem to have suffered no great harm, but you must stay quiet.'

Memory washed over me in a tide of

terror and bewilderment. I gripped her hand tightly.

'Tell me what happened!' I insisted. 'Who saved me from Rowan?'

'Thaddeus,' she replied softly. 'Fortunately, he came to Brennion this evening, saying he felt something was wrong, for he had spoken to Rowan earlier and found his manner strange. So I told him of Rowan's message to you; he said it was untrue, and he went at once to the quarry. I came here, in case you had not yet left the house, and I saw Jessie. She seemed alarmed at what I told her. She asked me to wait here in case you returned and insisted that she must go out and search for her son.'

She hesitated; a cold hand touched my heart.

'Thaddeus?' I whispered.

To my relief, she smiled.

'He saw that you were brought safely to Tremannion, though he could not cross its boundaries and waits by the bridge for news of you. He reached the quarry only just in time; there has been a landslide – the cottage is unsafe.'

'The landslide saved my life,' I whispered. I shivered, remembering, and asked:

'What has happened to Rowan?'

There was horror in her face, as she answered me.

'He is barely alive, Sara. He turned on

328

Thaddeus and tried to kill him. Thaddeus managed to restrain him, but Rowan broke free and he – flung himself over the edge of the quarry, Sara. Perhaps he was afraid of what he had done and the consequences he would face. The men who brought him up say he cannot live long because of his injuries.'

In spite of what he had done, I wept silently for Rowan. He had known himself to be despised; he had been cheated. It was an intolerable burden for any man to bear.

'Aunt Jessie?' I asked.

'She reached the quarry after Rowan had flung himself down; she is severely shocked, naturally. It is fortunate that Dr Evans was here this evening – your grandfather had a severe heart attack when he heard what had happened. Adam has ridden into Brecon for a nurse. Oh, what a house of tragedy this is!'

I could not do anything except agree with her; the shadows were deep and cold within the walls of Tremannion.

'Why did Rowan want to kill you?' Cathy asked curiously.

'Tomorrow I will tell you,' I said tiredly. 'Will you go and tell Thaddeus that I am recovered?'

She nodded; when she had gone, I closed my eyes and slept again.

When I awoke the second time, it was morning. Cathy was curled in a chair, fast asleep. She stirred as soon as I awoke and rang for Olwen to bring me some hot water.

Together, they bathed my face and hands, helped me to change my clothes and brush my hair. I saw both Olwen and Cathy look, wide-eyed, at the bruises on my arms and shoulders.

The imprint of Rowan's hands on my shoulders had left five purple indentations; my cheeks were swollen where he had struck me, my lips were cut and bruised.

When they had done, Olwen brought me a breakfast tray; I could not eat, but I drank the strong, sweet coffee gratefully. The curtains had been drawn back and the world outside the windows of Tremannion looked unbelievably tranquil. The events of last night seemed absurd and unreal...

I asked Olwen to send word to Daniel Pugh that I wished to see him; when he came to me, I said:

'The master of Tremannion is ill and Mr Rowan has been badly injured in an accident, as doubtless you know. Therefore, I would like you to take charge of all things concerning the land and the animals, seeing to it that everything is done as the master would wish.'

'Yes, Miss Pryce,' he said quietly. 'What is to be done, that I will do, as well as I am able.'

I went upstairs to the room where Meredith lay, propped against his pillows, his once ruddy-complexioned face the colour of ashes, only his magnificent eyes alive and burning fiercely. I sent the nurse away and sat down beside him.

'Well?' he said abruptly and with much of his old vigour. 'What is this strange and terrible tale of which I have been told only half?'

I told him the whole story, from beginning to end, omitting nothing. He looked angrily at me.

'Again you have disobeyed me; had you not done so, none of this would have happened.'

'No,' I agreed calmly. 'Instead, Rowan might well have carried out his plan to kill me, here at Tremannion! I owe Thaddeus my life.'

'Bad blood!' declared Meredith. 'Bad, gypsy blood from Seth Pryce; I have always known it ran in Rowan's veins! Well, what now? Do you plan to leave me and marry Flynn?'

'I do not; he is going away. I have instructed Daniel Pugh to take charge until you are well enough to do so. I will not leave you, Father.'

So I gave him, willingly, the gift he had so long desired; and I saw the sudden leap of joy in his eyes when I called him 'Father.'

Rachel had been told little of what had

happened; I left her in Megan's care, giving the servant precise instructions as to the amount of sedative she was to be given. Aunt Jessie was at Rowan's beside; I knew that my presence might well distress her, and so I left her to Cathy's ministrations.

'Where is Thaddeus?' I asked Cathy.

'At Brennion,' she said.

'I am going to him. I shall not be gone for very long, in case I am needed here.'

I put a cloak about my shoulders and walked to Brennion, glad of the fresh air that cleared my head. I seemed to be existing in a state of unnatural calm, as though I dwelt inside a glass sphere; the events of the previous evening had not yet made any impact upon me.

Adam met me at the door of Brennion, looking tired and worried.

'Sara?' he said concernedly.

'I am well enough, thank you, Adam, though I should be grateful if you would spare Cathy to us for a little longer; she is a great comfort to me. May I speak to Thaddeus?'

He nodded, and there was gentle affection in his smile; he ushered me into the drawing-room, leaving me alone there with the man who turned slowly from the window to face me.

Thaddeus walked across the room and looked at me; the morning sunlight put fire in his hair and his eyes; I looked at the beautiful, sensuous mouth, the clear-cut, arrogant splendour of his handsome face, willing myself to remain calm, despite the thunder of my pulses and the fever in my blood.

'Has he done THIS to you?' Thaddeus demanded with terrible fury, as he looked at the marks on my face.

'Yes; it is not important now. Had you not come when you did last night, he would have killed me. WHY were you there, Thaddeus? Cathy says you spoke to Rowan in the village yesterday.'

'HE spoke to *me!*' Thaddeus retorted. 'Early in the afternoon, outside the Brennion Arms. He was so eager to talk, to show friendliness, even trying – in vain – to persuade me to drink with him! He was interested in my movements, to a degree that made me highly suspicious! He wished to know when I proposed to leave the village; but his greatest anxiety concerned my plans for yesterday evening, so I told him that I was keeping a rendezvous in Brecon and the lie appeared to satisfy him. It was most obvious that he wished to be sure I was nowhere in the vicinity of Tremannion or Brennion last night!'

'Did he seem – strange?' I asked.

'Decidedly so; but I have always felt Rowan was unbalanced, that there were terrible fires banked down behind that quiet exterior of his! Yesterday, his manner and appearance gave me much thought; but I did not believe he planned to murder you. I walked up to Brennion, to see if Adam or Cathy could tell me anything concerning the whole extraordinary business, and she repeated what you had told her: that *I* was supposed to be meeting you at the quarry, according to Rowan. I thought, then, that he planned to lure you to the quarry for another purpose than murder.'

'And what purpose was that?' I asked, watching his face.

'You know quite well!' he retorted grimly. 'I thought that he planned to seduce you, with or without your consent!'

'Did that thought trouble you, Thaddeus?' I asked him gently.

'Why, yes!' he retorted, a gleam in his eye. 'I did not see why that should be HIS privilege!'

I was disappointed in his answer, and he knew; he smiled sardonically. I reminded myself that he had saved my life; but when I began to thank him, he cut me short.

'You are safe enough now, Sara. Let that suffice! The danger is over; as for me, I shall go my way, unhampered by any woman! No one binds *me;* understand that! I intend to pluck you from my thoughts and from my life, so that I am free to go where I please, and live as I choose, taking my pleasures where I find them, as I have always done! We should never have met. I admit that you have captured my imagination as no other woman has ever done! What more do you desire in the name of victory? You are Meredith Pryce's granddaughter – have I not told you that the very name of Pryce sickens me?'

'Then it can only distress you further to know that I am Meredith's daughter, not his granddaughter,' I answered.

Thaddeus listened to my tale in silence; those strange, unfathomable green eyes never left my face. When I had finished, he bent his head, and with great gentleness, he put his lips tenderly against my swollen ones, in the softest of caresses.

'That is to prove that I do not hate you,' he said lightly. 'Let it be your consolation, Sara. I AM going from here, and I shall forget you!'

'I did not come to persuade you to stay,' I replied, 'but only to thank you for my life; and to tell you that my one wish is for your happiness.'

'You must marry a man such as Adam!' he urged despairingly. 'Then you will know peace of mind!'

'I do not want peace of mind; I desire to LIVE! To tear myself to pieces for love, if it is necessary; to know its passion and pain and feel its torment as fiercely as I taste its exquisite joy! I shall never marry for less than that!' I replied proudly.

'Then you must stay unwed!' he cried angrily. 'Be mistress of Tremannion, then, growing old and lonely, as my sister did!'

When I walked away from him, out of the house, he made no move to follow me. I was still sustained in the calm of unreality; it was much later that I wept, lying alone in my room that night, and I could not stem the flow of scalding tears.

Thaddeus left Brennion the next day; and Rowan died that night. He made a full confession of all that he had done to me, before he died.

Aunt Jessie was utterly bereft; dry-eyed and tearless, with a terrifying stillness about her. She sat in his room, hands folded in her lap, and spoke to me.

'I did wrong, Sara; but not deliberately. I never sought to harm you, and I blame Meredith for the fact that my son behaved as he did. I do not want to see Meredith again; he is an evil man, a cheat, without conscience; and I cannot forget, Sara, that if you had not come here to live, my son would be alive today.'

Her voice was full of quiet bitterness; what could I say to her? I touched her hand fleetingly and left her alone at Rowan's bedside.

Cathy was a tower of strength; she accepted the story of my parentage without much surprise. Tremannion had produced too many dramas for this one to make any great impact upon her.

Meredith received the news of Rowan's death without comment; but his eyes were eloquent.

'You can tell Daniel Pugh that tomorrow the master of Tremannion will be in command again!' he said.

He dressed and came downstairs against Dr Evans' orders; I guessed how much the effort cost him. He insisted that I accompany him when he saw Daniel, for he declared that I must listen and learn, so that I would understand how Tremannion should be run. I think he accepted – for the time being, at least – that I would not marry Adam, even though I was now heiress to Tremannion.

In the days that followed, Aunt Jessie remained in her room, refusing to leave it, and one of the servants took her meals to her. I longed to talk to her and assure her she was not to blame for Lily's death, but she gave me no opportunity. With the death of her son, she had become like a clock with a broken spring.

A week after Rowan's funeral, she suddenly left Tremannion. I was at Brennion, that afternoon, seeking Adam's advice on a matter concerning the flocks; on my return, I discovered that Aunt Jessie had ordered the coach, as soon as I left the house, demanding that she be taken to Brecon. She had taken luggage with her, and when I went to her room, I found it stripped of her possessions.

Meredith declared we were well rid of her; but I made every effort to trace her. I discovered she had hired a conveyance at Brecon to take her to Tenby; and although I searched for news of her, and even visited Tenby on several occasions, afterwards she was never seen or heard of again. It grieves me, still, to reflect upon her sudden disappearance, in such an anguished frame of mind.

Soon after Aunt Jessie's flight, I heard that Bronwen had left the village, and the apothecary's shop was sold to someone else.

I felt very much alone in the weeks that followed, though Adam and Cathy could not have been kinder. Rachel, surprisingly, was docile and sensible enough, most of the time, though she showed no interest in Meredith nor he in her; they went their separate ways, as they had always done.

My father insisted upon taking an active part in the affairs of Tremannion, though I watched him becoming increasingly exhausted as the summer waned. He paid the price for his disobedience to Dr Evans' orders, sustaining another and very severe heart attack after a particularly arduous day spent riding around the Tremannion estates.

This time, as he lay against his pillows, he seemed to have no desire to pick up the reins again; his willingness to stay in his room saddened and alarmed me; we spent a great deal of time together, talking often of my mother. I reminded him of the last paragraph in her letter, concerning the quality of love, and he smiled at me.

'Is this your argument, Sara, for clinging to the memory of a waster and scoundrel such as Flynn?'

'It is the *only* argument,' I assured him.

'And memories will be cold comfort,' he retorted sharply.

'Pride, too, is cold comfort, Father; but many are well sustained by it.'

'You have a pert tongue,' he said, with a laugh. 'Ah, Sara, you are very like me; THAT is something you cannot escape!'

He taught me to play chess, as he had promised. The days grew colder, and autumn came early that year, with wild winds frolicking over the Beacons, driving the clouds like flocks of celestial sheep, and shaking down a golden snowstorm of leaves from the trees.

The air was sharp, and winter was hard on our heels; I wondered how I should endure it; I thought constantly of Thaddeus, imagining him warmed by the sun, a great distance away from Wales.

Yet, autumn was beautiful too; on a tranquil, golden afternoon in October, when the winds had shouted themselves hoarse and fallen asleep, when the bare trees spread mantillas of black lace against the pale sky, I sat companionably with my father, in his room.

He looked very tired, as he looked at his lands spread out before him, beyond the windows.

'There is a quotation from the Scriptures that comes to my mind, Sara,' he said suddenly.

'I cannot imagine that you have paid diligent attention to your Bible, Father!' I told him dryly.

'No, I have not. I did not live by the Scriptures, but as *I* thought best. I have little use for platitudes; the world will use a man hardly and unfairly – unless *he* learns to use it to his own ends. But there is one thing...'

'What is it?' I asked.

He turned his head and smiled at me, as he quoted:

'"This is My beloved son, in whom I am well pleased." I would say, rather: This is my beloved daughter, in whom I am well pleased.'

I felt the tears gather in my eyes. I could

not speak. When I looked up, he was sleeping.

I sat, watching the dusk make purple smudges of the Beacons; it was some time before I realised that my father had died, quietly, as he slept in his chair.

As I stood looking down upon him, I thought that he was like a mighty tree, felled in a forest of pygmies. Who shall judge such men as Meredith Pryce? None of us certainly; he has been judged elsewhere, and – I like to think – with compassion and mercy, this strange, ruthless, lonely man.

Some small part of me went with him that afternoon, for I was, as he had said, like him in many ways; and, because of that fact, death would never break the tie between us.

By the time winter came, I was truly mistress of Tremannion, having inherited everything that had belonged to my father; a fact that gave me little pleasure. The snows came, in a whirling, soundless storm, and left the Beacons lying still and cold, folded in their white shroud.

Adam and Daniel and I managed as best we could; the house seemed as grim as ever, full of ghosts, and Christmas was a mockery, though Cathy and Adam insisted on sharing it with me. Rachel was still vague and often strange, but she had never become violent since Meredith's death.

Late in February, when pockets of snow still filled the green hollows, I felt a strange excitement stir within me, like the promise of a quickening child. At first, I thought it was because I had lived alone too much with only the Brennions and Rachel for company; but a sense of waiting for some important event that would change my whole life still persisted strongly.

On a wild, wet February afternoon, Anne came back; she had walked up from the village, and I saw her first in the hall, drenched and windswept, her face pale as she took off her outdoor clothes. She looked up and saw me at the top of the stairs; I ran down to her and caught hold of her hands.

'I am glad you have come back!' I said.

She looked at me sombrely.

'I know HE is dead. They told me, in the village. So now you are the mistress here and hold us in the palm of your hand, as I said you would!'

'I do not wish to hold anyone in my hand! I am mistress because there is no one else. What has happened to you? Where is Philip?' I asked.

Her smile was curiously untroubled.

'He left me, Sara, more than a month since. We were living in Bristol. Bronwen searched until she finally found him, and then she persuaded him to return to her. It did not matter greatly; we had outlived our love, and I knew him for a weak and foolish man; but I regret nothing! For a little while I was free; I loved and was loved in return. Now I am free forever! I shall stay here with my mother as long as she lives and then I shall travel abroad, to visit all the places I have longed to see whilst I have been prisoner here. I can do as I please with the rest of my life; so I have no bitterness in my heart.'

It was true, I realised; the fierce fires of resentment and hatred, of jealousy and bitterness had finally burnt themselves out in Anne.

That evening I told her all that had happened. I also told her that she was Thaddeus Flynn's half-sister, and she received the news with pleasure, for she admitted that she had always liked him. I knew she would always hate the memory of Meredith Pryce; it satisfied her to know he was not her father.

I was glad to have Anne at Tremannion; we got along fairly well together. April came, and the air was soft. Our winter care of the flocks was rewarded by the sight of the lambs running with their mothers all over the green slopes, filling the air with the sound of their bleating. The strange happiness still filled my heart, and I knew it was nothing to do with the spring, and the prospect of summer when the foxgloves would bloom again.

Sometimes, knowledge of something about to happen, is hidden in the deepest recesses of our hearts and minds; it comes first as an awareness, no more; then it clamours for our whole attention. So, in the stillness of an April evening, I thought I heard someone call my name. I listened carefully, and I heard my name spoken again.

I went out of the house and down to the bridge. My feet seemed to scarcely touch the ground, my heart sang, and my blood was afire. Not once did I think: this is madness, of *course* he will not be there! My heart knew that he already waited for me by the stream.

He stood by the bridge; a tall, splendid figure, with tawny hair and eyes like emeralds; proud, arrogant, commanding.

'How did you know that I was here?' he demanded.

'I heard you call my name.'

'I have said nothing! *I* have not called you!' he retorted, looking at me with a strange expression on his face.

'Then why are you here?' I asked.

With one stride he covered the distance between us; he held me against his heart, kissing me with a hunger and longing to which every nerve in my body responded. When at last he released me, he held me at arm's length, searching my face, his own filled with such mingled fury and tenderness that I wanted to laugh aloud.

'Damn you, Sara Pryce!' he cried. 'You have disturbed my life, given me little joy in my travels, made a mockery of freedom! You let me go knowing full well that, in doing so, you would bind me more surely! I have painted – in Greece and Rome; I have written, in Paris–'

'I know,' I interrupted. 'Cathy has told me. She has had your letters. I know that your writings are all to be published.'

'Do you know also that it means nothing to me, without you? I have had mistresses since I left Brennion; tired of them and sought others. None of them contented me, because *you* have held me fast, without any chains! Very well, then; if you are still so stubborn and foolish as to wish to tear yourself to pieces for love, it shall be with no one but me! You will not find it easy, nor do I promise you a lifetime of faithfulness; you will certainly know the torment and pain, as well as the joy of loving, and I shall chafe often against the bond of marriage!'

'In that case, we had better not be wed!' I said demurely.

His arms tightened about me.

'We shall be!' he declared arrogantly. 'If I am not to be free of you, then you shall at least stay to give me comfort and pleasure!'

The green eyes were dark and sombre, as he said softly and passionately:

'I love YOU as I have never loved another human being!'

I thought how strange it was that he should use the words my mother had used about her love for Meredith; such was the fierce, compelling unearthly quality of the love that would bind Thaddeus and me together for all time.

'Do you wish you did NOT love me?' I asked, smiling up at him.

'Tease me like that, and you will pay the price!' he murmured wickedly. 'And do not look at me so, or you will regret that also! I am no saint, nor am I patient; it is as well we shall be married soon!'

He kissed me again, and the summer bloomed all about me as he did so; but, looking back, I realise how useless it is to look for words that are clumsy things to describe the most exquisite joy that exists on this earth.

EPILOGUE

Thaddeus and I were married a few weeks later, with Adam, Cathy, and Anne as the only witnesses to the simple ceremony, in the village church.

Since that day, thirteen years ago, we have not been back to Tremannion – until this summer. We have been wanderers, never staying long in one place, and I have not cared, for those years have been rich and splendid and full of great joy; they have not always been tranquil, for both Thaddeus and I are stubborn, independent spirits; I have never been a meek and docile wife, and he has not wished me to be so; we have quarrelled as fiercely as we have loved, known the pain and torment, as well as the bliss of loving deeply. Love has carried us to the highest peaks of joy; if there have been other women in the life of Thaddeus Flynn, since our marriage, I have not been aware of them. He has never become reconciled to the fact that I loved my father – the man who was responsible for his mother's death – and we still argue fiercely about it, until he closes my mouth with his kisses.

Thaddeus, today, is rich and successful; he

cares nothing for those facts. His writing and painting bring him deep pleasure; he loves our four children; our tall, red-haired son Patrick, now twelve, Edward, who is ten, Emma and Celia, the six-year-old twins.

Adam and Cathy were married a few years ago, and we rejoice in their happiness. Rachel lived for two years after I left Tremannion, and, after her death, Anne's travels often brought her to see us. Today, tired of travelling, she is back at Tremannion, a serene woman who has come to terms with life as it is, not as she would like it to be. I have made the Tremannion estates over to her, and she runs the place very successfully, with Daniel and Adam to help her.

We did not want to return to Tremannion, but on Patrick's twelfth birthday, Anne wrote that she saw all too little of her nieces and nephews, and the big house was lonely; come in the summer, she wrote, when the foxgloves bloom.

So we sit here, in the old Pryce pew, this fine Sunday morning, Thaddeus and I, our children, and Anne. From my window, I can see the Tremannion graves, and, again, I wonder: WHO was most to blame for all that happened? Was it Rachel, who turned from Meredith, and taunted him with Patrick Flynn? Was it my mother who had loved Meredith too well? David, with his longing to escape from Tremannion? Jessie, whose tale of the amethyst ring, told to Rowan, had led to tragedy? Rowan? Or Meredith, with his burning desire for power?

I know what Thaddeus would say, if I asked him.

'The past is done, Sara. The people who were part of it are dead. Do not grieve over yesterday, but rejoice in today and in the promise of tomorrow.'

I feel the reassuring pressure of his hand in mine; I see once more the quiet graves where the foxgloves blow in the breeze, their delicate pink bells seeming to toll silently for those who sleep beneath them. I think of the great, gaunt house that seems to sit on the roof of the world, under the wild and lonely Beacons. I remember the man who was master there; and, as I see the marble angel pointing skywards, I add to my prayers a silent plea that all who lived and loved and suffered in Tremannion may sleep in peace now.

349

This Large Print Book for the partially sighted, who cannot read normal print, is published under the auspices of

THE ULVERSCROFT FOUNDATION